P9-EIE-201

PRAISE FOR VICTORIA HELEN STONE

Evelyn, After

"Hands down, the best book I've read this year. Brilliant, compelling and haunting."

—Suzanne Brockmann, *New York Times* bestselling author

"Readers will cheer on Evelyn when the power dynamic with her lying, cheating husband shifts, even while they watch her flirting with disaster in her steamy affair with Noah. A solid choice for Liane Moriarty readers."

—*Library Journal*

"Stone (a nom de plume of romance writer Victoria Dahl) . . . ably switches to darker suspense in a compelling story exploring what lurks behind a seemingly perfect life."

—*Booklist*

"Stone pens a great story that will have readers wondering what will happen next to the characters involved in this mysterious tale . . . Fascinating tale told by a talented storyteller!"

—*RT Book Reviews*

"Victoria Helen Stone renders the obsessions and weaknesses of her characters with scorching insight. Her sterling prose creates a seamless atmosphere of anticipation and dread, while delivering devastating truths about the nature of sex, relationships, and lies, often with a humor that's rapier-sharp. *Evelyn, After* reads like *Gone Girl* with a bigger heart and a stronger moral core."

—Christopher Rice, *New York Times* bestselling author

Half Past

"A gripping, haunting exploration of the lengths to which we'll go to belong, *Half Past* will hold you in its thrall until the very last page. Stone's expert storytelling, vivid characterizations, and tantalizing dropping of clues left me utterly breathless, longing for more—and a newly minted Victoria Helen Stone fan!"

—Emily Carpenter, bestselling author of *Burying the Honeysuckle Girls* and *The Weight of Lies*

"A captivating, suspenseful tale of love and lies, mystery and self-discovery, *Half Past* kept me flipping the pages through the final, startling twist."

—A. J. Banner, #1 Amazon and *USA Today* bestselling author of *The Good Neighbor* and *The Twilight Wife*

"What would you do if you found out that your mother wasn't your biological mother? Would you go looking for the answer to how that happened if she couldn't provide an explanation? That's the intriguing question at the heart of *Half Past*, Stone's strong follow-up to *Evelyn, After*. [It's] both a mystery and an exploration of what family really means. Fans of Jodi Picoult will race through this."

—Catherine McKenzie, bestselling author of *Hidden* and *The Good Liar*

JANE DOE

ALSO BY VICTORIA HELEN STONE

Evelyn, After
Half Past

JANE DOE

A NOVEL

VICTORIA HELEN STONE

LAKE UNION
PUBLISHING

This is a work of fiction. Names, characters, organizations, places, events, and incidents are either products of the author's imagination or are used fictitiously. Any resemblance to actual persons, living or dead, or actual events is purely coincidental.

Published by Lake Union Publishing, Seattle

www.apub.com

ISBN-13: 9781503900899 (hardcover)
ISBN-10: 1503900894 (hardcover)
ISBN-13: 9781503901032 (paperback)
ISBN-10: 1503901033 (paperback)

Cover design by Faceout Studio, Derek Thornton

Printed in the United States of America

First edition

This book is for J. and anyone else who needs it.

CHAPTER 1

I see the moment he first notices me. The slight double take as he spots the new girl in the office. I don't notice him in return. I make sure of it.

He's a man who likes to think he's in charge. He's afraid of women who come on strong. How could you ever control a girl that bold? So I only watch through my lashes and keep my face turned toward my work.

My job doesn't require much concentration. There's no evidence of my true history on the résumé I submitted to this office, but I'm one law degree and six years of experience too qualified for this kind of work. Still, data entry is soothing. It's satisfying in a way that legal work isn't. I settle back into the rhythm of it and ignore him completely.

He isn't the boss. Steven Hepsworth is a classic middle manager. He shows respect to the bigwigs. He's decent at his job. He has an MBA and is Caucasian and classically good-looking, so he'll do fine in life. A great catch.

I noted his easy good looks during my orientation tour of the office yesterday. He uses too much gel in his hair, but he smiles a lot and the smiles feel genuine. The warmth of his brown eyes invites you closer. They distract from the weakness in his chin. People like him. The other women in the office flirt when he speaks to them. He's a nice guy.

Someone brings me a stack of records for input, and I put Steven Hepsworth out of my mind for the rest of the day.

I'll flirt with him like the other women do. But not yet.

CHAPTER 2

He finds me in the break room at lunchtime on my third day. It's possible he came upon me accidentally, but most of the managers use the break room upstairs, or so I've been told. Then again, Steven likely prefers being the big man in the room, so maybe he'd rather dine with us peons.

"Hi!" he says brightly. "I'm Steven."

"I'm Jane," I respond with a smile, offering my hand.

He shakes it gently, his fingers barely pressing mine. I despise men who shake a woman's hand as if their masculine power might crush her inferior bones, but I beam up at him.

"New girl in the office?"

"That's me!" I'm inclined to let my hand flop lifelessly onto the table when he lets it go, but instead I cross my arms beneath my breasts. His eyes flicker to my cleavage only briefly. He's interested but discreet.

The dress is soft and flowery, like all of my recent purchases. It could be demure, but I've unbuttoned one too many buttons. He's a breast man, our Steven. Mine aren't large, but they are there, and I've pushed them up to make them look more C than B. He likes the result. If he ever sees me naked, he'll be disappointed, but that will only work in my favor.

"What brings you to our little office?" he asks.

"Oh, you know. Same old story. I moved back to town a few weeks ago, and I heard you guys were always hiring for data entry. So here I am."

"Just finished college?"

I'm thirty, so I laugh at his flattery. "More along the lines of a bad breakup."

"I know what that's like," he says, settling in with a hip on the break room counter, his eyes sparking with interest. A girl coming off a bad breakup is vulnerable. He's calculating whether he can get me into bed. "Well, welcome back to Minneapolis."

Yes, it's been too long. Far too long. I should have come back a year ago. Two years ago.

The microwave dings behind him. My sad lunch is ready. He moves aside, and I let him see the cheap low-calorie brand name before I pick up the box I left on the counter and toss it in the recycling. I'm not doing well financially, and I'm trying to lose those last ten pounds. That's what he sees.

The truth is I'm almost certainly richer than he is, and my body is fine. It works, I'm fit enough, and no one needs a perfect body to get sex. Sex is the cheapest commodity, and any body at all is up for trade. I'm not interested in love, so I don't spend time worrying what my partners think of me. My lack of shame simplifies things.

But that kind of confidence would terrify Steven, so I smile self-consciously and take my low-fat beef stroganoff from the microwave.

"Looks good," he lies, as if I can't see the shit-colored pile of sauce atop noodles that are half-limp and half-overcooked.

"Wanna share?" I ask.

He laughs too hard at that. "I'm going to grab a meatball sandwich downstairs." Manly food. Meat and balls all at once. "But thank you!" he adds brightly. "Can I get you anything while I'm out? A coffee?"

"No, thanks. I brought some tea from home." The truth is I hate tea, but I'll drink it weak and tepid for him.

"Well, it was really nice to meet you, Jane. See you around?"

"I can almost guarantee it." When he laughs, I grin proudly at his response. He rewards me with a wink.

Once he's gone, I eat my low-fat beef stroganoff and open the paperback I had stashed in my purse. Reading is my favorite hobby. I don't have to fake that.

CHAPTER 3

It's not that I don't have feelings. I have some emotions. I do. It's just that I can usually choose when to feel them. More important, I choose when not to.

I don't think I was born this way. I suspect I used to feel things too deeply until my brain rewired itself to protect me.

My parents are still alive, still together, and they love me, I suppose. But they love me the way a careless child loves a pet. Too much attention one day, absolute neglect the next. The changes in current were too much for me to survive when I was young, so my brain learned to ride above them. It's not something I think about now. It's natural. I observe people's emotions, but I rarely participate.

I talk to my parents occasionally, but I only initiate contact on Christmas. If I happen to be in Oklahoma, I'll stop in for a visit—but, really, who ever happens to be in Oklahoma? I send money on each of their birthdays. They always need it.

I don't hate them; I just don't understand why people feel the need to try over and over with toxic family members. I know who my parents are. They're not the worst, but they're still awful, and I don't need their chaos spinning in and out of my life when I'm not expecting it. They used up all their chances to hurt me when I was very young, and they can't hurt me now even if they want to. That's all.

When I call them on Christmas, I listen to their tales of misadventure and bad luck, and I offer a couple of stories about living and working in Malaysia. They tell me what my brother, Ricky, is up to. I don't speak to him. I have nothing to say to a redneck asshole who's somehow managed to create five children with four women during his brief stints of freedom from incarceration.

That's my family.

As for friends . . . well, Meg was my best friend from the first day we met. She's dead now.

CHAPTER 4

A month ago I was still working as an American import-export attorney for a big Asian manufacturing conglomerate. I lived in a gorgeous apartment in a modern high-rise in Kuala Lumpur outfitted with Western luxuries. I've always found it funny that the expat Americans rarely cook anything but need the biggest, best kitchen appliances. I include myself in that observation. I loved my shiny six-burner stove.

I had a view of the whole city, which was rather brown and hazy during the day but sparkled like a universe at night. I went to parties. There were always parties. I bought designer dresses and shoes. I don't need beautiful things, but I like them fine.

Now I live in a run-down one-bedroom apartment three blocks from my new job. I rent it for its proximity to this office and because it has nice security measures for its price point—which is low. I could almost afford to live here on the pittance of an hourly wage I'm making now. The furniture is all cheaply rented.

My Malaysian employer thinks I'm caring for a dying relative. I now have less than fifty days for this little adventure. If I stay longer, I'll lose my job. And I like my job. I like my life. I like my condo in Kuala Lumpur. I want to get back to it—but not until I've finished this.

I like Minneapolis too, but I'll be happy to leave. There are too many memories of Meg here. Or should I want to stay so I can remember her and pretend I might run into her at any moment? I don't know how grief works. I have no idea what I should expect or even what I should want.

Regardless, my kind doesn't worry much about the future. If I lose my job, I can sell the place in Malaysia and move to New York. I've always loved Manhattan. Instead of depending on Meg's vibrancy to keep me human, maybe I could rely on the crazed heartbeat of that city. Melodramas playing out on every street and on every floor of every building. It might be good for me to be surrounded by that kind of emotion.

Kuala Lumpur is like that, but I don't speak enough Malay to truly sink into it. Minneapolis is fine during the summer but too empty during winter. And I have too much ice on the inside to live with the dark and cold.

Today I don't run into Steven in the break room, and I'm concerned that I haven't snagged his interest. When he joins a supervisor at a desk two rows from mine, I take off my cardigan and toy absently with the button at my dress's neckline. Unfasten, fasten. Unfasten, fasten. I let my fingertips rest against my bare skin. I drag them lower. When I look up, he's watching, and I gulp and smile and drop my face in shame.

A few moments later I glance through my lashes. He winks. I let him see me giggle.

All in all, it's a decent show. I hope it works.

I work until 5:30, then go home to my dingy apartment, which shares a wall with the apartment of a single dad who has custody three nights a week. Sometimes I like hearing the squeals and laughter of his kids, but tonight they're excited about going to the store to pick out Halloween costumes, and I hate them for their happiness and for my memories.

For our sophomore Halloween at the U, Meg made me dress up, the first time I'd bothered since I was ten. She went as a sexy nurse. I was a sexy teacher. The whole point of college costumes was the sexy, of course, and it worked. That night I got laid, and she met a boy who became her boyfriend. Kevin, I think. He was fine for a college boy, and I liked him. It only lasted three months, though.

Meg always fell hard and fast, and I was good at giving her the space for that. That was my role in her love life: to be there waiting when it all fell apart. To help her understand the logic of getting over it and moving on when she couldn't see past her torrent of tears.

Her role in my love life was to encourage me to give each guy a chance. *He's nice! He likes you! He's so cute!* Most of my college dating was just to humor her. To try it her way for a little while. I liked the physical closeness, the sex, but I could never get to the part where you opened up to the other person.

Why would I? People cause pain. Even good people hurt those they love. We all do it because we can't help it. Most of us aren't evil; we're just stupid and flawed and not careful with others. Meg thought the hurt was worth the goodness that came with it. Most people do. It's what keeps them going.

What keeps me going? I don't know. Small pleasures, I guess. Coffee. Chocolate. Competition. Silk dresses. A hot bath on a cold day. Winning. The satisfaction of shaping my life into exactly what I want.

Oh, and right now, my hatred for the muffled chatter of tiny children outside my door. I close my eyes and imagine they are Meg's children instead of a stranger's.

She wanted kids. She wanted a husband and a white picket fence and a swing set in the yard, and I wanted it all for her. She would have been an amazing mother, overflowing with love and attentiveness. She would have decorated for every holiday. She would have baked cookies and not cared how messy her kids got with the sprinkles and icing.

And she would never have disappeared for three days at a time to hit up the Choctaw casinos with her friends. She'd never have left her daughter home alone with strep throat and such a high fever that she hallucinated exotic animals. She'd never have let strange men rent a room.

Imagining Meg's love for the children she won't have fills me up with bittersweet yearning. It swells so tight in me that I briefly wonder if I could manage that kind of love myself. Maybe I could have a child and love it the way I loved Meg.

But no. Meg's childhood had been filled with motherly affection, so she'd been able to accept my cool logic as a soothing balm. But children can't thrive on calmness and remove. They need love too. Hugs and giggles and unfettered warmth. If that had ever been inside me, it isn't now. I'm empty.

But not empty. I'm filled with sorrow. As the children pass my door on their way out of the building, I cover my face with my hands and squeeze my eyes tightly shut, unwilling to share vulnerability with even my bare walls.

I need Meg, and she'll never be here again.

CHAPTER 5

On Monday, Steven finds me in the break room once more. He can't very well come by my desk to chat. It's in the middle of an open room full of desks and low cubicles, and health insurance administration is boring work. If he lingers, his interest will be noticed by the whole floor.

This works well for me. He's forced to time his approach carefully. He has to plan ahead. This makes me seem more desirable than I really am.

I pretend not to notice him standing in the doorway. Frankly, I'm deeply absorbed in my book and resent having to jump back into real life. Or unreal life. Whatever this is. But when he clears his throat, I look up and smile at the sight of him. "Oh, hi!"

"Hey, Jane. I was thinking we could grab a sandwich. I figure you're not familiar with the neighborhood, and my favorite place is just one block over. Gordo's. Have you tried it yet?"

"Oh, I'm sorry." I gesture toward the whirring microwave. "I already started cooking my lunch."

He checks the box on the counter. Spaghetti with low-fat meat sauce. "Sunk cost," he says. "Throw it in the trash and I'll buy you something better."

I laugh and shake my head. "I couldn't. But thank you."

"Tomorrow, then?"

Glancing down, I feign shyness, but I'm really calculating whether he'd be more interested in a yes or a no. I should probably keep up the chase, but I've been a little bored with all the planning. And I don't want to bruise his ego this early in the game. Decision made, I risk a yes, but I spice it with obvious hesitation.

"It's probably not a good idea . . ."

He smiles because he knows I'm giving in despite my gut instinct. "Nah, it's a great idea."

"You think so?"

"Definitely. Tomorrow?"

"Okay. All right. Tomorrow."

He stands taller, his chest puffing out before he inclines his head toward my book. "What are you reading?" I hold it up, showing him the name of a famous thriller author. Steven grimaces. "Genre fiction?"

"My favorite."

"I only read nonfiction." He wants me to feel self-conscious, but the truth is that a man like Steven doesn't want to immerse himself in someone else's world. It gives the author too much power. It makes Steven feel small.

I ignore all that and pretend I don't register the implied insult in his disapproval. "Nonfiction? What kind?"

"US history, mostly. Civil war stuff."

"Oh, cool. I watched that Ken Burns documentary."

"It was okay but pretty general." Neither my books nor my viewing habits are good enough for him. I have to bite back a grin. If this were a bar, I would've told him to sod off by now. But right now I'm supposed to believe he's better than I am. More discerning. I should probably apologize for my inferior preferences, but screw that. I don't have the patience today.

The microwave dings and I get up to open it, then set the meal on the counter and lean down to poke around at the plastic tray. The soft pink-and-tan fabric of my dress gapes to reveal a lacy white bra beneath.

I peel back the plastic wrap and frown as if the spaghetti is not quite done. When I look up, his eyes dart away from my cleavage.

"I'd better head out," he says. "Meet you at the elevator tomorrow at noon?"

"Sounds great!"

When he's gone, I'm relieved. Partly because I can get back to my reading, but mostly because I know he's on the hook. Goal achieved.

I've never had too much trouble getting dates, but I'm not beautiful, and people are unpredictable about attraction. Maybe his number one turn-on is an adorable button nose. Maybe he can only get hard for tan blondes. You can't tell these things from a distance.

But I know which emotional buttons to push. I know what he likes in a woman's personality. And manipulation is my specialty. Still, if he didn't even nibble at me as bait, I have backup plans, but there's no need yet. Apparently I'm good enough for Steven despite my subpar entertainment choices.

Snorting in amusement, I carry my lunch to the table and settle back in with my book. I love losing myself in someone else's world. I like learning how others' lives work even if I don't understand them.

Frankly, fictional people appeal far more to me than real people do. In fiction, the choices have to make sense. The timeline proceeds rationally. Emotions are explained to me. Characters feel the way they are supposed to feel in response to the actions of others. Nobody stays in a bad situation because of inertia or low self-esteem. That would make for a truly shitty story. But in real life . . . God, in real life people so rarely behave in ways that improve their circumstances.

Why?

Why, why, why? This is one of those things I'll never understand. All I know is books are better.

Just as I'm closing the paperback, my phone buzzes, surprising me. No one calls me. No one except—yeah, it's my mother, the call forwarded from my real phone number. I ignore her and let it go to voice mail. She knows what to do. I wouldn't want to actually answer her call and shock her into a heart attack or something. She hasn't lived a healthy lifestyle.

I toss the remains of my lunch, refill my water bottle, and wait for the message chime. I don't really need to listen to her voice mail, but I do. When I get back to my desk, I write a check for $800, then steal an envelope from the supply closet and beg a stamp from the receptionist. Five minutes later my mother and her broken-down car are out of my thoughts.

Ten years ago I would have called her back and grilled her to be sure the money was actually for car repairs and not bail for my brother, but I no longer care. It's worth the money to not have to bother with any of them.

Maybe I love them in some way, because I don't have to send money but I do. Or maybe I feel freakish for not feeling one damn thing for them and the money is an easy salve. I have no idea, and I don't waste time thinking about it. I have more data entry to do.

CHAPTER 6

"So did you grow up here?" he asks over his chopped-beef sandwich. It was either that or the meatball. No tuna and sprouts for this guy.

I finish chewing a small bite of my salad. "I went to high school here for a couple of years. We moved around a lot."

"Military family?"

"No, it was just me and my mom."

"Sounds like it may have been difficult."

"Oh, I don't know. It was okay when it was just us. But she was in and out of relationships. That part was hard. A lot of those guys were creeps."

"I'm sorry to hear that," he says. Maybe he even means it.

"What about you?" I ask. "Do you have family in Minneapolis?"

"Sure. My dad and his wife are here, and my mom's in Rochester. My sister moved to Milwaukee, but my younger brother is still nearby. We get together quite a bit."

"That sounds so nice. I don't have any other family."

"Your dad?"

"Oh. No." I shake my head and keep my eyes on my salad. "I don't really know him."

"That must be hard."

"I don't know. I hear he wasn't a good guy. What's your dad like?"

"My dad's the best. A really great man. He's a minister, in fact. He has his own church."

This salad is causing me heartburn. Or Steven is churning up the acid in my stomach. But I sit straight and force my face to light up. "You're a Christian?"

"Of course. Are you?"

"I am, but I kind of fell out of it. My ex wasn't a believer. I haven't been to church in years."

"You should get back to it!"

"Maybe I should. I have been feeling a little lost lately. I mean . . . gosh, you know what? I think you're right. Just thinking about it makes me feel a little better. Do you know a good church around here?"

"No, ours is out in the suburbs. It's a great place, though. You should definitely check it out."

"I don't have a car. But I'm sure I'll find something nice near here."

He glances around as if he's doubtful. I suspect this area isn't nearly white enough for him.

I've been to church plenty of times. When you grow up in rural Oklahoma, there's no avoiding it. My parents would occasionally find God for a few weeks and we'd attend services for a month or two, but Sunday mornings were rarely a convenient time for my family. Saturdays went pretty late at the trailer park . . . or at the casino or the bar.

Regardless, I know from experience that suburban churches are the most boring and least generous. We'd always been looking for generosity. We had no use for pull-yourself-up-by-your-bootstraps Christianity. If there wasn't a big potluck after services, what was the point of going? My mom always stayed late, putting on a show of helping clean up. I liked that part. There were lots of leftovers, and she usually smuggled out a couple of free serving bowls.

"Thank you for lunch," I say for the third time.

"It's nothing. I couldn't bear to watch you eat another of those microwave meals."

Way to make me feel shitty about myself, Steven.

"I'd love to take you out for dinner sometime," he adds.

I act flustered. I squirm and take too long to chew my food before answering.

"Steven, I . . . I just started at this job. Aren't there rules about dating subordinates?"

He waves a dismissive hand. "They wouldn't know."

"Someone might see us."

"Then come to my place and I'll make something."

"I couldn't come over to your place! On a first date? I'm not . . . I'm not like that!"

"Shit." He reaches out for my wrist to stop my flailing hand. "I'm sorry. Of course you're not. I didn't mean it like that. At all. Okay?"

I nod but let him see that I'm shaken by the very idea of putting out. A woman shouldn't have her own sexual needs. My role is to resist. That makes me a nice girl.

"Jane, I'm serious. That's not what I was thinking. I was just trying to protect you from prying eyes."

"I know."

"How about if I take you to a little hole-in-the-wall? Someplace we won't be seen. Then would you go to dinner with me?" He ducks his head a little, trying to meet my gaze. He raises his brows like a begging puppy, showing me his harmless brown eyes. "Please?"

I giggle. "I shouldn't be dating again so soon."

"We won't call it a date, then. Just two colleagues having dinner."

"You're a manager and I'm a data entry clerk. We're hardly colleagues."

"Then I'll be your mentor."

Laughing, I shake my head. "You're bad."

"Technically you don't even report to me. No conflict of interest."

Ridiculous, of course. He could still have me fired. I simper a little more. "Why do you even want to go out with me? You hardly know me."

"Come on. You're gorgeous."

I'm not gorgeous. I'm just a vulnerable girl who wears lacy bras. But I get it. Even a sociopath likes to hear that she's beautiful. "I'm not," I protest quietly, but I'm smiling.

"How about tomorrow?" he presses.

"All right. But only if you promise to mentor me."

He grins like a cat with too many teeth. "I'll teach you everything you need to know." Ha. Not everything *he* knows, but everything I need to know. Nice touch.

After lunch he walks me back to the building and rides up the elevator with me, so I don't have a chance to run to a newsstand and grab a protein bar. I hope to God there's a birthday on the floor today, or I might pass out from hunger.

CHAPTER 7

No birthday cake appears. I'm starving by the time I leave the office, so I hurry home and change into something more comfortable. Tight jeans, ankle boots, a black sweater. I wash off my colorful eye shadow and replace it with a few simple black lines, then pull back my hair into a tight bun. I've lightened my hair and I hate it. It's too soft-looking. I like it dark and straight, no highlights.

I want a meal, and I want a drink too. But, more than food and alcohol, I crave an end to my boredom, so I walk a few blocks into downtown and head into a high-end business hotel. I sit at the bar and order steak frites and a gin and tonic. Both are perfect.

There are several businessmen at the bar with me, all separated by at least one empty chair. Half of them watch me in the mirror above the bar. I watch the news channel behind the bartender's head.

As soothing as my easy new work is, my brain is starting to crave exercise. Business stories slide across the crawler, and it's news I haven't heard before. That never happened in Kuala Lumpur. I heard about most international trade news before it ever hit the business channels.

I finish my first drink, and before I set it down, a man in a suit approaches. "Buy you another?" he asks. I turn to look straight into his face. He's well over fifty and his cheeks and nose are already pink from alcohol. His suit is expensive and he's not bad-looking, but I imagine his face turning beet red as he pumps furiously above me.

I don't pretend to be insulted, nor am I flattered by his attention. This has nothing to do with me. I could be anyone. I am a woman with a hole he can fill. He might have a chance to screw me, so he may as well try. It's that simple. He didn't even bother slipping off his wedding ring.

"No." I turn back to the television and raise a hand to signal the bartender.

"Same?" the bartender asks. I nod. The man in the suit walks away.

"In town for work?" the barkeep asks as he makes my drink. It's nice of him to make conversation with a woman being bothered by men at his bar. He has the jaded air of a man who's been serving drinks for a long time, but he's still young. Twenty-eight, maybe, though he could have a baby face under that beard.

"I live here, actually."

His dark eyebrows fly high. "Really? We don't get many locals in here."

"I didn't want to go somewhere romantic and sit by myself." I don't really mean it, and the way he laughs says he's picked up on my dry tone. He fills a new bowl with pretzels and slides it toward me. He'll get a good tip for looking out for me.

Not that I need protection.

Now that one of their kind has been shot down, the men at the bar aren't studying me quite so closely. They likely thought I was a prostitute. You see them often in bars like this, even more often in the business hotels overseas. Women who look as professional as their clients but with open-necked blouses instead of loosened ties. Not that the men wouldn't like their whores to dress like classic streetwalkers, but the hotels can't have that kind of obviousness hanging around.

I watch the men now that their gazes have drifted hazily back to the second TV, which flashes the bright greens and whites of a football game. Two of the men, including the one who already approached, are middle-aged or better, their suits a little looser and more creased from travel.

A third man is younger, his suit pants cut slim, his widespread collar ostentatiously white against blue fabric. Cuff links glint when he raises his drink. He's handsome in a big-nosed kind of way, and his body is great, but I don't like the look of him. I imagine that he always watches himself in the mirror during sex, admiring the way his own ass clenches with each pistoning thrust.

My nose wrinkles at the thought. I'd bet he thinks his penis is all it takes to make a woman climax, and he continues to believe that no matter how many women tell him otherwise. I used to be better at giving men the benefit of the doubt, but it's hardly doubt after all these years. They're not difficult to figure out.

The fourth man, though . . . the fourth man has potential, and thank God for that. I'm so bored and restless tonight, I might have even given old Piston Ass a try.

But there's no need. The fourth man is dark skinned and handsome in a boyish way. Early thirties, maybe. His curly hair is cut close to his scalp. No wedding ring on his hand and no oversized Rolex either. He wears a simple white dress shirt with the sleeves rolled up, the fabric a gorgeous contrast to his brown skin. His long fingers loosely grip a bottle of domestic beer: no expensive brands for him. A man with no need to show off. In my estimation, that makes it a decent chance he's actually good in bed. Oh, lucky day.

His gaze leaves the game and slides along the mirror until I catch his eye. The right side of his mouth tips up and I grin at having been caught. When I don't look away, the quirk of his mouth widens into a smile. I raise my glass in greeting. He does the same.

I'm not shy about approaching men when the situation calls for it, but there's no need. He doesn't strike me as the kind of man who jumps into bed with every woman he meets, but he looks open and friendly, and there's no good reason not to chat up a single lady on a boring evening. Worst-case scenario is we won't hit it off and he'll be out a few minutes of conversation. But I'll make sure we hit it off.

To give him a little space, I check my email. I don't have an email address for this new identity, because this Jane doesn't need one. Who would write to a blank slate? The mail coming into my phone is from my real life. Business news, LinkedIn invitations, junk mail written in Malay, very exciting offers to meet Hot Asian Girls! Plus one actual personal email with a sender's name that makes my breath catch like a burr in my throat.

Cheryl Peterson. It's Meg's mother.

She's a hapless woman, and I've always resented the bad decisions she made during Meg's childhood, but even I can't deny that she'd loved her daughter. She'd loved her daughter almost as much as she'd loved having a man in her life. Almost. A pretty typical story.

With Meg gone, there's no reason to ever interact with Cheryl again; we have nothing concrete or logical in common. She's a mediocre hairstylist who adores kids, lets worthless men treat her like crap, and seems confused about why she's perpetually broke.

But emotion isn't logical, is it? Emotion is sticky as tar, and it's hard to get off you, which is why I've spent my whole life trying to avoid exposing my skin to it. But with Meg I was naked as a babe, and part of me is stuck to Cheryl now. I don't like it. I'll free myself as soon as I can.

Resigned to raw nerves and melancholy, I click on Cheryl's email. It's quick and to the point and still messy as hell.

> Jane, I haven't heard from you in a while, so I thought I'd check in. Meg's last letter asked me to take care of you. Are you doing ok?

God, Meg. Why were you so good? If you hadn't loved me so well, I wouldn't miss you this much.

Her last letter. I don't want to think about that. She sent me a letter as well. I get it out and read it when I need a hit of raw pain to cut through the dull throbbing of this grief.

"Hey." His voice interrupts my sorrow, and I'm so relieved, I turn to him with a blinding smile.

"Hey, yourself."

"Should I offer to buy you another drink or is that just irritating?"

I'm about to crack a joke about not needing a drink because I just started my current one, but a glance shows me an empty tumbler and I realize I can still taste gin on the back of my tongue. Sliding my phone into my purse, I look him up and down.

He's a little shorter than I thought, with the tight body of a runner. What's more appealing than his body is the way he stands at a polite distance, waiting for a signal that welcomes him closer. He understands women in that very simple way so many men never grasp. He knows we are raised in danger. He views our respect as a gift. He has sisters, probably. I like him.

"I'd love another," I finally answer, tipping my head toward the empty seat beside me.

He raises his hand to politely wave at the bartender, then slides onto the stool. "I'm Anthony." He offers a hand, and when I take it, the handshake is quick and firm.

"Jane," I respond. "Are you here for work?"

"I am. Pitching a new campaign. I work in advertising in Chicago. What about you?"

"I live nearby. Just wanted to get out of my place for a few hours."

"An extrovert?"

"Something like that. I like a little noise in the background, and I can only deal with twenty-four-hour news channels for so long."

"I get it. I don't particularly like sports, but I seem to find myself at sports bars all the time."

"Do you travel a lot?"

"A few times a month. Nothing too crazy."

I don't ask about his relationship status. He doesn't ask about mine. Our new drinks arrive and we gently clink glasses. "Thank you," I murmur.

"My pleasure."

We talk for an hour. You might think I'd be terrible at conversation, but I'm not. I enjoy small talk the way I enjoy books with an interesting narrator. The way other people live and love and think are cozy mysteries, though their stories are as two-dimensional to me as words on a page. I don't understand the stupid reactions of people. I don't understand their irrationality. But small talk is light entertainment.

On my side, I normally only have to mention Malaysia and the listener is hooked. But I'm treading cautiously here. My time in Minneapolis will not end well. How many questions will be asked, and who will be asking them? I have no idea, so I keep Malaysia to myself.

Still, there are stories to share, and I share them. Anthony is smart and funny, and he looks a little embarrassed when he finally asks if we should take our last round of drinks to his room.

He needn't feel embarrassed. I'm not. I pay my tab and leave a nice tip for the bartender before waving goodbye. The ruddy-faced businessman, eyes now bleary with booze, shoots me a scornful glare as I walk past with Anthony, and I resist the urge to tell him to fuck off and grow up. No matter how old he gets, he'll still want a woman my age, but he resents that I don't want him. Does he notice his own shitty hypocrisy? No. I'm a selfish bitch. It will always be my fault.

But who cares about him? Anthony and I step into the elevator, and even when we're alone he doesn't crowd me, but his eyes are warmer, the lids a little heavier as he lets his gaze slip over my body. I touch a fingertip to his wrist and draw a circle. "I like your arms," I say.

"My arms?" He's no weight-lifting type and he seems surprised.

"Stronger than mine, but not ostentatious."

He smiles as he eases closer. "You're an odd one." Boy, am I ever. His lips just touch mine when the doors of the elevator slide open. He hesitates, kisses me again.

"Come on," I whisper, and tug him into the hallway.

For a moment I'm a real person. I'm excited, happy, close to another human, nearly breathless with anticipation. He's kissing me before his hotel door is fully open, and I try not to think or plan or analyze. We're not frantic, but we waste no time in exploring, undressing each other as we kiss and touch.

Right now I could be any woman taking a chance with an attractive man. This could develop into something deeper. We could fall in love and marry and live the age-old dream. I like the brief fantasy of it as much as the sex, but after I climax, this intimacy will evaporate along with the sweat on my body. I learned this long ago.

The funny thing is a lot of people are sociopaths when it comes to sex, aren't they? And I'm the odd one? At least I'm consistent.

My instincts are good, and Anthony doesn't let me down. He gets me off before we have sex, then again at the end. I like his body all tight and slick with sweat, and he uses a condom without my having to ask. If he weren't flying out in the morning, I might come back again tomorrow night, but when he asks if I want to keep in touch, I reluctantly shake my head. He's said he only comes to town once or twice a year and I won't be here that long.

"You sure?" he asks. "I thought this was pretty nice."

"It was *really* nice," I reassure him, stroking a thankful hand over his arm and then his chest and stomach. My reassurance is so effective that he's hard again within minutes and we do it one more time, and this round is rougher, harder, and even better than really nice.

I leave his room with a grin, and I smile the whole way home. What a great night. The memory may even get me through a few days of playing with Steven.

CHAPTER 8

I'm thankful Steven avoids me for most of the day. Tonight we're going on a date, and he's likely being careful not to send signals to anyone in the office, but his distance helps me as well. My body is still moving with the warm lethargy of a satisfied woman, and I can't let him see that.

But let's be honest. Steven probably wouldn't recognize the cause or effect.

All in all, though, last night's fun was a good idea. Playing the submissive mouse is going to be a lot easier when I'm not tight with tension and always on the edge of snapping and telling Steven what I really think of him.

If there was any chance of regularly finding a partner of Anthony's caliber, I'd hit the bars every night, but Anthony was a long shot. Every one-night stand is a roll of the dice. I'm good enough at recognizing fellow monsters that I rarely put myself in danger, but no woman can avoid the risk of a seriously bad lay. It's like some of them are trying to be terrible in bed.

All those jokes about the clitoris being hard to find? Come on. It's right there near the top of the vulva every time. There's maybe one square inch of possibility, and they still can't work it out. The sheer incompetence astounds me.

Of course, there are plenty of men who don't even bother to try, but it's gotten easier and easier to spot them at first glance after years of practice. I'm pretty sure Steven is one of them, so I'll put off sleeping with him as long as I can. Luckily, resistance fits my narrative.

I want to spend my lunch hour reading, but I stupidly open my email and there is that note from Cheryl still waiting for me. I could just delete it. I don't care about Cheryl. But I do care about Meg, and Cheryl is the only link to my love for her. We could stay in touch. Have coffee. Talk about Meg.

Meg was the closest thing I had to a soul. She blew into my life like a hurricane. Is that too clichéd? It is, but the worse sin is that a hurricane is destructive, and Meg wasn't. So . . . she exploded my cold, quiet world with all the beauty of a fireworks show.

She was my sophomore roommate in college. My freshman roommate had been ignorable. We had nothing in common, but nothing that made us enemies either. That year was quiet. Forgettable.

But Meg . . . Meg was a new universe. There was no question we'd be friends, because Meg was friends with everyone. I didn't want to go out dancing with her the first night we met, but she had decided we'd go dancing, so we did. It was more fun than all of my freshman days smashed together.

But fun was just the start. With Meg I could almost imagine I was normal. She was hopeful, positive, and loving, and if I tried hard when I was with her, I could pretend to be those things too. Only for short moments, of course. I stole brief glimpses of the world through her eyes, and it was like reading the best book. I could lose myself in her story.

The most important thing about Meg, though—the thing that kept me tied to her—was her reliability. Meg was there for me every single time I needed her. She was the first person in the world I truly trusted. She was the *only* person. And she's gone.

I've never missed anyone before. What do I do with that? Without Meg, I'm no longer sure who I am. She was my connection to a future. To love and children and marriage.

One day Meg would get married. I'd be her maid of honor. She'd have kids and I'd be their aunt Jane. Meg was my only hope of loving children, even if that love was seasonal and sketchy. I'll never have my own. What would be the point in creating more people I'd barely connect with?

But I knew I'd love Meg's kids through her. Enough to be there on Christmases and birthdays. To celebrate with them. To have a link to family and traditions, even if they weren't my own.

Without Meg, my future is a cold march of nearly identical days. No true family. No holiday gatherings. Is that a reason to hang on to Cheryl? Is that what other people would do?

She promised Meg she'd take care of me, and I know she's a more-the-merrier type, so if I keep in touch I'll at least have the chance of a warm and raucous Christmas in the future.

But strangers aren't family. Meg will never be there. I'll never belong. I'll be a stranger everywhere I go for the rest of my life.

Still, I don't delete Cheryl's email. I have no idea what that means.

By the end of lunch I've lost a little of my glow, but that's a good thing. Hobbies are well and good, but I need to get back to the work of keeping Steven on my hook.

If I could get this all over with quickly, I would. Fall into bed with Steven and get close to him right away. Find out what makes him tick. This could all be over in days. But if I don't resist sex, I won't be worthy of love, and I need him to love me in his own little selfish way. I need him to show me his weaknesses.

So no sex tonight. Maybe a kiss. I'll keep my cardigan buttoned up to my neck until Steven talks me into having a glass of cheap wine with dinner. Then I'll get warm and unbutton it too far and he'll think he made that happen.

This relationship will be tedious and nearly unbearable, but the end will justify the means. Maybe I'll destroy his family. Maybe I'll set him up for embezzlement. Maybe I'll kill him.

I'll find what's most important to him and then I'll take it away. However that plays out is fine with me.

CHAPTER 9

I've never killed anyone. I'm not that kind of sociopath. But you never know. Desperate times . . .

CHAPTER 10

Steven promised a hole-in-the-wall and he delivered. It's a little Italian restaurant on a side street in downtown Minneapolis that's either going to serve the most amazing food I've ever had or food that will reveal why this place is slowly dying.

To ensure I look eager to please, I arrive early. The tables are topped with honest-to-God Chianti bottles dripping with old candle wax. The host leads me to a tiny table and pulls out my chair before lighting the candle on our bottle. I ask for a glass of water and sit primly.

I wrote back to Cheryl before leaving my apartment. I told her I was doing well aside from missing Meg. I didn't mention Minneapolis. Cheryl lives in Duluth now, and it would be an easy drive if I wanted to visit. I don't. But I ask how she's holding up and whether there's anything I can do for her. I don't tell her that the terrible example she set as a mother helped lead to Meg's death. Even I am not that cruel. She has enough guilt to carry. So do I.

Meg committed suicide. She became so hopeless and broken that she killed herself, so we're all to blame. Any one of us could have saved her, given the right timing.

But I wasn't here, was I? I'd only returned to Minneapolis once in the past two years. If I'd come back more often, would she still be alive?

What if I'd called more regularly? What if I'd been more empathetic, caring, human?

It had been a struggle to understand Meg's problems, yes, but I'd tried. I swear I had. Still, patience is not my virtue. Nor is sympathy. Maybe I was her weakest link. Maybe her mother deserves none of my anger and I deserve all of it. I've never experienced regret before, but I do now. Missing Meg for the rest of my life will be my penance.

We were both thirty when she killed herself, and she'll be thirty forever now. I will age and age and age without her.

Would I take her place if I could? Well, hell. I'm not given to selflessness, but I think I might. There's no hope for me, after all. I'm not going to someday blossom into a happy, whole person. But there was hope for Meg.

Or maybe there was no hope at all. Maybe she was destined to marry shitty men and put her children through divorce after divorce and boyfriend after boyfriend. My life will be less destructive than that.

Still, I wish I could bring her back.

Melancholy is draping over me like a spiderweb that drifted in on the breeze, and if Steven doesn't get here soon, I'm going to break character and order a carafe of table wine. If I'm quick, maybe I can drink it all before he arrives.

No such luck. Behind me I hear his loud, over-friendly greeting for the host. The host responds just as loudly. Everyone loves Steven! This could be a hilarious sitcom.

I stand and turn awkwardly to wait for him, as if I'm nervous. I'm probably overdoing this, but my instinct says to behave exactly the opposite of how I'd normally interact with a man. So far it's working.

"Jane!"

He walks over quickly and gives me a long hug. Too long. I'm very proud of myself for not shoving him onto his ass. I'm not a hugger.

"You look gorgeous," he whispers into my ear just as he's pulling back. The anger in my cheeks looks like a blush.

"It's just my work clothes," I protest.

"You always look gorgeous." I can see how women fall for him. He's attentive.

"You drink red wine, I hope?" he asks as we both sit down.

"Not often."

He ignores that and calls out to the host for a bottle of his favorite red. That's when I realize this is a place he brings people so he can show off. Be the big man. It's perfect.

"I'm glad you came," he says.

"Did you think I'd chicken out?"

"You did seem pretty nervous."

"I *am* nervous. I can't afford to lose this job."

"Don't worry about it. Come on. No one really cares. As far as I know, nobody's ever been disciplined for interoffice dating. It's fine."

"Do you think so?"

He reaches across the table to take my hand and tug it closer. "Trust me."

His smile is meant to reassure me, but his words have the opposite effect. Why would I trust a man I'd just met? It's a warning sign that he'd even *ask* me to. I give his hand a little squeeze as if I need someone to hold on to. When a waiter appears with a menu, I act embarrassed to have been caught in an intimate moment.

I fully expect the waiter to hand the menu to Steven so he can order for both of us, but he hands it to me instead. Steven winks. "I already know what I'm getting. Everything is good, by the way. You can't make a bad choice."

Oh, what a relief.

The waiter arrives. I order spaghetti Bolognese and my mouth waters at the thought of it. Please let this place be a hidden gem. This relationship doesn't have to be all work and no play. I may as well enjoy what I can.

Garlic bread arrives. Honest-to-goodness hot, toasted garlic bread, and in that moment the future bad sex with Steven is all worth it. I grab a piece of bread, close my eyes, and bite.

"It's good, right?" he asks.

"Oh my gosh, it's so good."

His smile lights up his whole face and I see his charm on full display. I see what someone could love about him if they didn't look too closely. Sometimes I wish I didn't always look so closely. I wish I could lose myself like other people do. But there's no point in wishing for something that can never be. It's a waste of energy.

"Is everything this good here?" I ask.

"Everything."

"Then thank you for bringing me."

The host brings a bottle of wine and pours us each a modest glass. Maybe I'll walk here by myself one evening after work so I can overindulge in everything, but tonight I take a small sip. Patience. Self-control. The payoff will be worth it.

"Tell me about your family," he says.

"You've heard most of it. I grew up with my mom. My dad wasn't in the picture. My grandparents died recently, but I used to stay with them during the summer so Mom could work. And you know . . . I hated it then, but now I'm glad I got to spend so much time with them." An acquaintance had once told me this story.

I had a grandmother, but she was mean and drunk most of the time. She had a weakness for Twinkies, though, and I appreciated the supply whenever my family dropped by her house to beg for money.

"So you went to high school here?"

"Only for three years, but for some reason it feels like home. That was the most stable time of my life, I guess." I made sure to lose my Okie accent in college, so he'll never guess my real roots. "What about your family? It sounds like you're really close."

"Absolutely. Well, to be clear . . . I'm close to my dad. My mom left when I was fifteen. It got pretty ugly."

"Oh no."

"She cheated on him," he says tightly, and I have to stop my grin. Jackpot.

Instead of laughing, I whisper, "I'm sorry."

One of his shoulders rises in a jerky shrug. "My dad is a pastor, so you can imagine how humiliating it was for him."

And you, I think.

So his dad is a saint and his mom is a whore. If I were a normal person, I'd feel sorry for him. Nothing good ever comes of an ugly divorce. But I'm not a normal person and I know the kind of adult he's become, so I feel nothing but contempt.

Regardless, I reach for him. His hand is tight beneath my touch. "It must have been awful."

"Yeah."

"Are you on good terms with her now?"

His lip lifts in a small sneer, but he shrugs again. "We're fine. I got over it." Even the most trusting person could spot that lie, and I trust no one. He hates his mother. Not a good prospect in a boyfriend.

He flips his fist over and engulfs my fingers in his grip. "Anyway, that's all in the past. My dad and I are still close. I go to his church every Sunday. I do some work for him. My brother has two great kids, and I love being an uncle."

"So do you want kids of your own?"

"Someday." He winks as if he's handed me a little treat. I'll tuck it in my pocket and put it in my Big Book of Dreams when I get home.

"Where is your dad's church? Is it big?"

He tells me about United in Christ Church as I do away with another piece of garlic bread. The place is out in the white-bread suburb of Apple Valley, where the Christians have money.

"It's grown quite a bit lately. The world is chaotic. People are coming back to God. We've got almost twenty-five hundred members now."

"That's huge. And you work there?"

"I'm a deacon."

"Wow. I didn't think there were any good guys around anymore."

He swallows that hook, line, and sinker. He knows he's a good guy because he goes to church. It doesn't matter how he treats people. It doesn't matter if he's cruel. He's a God-fearing man, so he's *good.* I swallow my anger down with my wine. He refills my glass without asking. Flushed from temper and alcohol, I take off my cardigan.

Today my bra is lavender lace and it peeks up above the last straining button of my dress. Steven has finished his glass of wine too, and he can't stop his eyes from dropping. And staying. He might fear God, but he still loves boobs, and I know for a fact that he's a big believer in fornication.

Our salads arrive and he digs in with gusto.

The nice thing about bad men is they're easy to manipulate. If he were truly a good guy, I'd be lost. How could I know what motivates nice people? How would I get him to do what I want? But this isn't a matter of hoping Steven notices me and wants to start a relationship. I'm good at manipulation because I've had to study and learn how people behave.

Before I knew what was wrong with me, I felt like an alien. I didn't fit in anywhere with anyone. It was typical teenage angst . . . except I honestly didn't fit in. I was so damn alone.

The first time my brother was sent to prison, I was sixteen, and I still remember my deep, disturbing confusion at the emotional reaction of my family. My mom wailed about how unfair it all was and that the system was rigged and he would never get a decent job now. My father actually cried for his "baby boy." Wept like a child. My grandmother threw in a couple of racial epithets and complaints that a hardworking white boy couldn't get anywhere these days.

It was all complete nonsense. He'd *deserved* to go to prison. He'd finally gotten caught selling stolen goods out of the back of his raggedy truck, and—lucky for him—he was only doing time for what he'd been caught with and not the hundreds of other things he'd stolen and sold over the years. Everyone knew white people got the best breaks in the criminal justice system. He'd gotten way less time than he should have.

Plus he was a lazy asshole and always had been, and a decent job had never been in his future.

So why the grief and surprise?

When I pointed out that he was, in fact, guilty and deserved to do time, my grandma called me a nasty little bitch. I'd heard it before, of course, usually from my mother. A nasty, cold-blooded, selfish, grasping, uppity, ungrateful goddamn little bitch. And I knew that to be true. I could feel the coldness in my own veins.

What was wrong with me? Why couldn't I be normal? Like any other teenage girl, I just wanted to fit in. I hadn't been good at faking it back then because I hadn't understood what I was trying to fake: a soul.

My senior year of high school, I took psychology as an elective, and boom, there it was. A description of me right in our textbook. That first time I read about sociopaths, I felt filled up with a bright light that was equal parts terror and joy. Finally—*finally!*—I understood. It was scary to know the truth, yes, but not nearly as frightening as ignorance.

I didn't feel doubt. I didn't feel guilt. And empathy was mostly beyond my grasp.

Of course, that was the golden age of serial killer true crime books, and for a while I thought being a sociopath meant I was destined for an existence of psychopathic evil. I thought it was the inevitable progression of my life. After all, I'd slept with my married English teacher and felt not one ounce of regret despite that his wife was my very kind calculus teacher. He, on the other hand, had sobbed with shame and guilt. *Afterward*, of course. Always afterward. Erections and guilt can't exist in the same plane. One makes way for the other.

I'd watched him weeping, his penis flaccid and wet, and I'd thought, *Well, that was my first act of true evil.* I'd seduced my teacher just because I hated the homework so much and I wanted to blackmail him into an A. I figured I was heading into serial killer territory soon. I set my next-door neighbor's pet rabbit free in the woods, because I was sure I'd wake up one morning tempted to kill it. I wanted to put off my degeneration as long as possible.

But, happily, later research at the county library assured me that most people like me don't grow up to be killers. We lie and manipulate and take advantage, but usually that just makes us great at business. Yay for capitalism.

From then on, I worked on navigating my way through life with this . . . disability. I even learned to appreciate my affliction, to see the decency of living with logic instead of being buffeted by the whims of a fickle heart.

I've felt different my whole life, because I am. Still, I'm not as different as you'd think. There are a lot of us. More than I even realized back then. Most of us are just trying to get through the day, like aliens living secretly among humans. And we're great for the economy. It's easy to turn a profit when you have no self-doubt.

"You're a healthy eater," Steven says. He could be complimenting that I've eaten all my greens, but he isn't. He means I'm keeping up with him.

"Thanks," I respond.

He laughs in surprise at that, and then our entrées arrive, and, boy, I'm going to health the heck out of that plate. The Bolognese smells amazing, and I'm suddenly thankful for this night with Steven. The waiter adds Parmesan with a flourish, and Steven watches as I take my first bite.

Oh my God, it's perfect. He grins at my happy groan and I relax into the pleasure.

He mentions judo, and I know if a grown man is practicing martial arts, it's important to him, so I ask questions and let him talk about it for a full half an hour to make him feel important. I don't mention that I've seen elite karate and jujitsu matches all over Asia. It's not something I'm interested in; it's just part of business networking there.

By the end of the meal, I'm stuffed, half-drunk, and thinking the best ending to the night would be sex. Hell, I'd even go for sex with Steven at this point. He's been entirely pleasant, but pleasant or not, sleeping with him now would be a tactical error. He'll lose all respect for me. I'll just be the slut at the office who puts out too easily. He'll avoid me. He won't invite me over. He won't be vulnerable.

I need him vulnerable.

I could have just gotten rid of him, of course. I could have flown into town, poisoned him, shot him, stabbed him, whatever, and been on my way, a complete stranger with no connection to the crime. The perfect murder.

But I want to hurt him in the worst way possible. Death, after all, is one moment in time. But what if I can find a way for him to live in misery for years? I need to get closer to find out his weakest point, and if I have sex with him now, I'll be trash.

Women have to worry about that kind of bullshit when they're dating *and* when they're plotting a crime. Hardly seems fair, does it?

Oh, well. I've already decided Steven won't be good in bed, so I play coy even as I giggle drunkenly at his flirting. He's sure he has a chance tonight. I'm tipsy and I'm wearing a lacy bra and I'm on the rebound. He thinks he can get in my pants, which means he'll want it even more when I don't put out.

Steven throws some twenties on the table, then stands up to pull out my chair. He even helps me back into my sweater. His hands smooth over my shoulders and squeeze my arms. "I'll give you a ride home," he murmurs into my ear.

I loop my arm through his as we walk out the door of the restaurant and into the cool night. The gorgeous scent of dead leaves wraps around us on the breeze. I shiver and tuck myself a little closer to his body warmth, and I'm more than willing to let him wrap his arm around my shoulders for the sake of comfort. His cologne swamps the delicate smell of autumn, but I can still hear the dry leaves shaking overhead.

Fall is my favorite season. It reminds me of myself, all hollow and cool. And despite the dying crispness of it, people still find it beautiful. Maybe they could feel that way about me too.

I think I had too much wine.

He opens the passenger door of a big silver SUV that looks as if it's never touched mud. For a moment after he closes the door I'm alone, and I want to open the glove compartment and look for a sign or a clue of who's been here before. A hair clip. A lipstick tube. Maybe even an actual glove. But then he's opening the driver's-side door and I'm smiling at him again.

"My place is only a mile away," I say before I give him directions. The seat heater kicks in quickly, and now I'm cozy and tipsy and full of good food and I can't wait to get home and go to sleep. I don't like cuddling, but a warm body would be nice right now. Not Steven, though.

Maybe I should get a cat.

The thought invades my head fully formed and utterly obvious. A cat. Another little sociopath to curl up beside me at night and keep me warm.

The idea is a sudden, desperate need in me. And it's an awful idea. I won't be here long, my apartment doesn't allow pets, and I'm heading out of the country after this. But I'm terrible at denying myself what I want, and I'm already wondering where the nearest animal shelter is.

"Right here?" Steven asks, and I realize we're on my street.

I point to my run-down 1920s apartment building. "This one."

"I'll walk you up," he says as he pulls to the curb.

I'm irritated that I have to stop making plans for my new cat and pay attention to him again, but I wait like a nice, patient girl as he walks around to open my door.

He walks me up the stoop, waiting while I unlock the main door with an old-fashioned metal key. There must be hundreds of these floating around. I can't imagine when they last bothered changing the locks. I glance at him. "Thank you for walking me up."

"I'll take you to your door. This doesn't look like the best neighborhood."

"You don't have to."

But he holds the door open and follows me into the dingy lobby and past the mailboxes to the stairs beyond. My place is on the second floor, right at the top of the stairs. I've heard it's better to be farther from the entry for security reasons, but I like watching my unsuspecting neighbors come and go through the peephole. The woman three doors down is an old barfly who brings home a different drunk codger every night, and she's my favorite. Everyone needs a hobby, and I'm glad she's found hers.

But tonight I'm the scandal in the hallway. I stop at my door. "This is me."

"Must be noisy here by the stairs."

I let him get his dig in. Yes, I was too stupid or poor or weak to demand a better apartment. Another barely noticeable insult to grind me down, but I know his game and I hear exactly what he means.

"Thanks for dinner," I murmur shyly. "It was really, really good."

"I had an amazing time. You're a fun girl."

But how much fun? That's the question.

He moves closer and tips my head up with a gentle nudge. I let him kiss me. He's not bad at it. Careful but firm. Not asking so much as suggesting. His tongue slips quickly in, claiming my mouth. I settle in against my door and try to enjoy it.

He's already excited. Excited that I'm *letting* him. His fingers curve around my waist and grip me. He's breathing harder, kissing me more deeply, sliding his tongue in a suggestive rhythm over mine.

I pull back a little and pretend to be breathless too.

"Maybe I should come in," he whispers against my mouth.

I shake my head.

"I don't mean that. We can have a drink."

"No. I . . . I can't."

He growls a little and presses his hips to mine. "God, you're so damn hot." His mouth is wet on my throat now, his erection poking my stomach. I breathe with little panting sighs that make me sound helpless.

His hand slides up to palm my breast and he groans. I was eleven the first time I let a boy touch my breasts. I was so ready for it, and then when it happened I thought, *That's it? That's what I was waiting for? It feels like he's honking a horn.* Such a letdown after all those stolen copies of *Penthouse Forum*.

Steven's technique isn't much better. He's rubbing and squeezing and getting mostly padded bra. I let him go on for a little while before I finally say "No" and push him gently away. "I can't do this. It isn't right."

"It feels pretty right," he says with a sly smile.

"What kind of girl would I be if I slept with you on our first date?"

We both know the answer to that.

If we were already in my apartment, he'd push harder, of course. Here on the landing he has no choice but to give in gracefully, so he chuckles and tries to pretend his face isn't flushed with lust. "I know. But what kind of guy would I be if I didn't try?"

In deference to my role, I don't answer "A born-again Christian with sincere beliefs and a genuine respect for women?" but it's a close one. Instead, I ask, "Will you call me this weekend?" and give him a little power back.

"Yeah, if I can. Weekends are pretty busy."

"Sure. Well, I had a good time. Thank you again."

He winks and gives a little wave as he backs away. I open my door and slip inside and feel confident we'll be going out again soon.

CHAPTER 11

The nearest animal shelter is twelve blocks away, but it's a gorgeous day for a walk, so I set off with enthusiasm. I've never had a pet before. Oh, my family cycled through a couple of mangy guard dogs chained in the front yard, but they were vicious and flea-ridden. Just another dreary part of my childhood landscape.

My future hasn't become any more solid, but my determination has. I want a cat. And when it's time to move back to Malaysia, I'll deal with the issue then. It isn't a real problem yet.

I pass close to the Italian place and make a detour thinking I can stop in later, but they're not open for lunch. The neighborhood deteriorates further as I approach the shelter. I'm entering a quasi-industrial zone near the railroad tracks, and there aren't many pedestrians around. I'm just considering reaching for my pocketknife when I see the shelter sign ahead and perk up. I can already hear dogs barking.

The parking lot is small and nearly full. Saturday must be a busy day for this place. As soon as I enter, I'm in the middle of two families with kids who are here to pick out dogs. I weave my way through their jumpy little bodies and approach the counter.

"I'm looking for a cat."

The clerk is a pale young man who looks like he suffered a terrible haircut nine months ago and decided to never try again. He finishes writing something on a paper and sighs. "You're looking for a cat you've lost?"

"No, I'd like to adopt a cat."

"Okay. Cats are through there." He points without once looking up at me. He's being rude, so I steal a tiny metal dog figurine from the edge of his tall desk. I don't want it; I just don't like his attitude.

Turning in the direction he indicated, I push through the glass door, and the sounds of dogs and little kids fade to a low roar when the door closes behind me. I expect tiny cages, and there are lots of those, but most of the cats are portioned into group living for the day. Five or six cats wander rooms filled with carpeted trees to climb or sleep on. They don't look miserable. Most seem perfectly content. Like me, they don't need constant human contact.

I walk up and down the hallway, noticing which cats immediately rush to the gates and meow. They're cute, but they are not the cats for me.

A small black cat sticks its paw through the metal grating, reaching for me. I touch the tiny pink pads of her foot, but then I move on down the short hallway. At the next partition, two cats are waiting for me. Two are asleep. The fifth cat watches from the middle of the floor, her golden eyes meeting my gaze with a haughty coolness. I like her immediately. I know I'm anthropomorphizing, but I'm sure she's female because of the regal stretch of her neck and the occasional elegant flick of her tail. She has short gray fur that looks tipped with silver. There's no question her body will be a soft, warm comfort.

I watch her. She watches me. She blinks slowly. Looks away. Then she yawns as if she's bored with the whole situation. I grin at the way she stretches her body long and hard before rising to her feet to approach me.

Instead of coming all the way to the grate, she sits down six inches away. I press my fingers to the metal and she stretches out to smell my skin. After a moment's investigation, she rubs her cheek against my fingertips in one quick stroke, then settles back on her haunches as if the interview is over.

She's marked me, but she doesn't need me.

I want her with all the fullness of my dark and twisted heart.

A door opens at the far end of the hall and a young Hispanic woman with a bouncy black ponytail rolls a mop pail into the space. Her name tag just says VOLUNTEER. "Hello! Did you want to see one of the cats?"

"I've found one I like. This gray one."

The girl ditches her mop and hurries over. "Oh, that's Bunny! She's gorgeous."

Bunny? Good God, the indignity this poor queen has suffered.

"Have you filled out the adoption paperwork?" she asks. When I shake my head, she claps her hands. "Then let's get you started!"

Started? How much paperwork is involved in taking home a cat that no one else wants?

A lot, apparently. The paperwork isn't a problem. I had to set up this false identity to get a job, and I kept it close enough to my true information that everything is easy to recall. The background check won't show anything suspicious, but I'm intensely irritated that I can't take the cat home right now. She's mine.

But, mine or not, I have to wait until tomorrow so they can be sure I'm not running an international stray cat smuggling ring, I guess. I do my very best to act grateful for their careful stewardship when I just want to shove past this woman to grab my cat and go.

I pay $35 and tell myself this delay will give me a chance to buy what I need. The shelter has a printed sheet for what a "Good Cat Owner" should have on hand. They don't have a handout for a "Bad Cat Owner," so I take the offered paper and push through the exit door, hoping my cat won't change her mind about me by tomorrow.

According to my phone, there's a small pet store just a quick detour from the path home, so I head in that direction. The route takes me out of the way of the Italian restaurant and down a little tree-lined street where gentrification has crept in. Lots of people are eating brunch at outdoor café tables nestled under propane heaters.

I stop to gaze wistfully through a boutique window at a pair of black leather boots I'd love to own, but this Jane isn't a knee-high, stiletto-heeled-boot kind of girl. Well, she might be that kind of girl in the bedroom if Steven tells her to slut it up a little and stop being such a cold fish all the time. But we won't be together long enough to reach that point.

I'm busy imagining which of my old outfits would go best with these boots when I hear a man say my name. My actual name, including my real surname—not the fake one I'm currently using.

"Jane?" he calls more loudly. "Is that you?"

I'm so startled that I turn toward the voice instead of pretending not to hear. Damn it.

"Hey!" he says.

A man is approaching from a few doors down. He's white, about my age, brown hair, average height. He extends his hand as if he's trying to get my attention or stop my flight. I don't recognize him until he smiles. That's when I know him.

My kind aren't easily alarmed, but I definitely feel surprised. "Luke?"

"It *is* you!" he says, seeming more delighted to see me than anyone else ever has been.

"Yes," I say. "Hi." His friendliness has cast me into an uncertainty I'm not used to. Luke is an old friend. Or something like that. We dated for a couple of months in college, just before I left Minneapolis for a summer internship before law school. I liked him just fine then, though I haven't thought of him since. But now here he is.

He gathers me into a hug and I return the embrace even as I blink rapidly in confusion. It feels like I've been flung back into my past.

"What are you doing here?" he asks as he sets me back on my heels.

"Here? I just adopted a cat."

He laughs. "No, I mean here in *Minneapolis*!"

"Oh. I . . . I'm working on a temporary project."

"Temporary?"

"Yeah. I won't be in town long."

"Long enough to grab a drink, I hope."

I shouldn't. It's not smart. If my stay here ends badly, Luke can identify me. But he was always going to be able to identify me, it seems. I may as well be friendly and get him on my side. Maybe I can earn his loyalty.

"Actually"—he swipes a hand through his hair as if he's nervous—"how about lunch right now? I'd love to catch up."

I should say no and walk away and hope he has short-term-memory issues. I can't form any real connections while I'm here. Not that I ever form real connections. No one is ever thrilled to see me now that Meg is gone. No one wants to catch up. But Luke does. Which is . . . an odd experience for me. But he was the nicest guy I ever dated, so maybe warm and welcoming is his default.

He's not a very good judge of character, obviously. But, unwise or not, I suddenly want to have lunch with him, and I always do what I want.

"I'd love to, actually," I say, and his face lights up. Nobody has looked at me like that since the last time I saw Meg. My throat tightens in a strange way.

"The place on the corner is one of my favorites," he suggests. "We could sit outside and enjoy the nice weather."

I'd just been walking past people sitting outside with friends and enjoying the day, and now I'll be one of them. I nod, trying to swallow the strange obstruction in my throat, and we turn toward the corner.

"So you said you just adopted a cat?"

"Yes. A terrible idea when I'm here temporarily, but I couldn't resist."

"Why should you? It's a noble cause. When do you get to pick it up?"

"Tomorrow. I wanted to take her home today, but I guess this will give me time to buy everything I need."

"You always were good at quick decisions."

I smile at his wording. That's the nicest way anyone has ever said it. "I think you mean I'm impulsive."

Luke shrugs. "Let's just agree that you know your own mind."

I laugh. Genuinely laugh. And I remember how much I liked him in college. He was funny. And he was decent in bed. I thought he was naïve, of course. Time hasn't toughened him up much. Meg was like that too. Always seeing the good in people, even when she shouldn't. *Especially* when she shouldn't.

Luke leads us to the outdoor hostess station and the woman greets him with surprise. "Hey, welcome back!"

Luke's cheeks tinge with pink. "I met a friend here for coffee earlier," he explains.

"Oh," I drawl. "A lady friend?"

"Yes, but not a *girl*friend."

"Such a player." I sigh and shake my head at the hostess, and the color in Luke's cheeks deepens when we both laugh.

"Come on, player," the woman says, grabbing two menus before leading us to a little wrought-iron table.

We sit and she hands us the menus, and my mouth is already watering at the breakfast selections. I like food more than people.

Luke clears his throat. "I honestly wasn't here on a date."

He's very eager to make that clear. I drop the menu a little and stare at him over it. "Are you saying you're still single, Luke?"

"Not *still* single. I mean, I'm not in a relationship right now, but I have been. Obviously." He shakes his head and mutters, "Jesus," and I'm laughing again. Then he's laughing at himself, a self-deprecating chuckle, and I'm struck by how absolutely different he is from Steven.

I didn't miss him when I left Minneapolis. I had an internship to complete and then I was going to law school, so that was that. But I feel happy to be sitting with him now.

"So what did you do after college?" I ask.

"I went straight into IT."

"No reason not to in this economy."

"Exactly. I decided I could always go back for a master's later. But, to be honest, I haven't thought much about it since. Too busy."

A waiter brings us water and I order a latte, then fall silent to look at the menu. It never takes me long to decide, and I know immediately that I'll have the French toast and bacon. In general, I do what I want and worry about consequences later. If I gain more weight than I like, I start a workout regimen, but it's usually not a problem. I don't stress-eat or try to smother pain with food. Whatever pain I have I ignore until it goes away. I tried that for months after Meg. It didn't work.

"What about you?" Luke asks. "What did you do after law school?"

"I jumped right into trade law. I've been overseas for a few years. Malaysia."

"Wow! Now I feel provincial. I never left Minneapolis."

"Honestly, it's still one of my favorite places." I spent four good years here. And my soul lived here with Meg.

The waiter appears to take our orders, and then Luke and I study each other for a moment.

"You're really only here temporarily?" he asks.

"I'm doing work on a confidential contract." The lie comes easily to me, as they always do. "A merger with lots of moving parts overseas. I'm not sure how long it will take. A couple months at most."

"Well," he says as his cheeks color again, "I'll just jump right in, then. Are you single?"

I'm about to say yes when I realize this is a problem. If he's going to ask me out—and he is—I can't be seen in a romantic situation with him. And there's still that little issue of how my plans will culminate and whether I'll need to flee an investigation.

He's watching with one raised brow, his gaze direct and patient. Shit.

"I am dating someone," I answer.

"Oh."

"Not exclusively."

He smiles. "Oh."

"It's complicated," I add, but he doesn't care. I've made clear that I'm open to something and he'll take that. He's a man. "Why are you so interested?" I challenge him with a small smile, just to see how he'll react.

"Because," he answers, "you're the one who got away."

I almost choke on my latte. He's surprised me again. "What? Me?"

"Yes."

"Like a fish that escaped?"

"No!" He shakes his head hard. "No, not like that. I just liked you a lot, and then you were gone."

I honestly had no idea I was anything special to him. As far as I can remember, we dated for about two months, we both knew I was leaving, and we said goodbye with little fanfare. "Really?" I press.

"Really really."

I stare at him. I don't like knowing that I missed signals, even if they wouldn't have meant much to me at the time. But as I study his face, I remember that he made a couple of jokes about long-distance relationships and I ignored them. What's the point of a boyfriend if you can't have sex?

He winces at my continued silence. "And now I'm getting the idea you didn't feel the same connection." When I smile, he laughs again, easy and unperturbed.

"No, it's not that I didn't like you," I say, "but I was moving, so I guess I never thought of it as something long term."

"I get that. Maybe that was what made you so appealing to a twenty-two-year-old guy. You were elusive. Unattainable."

I laugh at that. "If I remember correctly, you attained me quite a few times."

The joke wasn't that funny, but he laughs until tears leak from his eyes. I remember he always had a way of making me feel special. Or the opposite of special, maybe: just *normal.*

"So you're not seeing anyone?" I ask, even though I don't particularly care one way or the other.

"No one serious," he answers, and I know I can have him if I want. And I might want. He's a nice palate cleanser after spending time with Steven.

We fall into a comfortable conversation, reminiscing about our college days. We're just digging into our food when he asks how Meg is doing.

"She died," I say before I remember I'm supposed to soften it up.

His fork clatters against the plate. "What?"

"Meg died. In February."

"But . . . how?"

"She killed herself."

His face has drained of color, and I slowly set my fork down because if I take another bite that would seem callous. I feel genuine grief, but it's muffled in a way that others wouldn't understand. It's there, but I can always function just fine.

"My God," Luke whispers. "Were you still in touch with her?"

"Yes. She was my best friend."

"Jane, I'm so, so sorry."

He's the only person I've told. No one else would have cared. But he knew Meg, and he knew what she meant to me. "She took pills," I say, though he didn't ask.

"I'm sorry. I didn't know. You must be . . ." But Luke doesn't know how to finish that sentence, and I can't finish it either. I'm not sure what

I must be. In pain, yes. Lonely. But angry too. Vengeful. And always, always cold. I'll go on with my life; there's no question of that. I'll be fine. But everything has shifted.

"That's how I ended up here," I say, and that small part is the truth, at least. "I just . . . I needed a change. When I saw an opportunity in Minneapolis, I took it as a sign."

"I'm so sorry you lost her."

Lost her? Did I lose her? It's more like she made herself disappear. I know exactly where she is. She's *not here*. And that was what she wanted. Should I even be sad about her when she got her wish?

I pick up my fork and dig into the French toast again before it gets cold. It belatedly occurs to me that I should have cried or broken down in some way, but it's too late now, and frankly Luke seems relieved.

"She was so kind," he says after a minute of silence. "I should send flowers to her grave."

It makes no sense to me. Meg won't know the difference. But I tell him the name of the cemetery, because I've learned to keep thoughts like that to myself. There are so many human rituals I don't understand.

My grandmother died when I was twenty, and I managed not to tell my mother she'd be better off using the funeral money on anything aside from putting a corpse in the ground. Groceries, car repairs, bail money for my worthless brother. Hell, she could even have contributed one goddamn dollar to my education instead of throwing money at a dead harridan.

While I managed not to tell my mother, I did spill my contempt for the burial rites to the funeral home director. I told him we should just cremate the body and get it over with. His mask of polite respect slipped for a moment to reveal arrogance and revulsion, but I wasn't the one bilking grief-stricken idiots out of thousands of dollars. Of course, the joke was on him. The check bounced, and Grandma was already embalmed and interred. No taking that back.

"Are you okay?" Luke asks, and I am. But now I'm thinking about Meg dead and decaying in the ground, and I don't want to think about that. I didn't come home for the funeral. There was no point. I would've felt nothing but selfish rage. I didn't want to see her strange, rubbery face in the casket. I didn't want to see her being lowered into dirt.

Now I'm thinking about it even though I was so careful to avoid it. I don't want this.

"Do you live nearby?" I ask suddenly.

"In St. Paul. It's not too far. A condo on the river."

"Can we go there?"

"Go there?" He's confused, a puzzled half smile on his mouth.

"Yes," I say. "Now."

And he gets it then. His eyes flare wide, his lips part. He doesn't answer.

"Do you live with someone?"

"No, of course not. It's just . . . I mean . . ."

I shrug one shoulder. "Just for old times' sake?"

"Jane." I'm not sure if he's scolding me or just reminding himself of my name. It makes no difference to me. I watch him the way my cat watched me today. I want what I want when I want it. He leans back a little, trying to figure me out.

"Come on, player," I finally drawl, and Luke smiles. Then he laughs. "My car's around the corner."

And that's all the answer I need.

CHAPTER 12

The boy has learned a thing or two since college. He had been fine, but now he's *good.* He took me enthusiastically—just what I needed. Then he went down on me and worked us both up to another round.

"I am *so* glad I ran into you," he says breathlessly as the sweat cools on our skin. He seems to remember that I don't like to cuddle afterward and settles for splaying one hand on my hip. I don't even mind. In fact, I kind of like it.

"That was slightly better than shopping for cat litter."

His low, satisfied rumble of laughter shakes the bed. I stretch hard and then rise naked to walk to the row of windows overlooking the river. I know he's watching my ass, the sway of my hips. I like that. Men love a show and I love an audience. I stretch again, half hoping someone on the street is watching too.

"You're sexy as hell," he says. Lots of men have said this to me. They like a woman with no shame. We're rare, you see, because we're told to be ashamed of everything every day by everyone. Ashamed to give them what they want, ashamed not to want to give it to them. Ashamed to show our average bodies, ashamed not to have a perfect one. I have no idea how normal women date. The world seems like it'd be an unbearable place for people with real feelings.

But it's simpler for me, so I watch a sailboat skim the water below and wonder when Luke will be up for another round. Probably not for hours, sadly.

"I should go," I murmur.

I hear the bed shift, the sheets rustling. "I'll drive you."

"No, I'll grab a car."

"I can drop you at the pet store," he offers.

I shake my head and turn to watch him pull on his jeans. "Better not. It's complicated."

"Ah. Right."

"Can I get your number, though?"

"Yes. Can I get yours?"

Better if he doesn't have it, but I'm riding a mellow wave of satisfaction, and I know I'll want to do this again. "Okay, but text instead of call. I'm in meetings a lot."

That's bullshit and he knows it, but he doesn't protest. Of course he doesn't. He'll screw me at least a few more times before he decides to press the issue. Why look a gift whore in the mouth?

I order my car, then dress slowly, letting him watch. I'm glad I'm not wearing one of those stupid flowery dresses today. The lavender bra looks nice, though. I'll wear it again on Monday so Steven can leer at it while I remember another man stripping it off me with rough lust.

"That's a naughty smile," Luke says.

"Yes," I answer.

My car arrives in no time, and Luke kisses my mouth and reminds me to call him. I'm sure I will. I want what I want when I want it. I carry my naughty smile with me all the way across the river. Maybe I'll call him tomorrow. Maybe I'll have sex with Luke while Steven is at church pretending to be a good man.

A new lover and a cat. This was quite a worthwhile Saturday.

I'm just leaving the pet store with two giant bags of goodies when I get a text. I'm half hoping it's Luke asking if he can see me again tonight, so I set my purchases down on the street and dig out my phone.

No luck. It's Steven, stepping in to ruin my lovely day. I sigh at the sight of his name, but it's honestly a good thing it's not Luke. I know myself, and if he's too eager, I won't want him anymore. Still, I'm a little disappointed. I'm even more disappointed when I open the actual text.

Are you up for church tomorrow?

The least arousing words I've ever read. Thank God he's not here to see my expression.

At your church? I respond. I don't have a car.

I'll pick you up. 8 AM.

This is exactly what I need to happen, but I'm highly irritated that he's interfering with what I want. If not another round with Luke, I could at least pick up my cat. But the shelter doesn't open until noon, and going to church with Steven is a huge step in the right direction.

I didn't put out, so I might be worthy of more. Going to church will bring us closer together, and I need him close.

I roll my eyes as I text back a bright-eyed smiley face. That would be great! I can't wait!

And I can't. Now that I've set my more immediate impulses aside, I'm excited.

I can't wait to meet his family. His friends. To bathe myself in his most sacred beliefs. Tomorrow he'll be in his element, and I'll find out firsthand what Steven Hepsworth holds dear.

Then I'll figure out how to take it all away from him.

CHAPTER 13

I didn't pay much attention to her new boyfriend at first. Meg was always gaga over new boyfriends. I just asked how they were in bed and I moved on.

She would eventually get married, but it didn't matter to me which man became her husband as long as he helped complete the fantasy I had for Meg's future family. The sooner Meg got married and had kids, the sooner I could pretend I belonged too.

She dated the new guy for three months. It was a whirlwind romance, they were already talking marriage, and then they broke up. I barely registered it. He told her she was immature and unstable. I told her he was shitty and mean. He was.

When they got back together a week later, I said, *As long as he's good in bed.* She laughed it off. She was so happy.

A month later she called me, sobbing. Her boyfriend had told her he'd never have kids with her because she would be a terrible, worthless mother. I honestly didn't understand her tears, because this was a ridiculous insult. Meg wasn't terrible or worthless.

She might be a little flighty and she was definitely too trusting, but Meg was amazing with kids. Caring, kind, supportive. But she somehow bought into his bullshit, because, despite her degree in English, she was still working as a waitress and she occasionally drank too much at clubs.

"He's an asshole," I said. "Be relieved that you're seeing this now and walk away." It seemed simple enough to me.

He asked her to move in a month later. She did.

This was a secret, of course. He wanted her there and available twenty-four hours a day, but he didn't want his family or church to know that he was a sinner. I mean, that was Meg's fault anyway for putting out, wasn't it?

I told her she was being stupid. I actually told her that. "Don't be stupid, Meg. This guy is a dick." She told me he was a great guy and I should be happy for her; then she made an excuse to get off the phone.

We didn't speak for three weeks. I was secretly relieved when she called, sobbing again, to tell me he'd kicked her out. She was homeless and heartbroken and all I could think was *Thank God that's over*.

It wasn't over. Not by a long shot. Steven Hepsworth had found a hot girl who'd put up with his abuse, and he was just getting started.

CHAPTER 14

Today my flowery dress is buttoned up and my bosom is further shielded by a cardigan. Today is not a day for seducing Steven; it's a day to observe and learn.

He arrives at eight, and even though I'm ready, I ask if he can wait in the hallway for one minute; then I close the door and move frantically around my apartment, as if I'm running behind. Three minutes later I rush through the door and apologize several times for my tardiness. "I'm sorry. I hit my snooze button too many times!"

"Never use a snooze button," he instructs. "It signals your brain that an alarm is just an excuse to sleep more. That's why you couldn't wake up."

"That's smart."

"Let's go. We're going to be late now."

"I'm so sorry!" I chirp as I follow him down the stairs. It's 8:05 now and Jesus waits for no man, I guess.

We talk about the weather and the city as we drive to church. Steven doesn't like my urban neighborhood, of course. He assures me I can do better once I apply myself. "You're going to have to find better work than data entry, though. What did you do before?"

"Various things. My last job was working as a secretary at an accounting firm, but my . . . my ex was an accountant there."

"So you couldn't stay?"

I shrug and shrink a little in my seat. "He had a jealous streak. He was always accusing me of flirting with other men in the office."

"Were you?"

"No!"

"Hey, I was just asking. Sometimes women can be flirtatious without even realizing it."

Instead of explaining that jealousy is rooted in deep feelings of inadequacy, I pout. "I'm friendly with everyone, whatever gender they are. That was my whole *job*."

He pats my hand. "I know, but sometimes men just don't get it. You have to be careful."

"I know. I am." After all, everyone knows that women are responsible for how men behave. If we're not careful, they might decide to take what they want. They can't help it. But somehow I'm the one with the psychological impairment.

We get to the church by 8:35, so I guess my irresponsible use of the snooze button didn't ruin everything. The service isn't until 9, but, as a deacon, Steven has responsibilities. "I'll introduce you to my dad after the service. He'll be putting the finishing touches on his sermon right now. Are you okay on your own?"

I haven't burst into flames yet, so I assure him I'm fine, and he leaves me to wander the giant church hall. There are plenty of people already in the pews, mostly older couples who don't have to worry about entertaining small children through the service.

The lines of the church are modern and sleek, but the décor adds more than a hint of ostentation. The lectern is carved wood painted gold, and behind it a giant stained-glass window rises up to heaven. The window is a beautiful scene of worshippers in brightly colored robes gathered around a hill to hear the Savior speak. Jesus looms over all of us, arms spread in what might have been a gesture of welcome but looks more like an open-armed invitation for adoration.

In case it's unclear, I'm not a believer.

Where I grew up, everyone believed in God. Everyone worshipped Jesus. And they were all poor and miserable and suffering. They lost jobs and children and dignity, but that only made them pray harder. I recognize a con when I see one.

But the people here have more to be thankful for. I spot a very expensive Louis Vuitton bag sitting next to a woman perched at the end of a pew. She got here early, but instead of moving to a seat in the center she'll make everyone step over her and her expensive purse on their way in. She wants them to see it and be envious or at least recognize that she is better than they are.

If I weren't here to be placid and innocent, I'd sit behind her and wait for her to be distracted. When she stood to catch up with an old friend, I'd slide her purse from the seat and sneak it up the aisle. I'd put it in the bathroom. Set it on the floor of a stall, as if she'd retreated to the restroom and left it there herself.

Within a few minutes she'd be frantically looking for her very important purse. She'd be furious. She'd interrupt the service. She'd cry. Then she'd accuse her godly neighbors of stealing her precious bag. Someone would eventually find the missing purse in the bathroom, the contents still intact and unmolested. The purse would be returned, but no one would ever forget her nasty carrying-on. What kind of woman would forget her bag in the bathroom and then accuse others of stealing it?

I grin with delight at the damage I could do to this woman. But, alas, I'm not here to take risks. Not today.

A few people notice my delighted smile and greet me warmly. I am obviously filled up with the Spirit.

More people are flowing in, so I find a seat in the tenth row and settle in for the show. Steven's duties seem to be complete, and he emerges from a side door and takes a seat in the front pew with several other men wearing suits. I see him glance down the pew to the other end, where a woman sits stiffly in a bright-raspberry suit. Icy blond curls tumble down her back.

She doesn't return Steven's glance but stares straight ahead. The women nearby watch her. Occasionally one approaches to greet her and shake her hand. I'm almost certain she is the pastor's wife.

A great wave of red enters the room. Men and women in satiny scarlet robes flow in until they fill the entire floor behind the lectern. Everyone rises.

I expect a band to lead us off with a bass line and some drums, but this isn't a Southern church. Instead, everyone opens their hymnals and the choir starts with a staid hymn about God's love. I try not to let my lip curl. Not only is the music terrible, but it promises no spectacle for me to watch. At Southern Baptist churches, people dance and carry on. Sometimes they fall into the aisle and twitch. It was my reward for the times we got up early for church on Sunday morning.

But at least there's no danger of my grandmother jabbing her elbow into my ribs and snarling at me to stop *grinning like some whore devil.* That was when I was nine. A precocious whore devil, apparently. By twelve I told my mother I'd poison her Dr Pepper with Visine if she made me go to one more service. Since she'd had diarrhea the Sunday before, she believed me. That wasn't me, though. That was a result of bad handwashing habits. The Lord works in mysterious ways.

The terrible song ends, and they start another. I watch the people singing around me. Steven raises his face and sings loudly, of course. The woman I assume is his stepmother smiles as she sings, but it looks weird and fake to me, and I'm good at recognizing weird and fake.

Finally the pastor climbs the stairs at the side of the stage. He doesn't look much like Steven. He's gray and balding and a little pudgy, and his face is much softer than his son's, but when he smiles condescendingly at all of us, I immediately see the resemblance.

"Friends!" He lets the word boom out over the congregation, and it hangs there amid the greetings the parishioners call back. "Friends," he repeats once everyone has quieted down, "welcome to our church on this blessed day!"

A smattering of amens drift to him. In Oklahoma, half the people would've already been on their feet, but things are different in Minnesota.

"And this *is* a blessed day in a blessed place."

"Yes, sir! Yes!"

"But not every place is blessed, is it? Not in this country. Not in this age. And we need to talk about the less fortunate."

I raise my eyebrows, surprised that this man in this church is going to speak about the poor. I have to admit it's not what I expected from Steven's father. Maybe Steven is more nuanced than I thought he was. Maybe my view of the story from Meg's side was skewed and twisted.

But the faces around me look self-righteous instead of sympathetic, and Pastor Hepsworth's next words prove why. "Not everyone is blessed, because not everyone is fortunate enough to have found the Lord the way we have, friends. Not everyone understands the *right* way to live."

Oh, here we go.

"The *right* way to live," he repeats, the words deeper and louder and now whetted with hate. People around me begin to stir with excitement. "Because there *is* a right way, isn't there, folks? Despite what you see on TV and in the movies and all over the internet, there is a *right* way to live, and people who don't live it pay a price."

Amens ring out. Everyone likes to be told they are right, because that means someone else is deliciously, fantastically wrong, and that is a joy that never gets old. I like it too.

"Times change," he says. "Laws change. Cultures change. But God's law . . . God's law never changes, does it?"

"No!"

"God's law is right there for us to follow, and if you follow it in heart and in deed, you will be rewarded."

"Yes, sir!"

"You'll be rewarded with work, with dignity, with food, with money, with love, and with the knowledge that you are *living in the right.*"

Steven holds up a hand of praise and shouts, "Yes!"

"Now, that doesn't mean there won't be trials and tribulations. We all have them. God tests us. He tests us with job layoffs. He tests us with gay, promiscuous children. He tests us with *temptation.*"

And slutty, cheating wives, I add silently.

"It's up to you to pass those tests, my friends."

"Amen!" someone calls from behind me.

I've heard this all before, but I'm still a little dumbfounded by what people will accept. When *other* people are suffering, it's because they're not righteous. But when *our* people suffer, it's only a test of faith.

It's all so blatant and misguided, but it works out great for me. These human foibles make it easy for me to navigate the world. Say the right thing, push the right button, and I get what I want every time.

He launches into the meat of the sermon, and—lucky me—today he's focusing on promiscuity with a dash of homophobia. I have a feeling the homophobia sneaks in every week no matter the topic.

I listen, because this is important for me to know, but I also look around at the faces of the people taking this in. They seem to love the idea that women and children are abused and hungry because women can't keep their legs closed. They nod along when he explains that poor women choose fornication over hard work. They shake their heads at the idea that upstanding, God-fearing people like them have to pay taxes to support these lifestyles.

"When children are taught that there is always a free lunch, how will they ever learn the dignity and blessings of hard work? A *free lunch,*" he sputters. "Free lunch and free love and free health care? I say we have free *will!* Free will to live the way our Lord intended. To marry and work and live in God's grace! To keep your legs closed and your hearts open to the Lord!"

Several people are shouting approval now.

"Women used to have shame! They weren't rewarded for promiscuity! They weren't given food stamps and free abortions and an apartment with cable!"

The crowd is bright-eyed now. They are tired of paying taxes so little bastards can have a decent meal and a place to sleep.

Of course, I don't have sympathy either. My sociopathy separates me from others and muffles me from their suffering. But it doesn't make me blind.

I may not feel bad for women who work full-time and still can't afford to feed their kids, but I can see what's being done to them. I can see that the sociopaths heading up huge corporations take as much money as they can, and our tax money pays for their employees' food stamps. We subsidize the corporate profits. It's genius, really. A fabulous con. And all of these smug parishioners think they're the smart ones. I'd fleece them too given the chance.

The lecture goes on and on, and I'm thoroughly bored by the end of it and mystified by the women nodding along to all the scolding.

In my experience, men try to talk women into opening their legs from the moment girls can walk on them. Men stand in for the Lord in this scenario. Always testing us to see if we choose right or wrong. But it's a trick. There is no right. You're a tease or a whore. A heartless denier or a Jezebel. Their penises are God's divining rods, searching out evil.

I smile at this, and the pastor's eyes light on me. I have no idea what he's said that he thinks I'm responding to, but I'm definitely not supposed to be smiling. I press my lips tight together and bite them to stop my giggles. He watches me for a moment, trying to suss me out.

He's intrigued.

I'm intrigued as well. Pastor Hepsworth has some intense thoughts about fornication. He thinks about it a lot. He likely has a secret I could use against him.

It would be a decent revenge. Painful and sordid.

Decent but not perfect, because Steven would just blame it on women being whores and he'd forgive his father and learn nothing from it. The wound wouldn't be fatal, maybe not even disabling.

Still, it's a fun idea. I'll keep it in mind as a sort of . . . appetizer. Something to accentuate the main dish.

There are two more uplifting songs to help end the judgment and hypocrisy on a positive note. Baskets make their way around during the music, and I could easily slip a few hundred dollars out as I pass them along. I don't need the money, but I love a good thrill. I mentally slap my sticky fingers and smile benignly at my neighbor as I hand over the basket. Patience is a virtue.

When the service ends, the place erupts into a low roar of conversation as parishioners stand and make their way to friends. Steven is in a scrum of people near the lectern, shaking hands and slapping backs. He's a minor celebrity here. Son of the chief. He catches my eye and waves. I wave frantically back, thrilled that he's bothered to notice me. He doesn't call me over, so I hang back and try to look uncertain about all these strangers.

His father is in an even larger group of worshippers, but I notice that the woman I've pegged as Steven's stepmother is only talking to a few women. I move closer.

She has a lot of makeup on, but I try to look past it to the woman beneath. Steven's father looks about sixty, but his wife looks younger than forty. No big surprise, as I already know it's a second marriage.

The women begin to drift off and I make my move. Keeping my hands clasped uncertainly together, I sidle over. "Hi! I'm Jane. I work with Steven."

"Hello. I'm Rhonda Hepsworth."

"Nice to meet you, Mrs. Hepsworth. Steven invited me to attend the service, since I'm new in town. It was lovely."

"Oh, thank you so much!" The bright words and big smile don't match the coolness in her eyes.

"You must be so proud of this church," I say. "Your husband is a great man."

Her stiff smile doesn't budge. "Thank you."

"And your stepchildren. Well, I only know Steven, but I've heard all about his brother and sister."

She clears her throat, and I wonder if she's uncomfortable with the stepmother title. She's only a few years older than Steven, after all.

After glancing around as if she'd like to escape, she clears her throat again. "Are you . . . ah, are you and Steven dating?"

I drop my head in embarrassment. "I wouldn't say that. We're just friends."

"Well, it was really sweet of you to come to the service. I'd better go check on—"

She's cut off when Steven approaches. "Jane! Hi!"

"Hi!"

He looks from me to Rhonda but doesn't introduce us. "What do you think of the church?"

"It's beautiful! And everyone's been so nice."

"I was just saying I'd better go . . ." Rhonda lifts both hands to show that she's helpless. "But it was lovely meeting you, Jane."

Once she's out of earshot, I turn to Steven. "She's really nice."

He shrugs.

"What? You don't like her? She seems like such a great lady."

"Yeah. Yeah, she's great." That's all he says. His lips twist a little. Boy, am I intrigued. Does he think she's a gold digger? A social climber? I hope I'll see her interact with her husband, so I can figure out these dynamics.

"Steven!" the pastor booms from behind us. We both swing around and Steven greets his father warmly, hugging him with a few loud claps on the back as if they haven't seen each other in weeks.

"Great sermon, Dad." A little father-son bonding over the failings of women. Touching.

The pastor's eyes slide to me and widen with curiosity.

"Dad, this is Jane. We work together. I brought her to check out the church today."

"Pastor Robert Hepsworth." He shakes my hand gently and doesn't ask me to call him Bob. "A pleasure to meet you, Jane."

"It was a lovely service. Thank you. And it's such a beautiful church. Everyone is so nice."

"We started this church when Steven was only six. It was just a little storefront back then. The Lord has blessed us."

"He truly has," I gush; then I pull out a prosperity gospel quote for him. "'Whatever you ask in prayer, believing, you shall receive.'"

He lights up. "Oh my, yes. Yes indeed. A very impressive coworker, Steven. Impressive *and* pretty."

Even Steven looks surprised that I know my Bible, but his eyes dart up and down my body at his father's compliment.

I bite my lip and look down. Of course I know my Bible. I grew up in rural Oklahoma and I had to blend in.

"So are you two going out for lunch after this?"

Steven chuckles. "I haven't asked her yet. You're stepping on my toes, Dad."

"She's a nice churchgoing girl. You can't take that for granted these days."

Steven sighs and smiles sheepishly at me.

Pastor Hepsworth slaps his son's back. "Well, I'm happy to see you make such a pretty new friend. Especially after all that unpleasantness."

I glance quickly down because I can feel my eyes flash with hatred at his words. *Unpleasantness.* He's talking about Meg. Dead Meg. As if she were an unfortunate bout of diarrhea that passed through the family during a road trip.

I'm suddenly filled with the joyful idea of killing Steven's father as a way to take revenge. Kill him for so callously sweeping Meg and her pain aside. Kill him for being so self-righteous about it.

I could trick Pastor Hepsworth into going to a motel room. Bring condoms and blow. Shoot him up with enough drugs to kill him. Scatter a few sex toys. Then Steven can live with that for the rest of his life.

The fantasy is enough to relax my expression. I glance up at Steven with a question in my eyes, pretending I'm not sure what his dad means by *unpleasantness*. He shakes his head a little.

"You know, Jane," the pastor continues, "we're having a small birthday party for my wife next week. Maybe you'd like to drop by?"

"Dad!" Steven scolds, but he's laughing again. He adores this man.

"I'm just putting it out there!"

"You're very kind to offer, Pastor Hepsworth," I say. "But I'm sure Steven wants his family all to himself. I wouldn't want to intrude on such an important event."

"We'll see," Steven says with a wink. I guess I'd better be on my best behavior until the party if I want an invitation from Steven. "I need to drive Jane home, but I'll be back for afternoon Bible study."

I should ask to stay. I really don't want to, but I open my mouth and try to force myself to volunteer. "Oh, I wouldn't mind—"

"It's a men's group," he clarifies. "We thought a dedicated time to focus on men's spiritual needs would really strengthen our families."

Ah. Thank God for the scourge of internet porn. I'll escape Bible study this time.

"Can you hold down the fort without me?" Steven asks his dad, and then they slap each other's backs again in parting.

CHAPTER 15

There are very few people left in the church by the time we leave, but Steven bids farewell to every straggler we pass. They call him Deacon Hepsworth and seem honored when he knows their names. He loves it.

"Are you hungry?" he asks as we walk across the parking lot toward his car.

"A little, but I'm trying to lose weight, so . . . maybe just coffee?"

He doesn't argue. "Sure. There's a Starbucks down the street."

"Perfect."

Once we're pulling out of the parking lot, Steven reaches for my hand. "My dad really liked you."

"I was so nervous!"

"You were great."

"That's really sweet, Steven. Thank you. I just didn't want to embarrass you. Do you . . . do you bring a lot of girls to church?"

"Only if I'm thinking about dating them. I wouldn't want to start something with a woman who couldn't fit into my life."

"So . . ." I glance at him and then quickly away. "We're dating?"

His fingers squeeze mine. "Are you leaving it up to me?"

I smile and shrug. In the first years of our friendship, I was fascinated by the way Meg interacted with men. She always made herself smaller, and they always loved it. At first I admired it as manipulation, but I later realized that once she'd established herself as small, she couldn't make herself bigger again.

With me she was larger-than-life and bursting with goodness. I never understood this other side of her. She would shrug and say she felt shy with men she liked, but that wasn't it. It wasn't shyness. It was *fading*. She dimmed her light to make a certain kind of man feel vibrant.

And it worked.

Steven brings my hand to his mouth and kisses my knuckles. "If it's up to me, I'd love to try. Maybe we could have dinner again?"

"Tonight?"

"My dad is giving a sermon at a homeless shelter, and I'm helping him out there."

"Oh, I see. Sometime next week?" He wants to take me to dinner, but now I'm the one asking for it.

"Sure. How about Thursday? I'll pick you up at your place this time."

"That would be really nice," I say.

We reach the Starbucks quickly and I order a nonfat latte and a mini-scone. Steven raises his eyebrows. "What?" I protest. "It's tiny!"

"Sure," he answers, but his eyebrows stay high. I eat the whole thing before our drinks are ready. It's only two bites.

The wind has picked up since this morning. A cold front is moving in and we can't find an inside table in the post-church crowd, so we take our drinks back to the vehicle and set off for my apartment.

My phone buzzes and I see it's a text from Luke. Maybe I'll get lucky tonight after all.

I fell asleep and forgot to check if you made it home okay.

I did, thanks, I write back.

"Who's that?" Steven asks and I realize I'm smiling. Oops.

"It's the animal shelter. My cat is ready!"

"You have a *cat*?" This isn't a question. It's disgust.

"I adopted her yesterday."

"Cats are disgusting."

"They are not! They're great!"

"They walk through feces and then jump onto countertops."

"Cats are very clean. Their saliva has antibacterial properties and they constantly clean themselves."

He shudders. "Right."

"I like cats," I whine defensively.

He laughs. "Yeah, you'd better be careful. You're on your way to being a fat cat lady."

Even I'm surprised by how quickly he's turned from flirting to insulting me. I cross my arms as if to protect myself. "It's one cat. And I'm not fat."

He snorts. I look out the side window.

"It was just a joke," he eventually says. When I don't answer, he huffs. "Come on. Don't pout. I was kidding."

"That was really rude."

"I'm sorry. You surprised me, that's all. I don't like cats."

He's sorry, but apparently it was my fault the whole time. I should have known he hated cats and conformed to his preferences. Shifty or not, it's a peace offering, and I'm supposed to take it. Accept the blame and swallow my hurt and be ashamed of my weight and my cat.

"I'm sorry," I respond quietly.

He pats my hand. Everything is fine now. "You're not still pouting, are you?"

I sit straighter and force a laugh. "I'm not pouting."

"Good. It was a really nice day."

It was. And I came so close to ruining it.

"How about lunch tomorrow?" he offers.

I smile in response. "That would be nice."

He drops me off and I wave as I let myself into the lobby. As soon as the door closes behind me, my bright smile twists into a sneer.

I can't wait to take him down.

CHAPTER 16

She's finally here. My cat.

They gave her to me in a cardboard cat carrier, and during the walk I imagine her crouching inside, furious and ready to attack. Certainly that's how I would react to being dropped into a box with only a few holes to see out of.

I set her carefully on the floor and pop open the little tabs keeping the cardboard handle closed. I ease the flaps open and step back, trying to avoid an attack. But she doesn't leap out. She only stretches her head through the opening and looks around, alert but faintly bored. She's so incredibly cool.

Once she's assessed the room and deigned to glance in my direction, she hops elegantly up and out to land silently on the floor. She swipes her tongue over her gorgeous gray fur a few times and then, blatantly ignoring me, begins to explore the room. I love her already.

It's common knowledge that sociopaths can't love. I've known this since I was seventeen. But this fact no longer feels sure to me. I feel like I loved Meg. I may not have been empathetic or understanding, but I cared about what happened to her, and I liked the way I felt when I was with her.

Was I just using her for what she brought to my life? Maybe. But how is that different from how most people love? I look around and see people loving others because it feels good to be with them. Isn't that mercenary? Isn't that selfish? How am I so different?

After she died, it hurt so much that I looked up *love* and *sociopathy* online. I was surprised to find new opinions from experts who theorize that even people like me can form connections. We may not have souls, but maybe we're not completely hollow. There's something knocking around in there. Unfortunately, that something hurts.

So maybe I love this cat and maybe I don't, but I at least have a burning crush on her. She stalks the space of my apartment, her muscles bunching and relaxing in a mesmerizing rhythm. She's a hunter, hyper-aware, eyes wide and ears forward.

I sit down on the couch and watch as she discovers the litter box and immediately crouches to pee, marking it as hers. She hops out and gives herself a quick bath before disappearing into my tiny bedroom.

A few minutes later she returns and jumps onto my small kitchen counter. I should take a picture and text it to Steven. I'm still laughing at my own joke when she leaps nearly all the way to the ceiling to explore the top of the cabinets. She settles into a crouch there and finally turns her gaze on me, surveying me from her position of power.

"You little bitch," I whisper in admiration. She blinks sleepily in response. She's the best cat in the whole world.

CHAPTER 17

She did a good job of keeping her distance for a few days, only approaching me on the couch for occasional attention. But when I woke up this morning, my cat was curled against my hip, and she was as warm and soft as I imagined she'd be. I stayed in bed an extra ten minutes, just feeling her there. I stroked her back and she purred her approval.

That was by far the highlight of my day. Now I'm off work and an hour into this dinner with Steven and I just want to get home and see what she's doing.

"Steven?" I ask tentatively as I pick at the last of my french fries. "Do you believe all that stuff your dad said on Sunday?"

"What stuff?"

"About women."

"I'm not sure what you mean."

We had lunch twice this week, but I've been waiting to have this conversation as if I'm embarrassed to even bring it up. Finally, I spit out the horrible truth. *"I'm not a virgin."*

He blinks in shock at my sudden confession while I hold my breath a little, hoping to make my cheeks go red. "I mean"—I stop to grimace—"you wouldn't expect me to be, would you? After what your dad said . . ."

"No," he says quickly. "No, of course not."

"But all that stuff about women keeping their legs closed to be more godly . . . I just worried . . . We're supposed to be dating, and I started thinking you wouldn't like me if . . . I don't know! I mean, I assume you're not a virgin either!"

He flashes a smile. "No. Of course, it's different for men, obviously."

I nod as if I agree. "I know."

"But, no, Jane, I don't expect you to be a virgin. As long as you're not some slut who's slept with fifteen different guys."

I'd slept with fifteen guys by the time I was . . . twenty? Twenty-one? Who knows. But since his guess is way off my current number, I shake my head hard. "No. Definitely not fifteen."

He settles back in his chair and watches me for a moment. "Okay. So how many guys have you slept with?"

I cover my eyes with my hands. "Steven! That's . . . that's really personal."

"Does that mean it's too many?"

"No!" I wonder what his ideal number is. One, maybe. Not a slut, but he doesn't have to worry about being the first time. Or maybe he'd like that. I bet he would. A little pain and blood to prove he's having sex with a good girl.

"Come on," he coaxes. "How many?"

"I don't think it's . . . God! Why do you want to know?"

"I'm just curious. Shouldn't we know these things about each other? We've been dating nearly two weeks now." When I shrug, he says, "You brought it up."

"I . . ." I wilt a little and keep my eyes covered.

"I'm not going to judge you."

That's the most ridiculous lie I've ever heard, but I pretend to believe him. "Eight," I say quietly.

"Eight?" He sounds incredulous. He couldn't even make it one second without judging me.

"Maybe seven and a half," I correct.

"Wait—how do you have half sex with someone?"

"It wasn't . . . I mean, I didn't really want to do it."

"He raped you?"

"I don't know. We were making out and I didn't really want to do more, but . . ."

"But he was already excited?" He says it like it makes total sense to him.

"Yeah."

"Eight guys," he says, discounting my adjustment. "Wow. That's a lot."

"I don't know. Most of them were relationships, not just . . . you know, one-night stands."

"But some of them were?"

I shrug.

"How many?"

"How many what?"

"How many were just strange men you picked up at a bar?" God, this color commentary.

I grab a number out of the air. "Three."

"Jesus."

"What?" I cry. "You said you wouldn't judge me. And that's not so many. I'm thirty! What's your number?"

He laughs. "I'm a guy. It's higher."

"Then I don't know why you're judging me," I grumble.

"It's just a lot for a girl, that's all. You're almost into double digits."

"But I'm not!"

"Okay, okay." He holds up his hands to try to calm my sensitive feelings. "You don't want dessert, do you?"

I do, of course, but I shake my head.

He pays the bill and we walk to the car. He's silent on the drive to my place, and I'm still pretending to feel bad about what he said, so I stay quiet too. The days are getting shorter and it's full dark even though it's only 7:30.

I haven't seen Luke at all this week and I'm getting bored with this long game. To entertain myself as we drive, I try to predict where my cat will be when I get home. Her favorite place is the highest place, of course, on top of the cabinets. But she doesn't have to convey superiority when I'm not there, so maybe she'll be sprawled on the couch or curled on the bed.

The silence holds until Steven slides into a parking space a few doors from my building and shuts off the engine. "My dad is really old-fashioned. I don't believe all that stuff."

Ah, right. I'm supposed to be worrying about my sexual worthiness. "But you believe some of it?" I press.

"Look, I think premarital sex is a sin, yes. But nowadays people don't get married at sixteen, and men have needs. Women have needs too," he adds hastily. "I get that."

"Okay. Sure. I'd better get inside. I need to check on my cat."

"The cat." He groans, letting his head fall back against the seat as the interior lights fade to dark. "I forgot about that. There's probably cat hair everywhere already."

"There's not."

"Whatever. I can't risk it with my allergies."

"Oh. Okay." It's the first time he's mentioned being allergic.

"I guess we'll have to say good night now." He smiles and reaches to slide his hand behind my neck. "Come 'ere."

I let him pull me toward him for a kiss. He kisses me hard and deep, as if he's already turned on. I'm not, but I let him devour me and I gasp when I feel his hand on my breast.

He tugs me even closer, twisting me over the console in a way that would've turned me off if I'd been anywhere near excited. Then he grabs my wrist and lowers my hand to his crotch. He's hard, and I wonder if I'm supposed to be impressed that I've caused an erection.

"Oh God," he groans. "You're so fucking hot."

I haven't really done anything except confirm that I'm a slut, so I guess that's his thing. I cup his penis for a moment. I even rub it a little and he thrusts up into my hand.

"Steven . . ."

"Oh yeah. Touch me, baby."

"Steven, I can't."

"You've got me so hard."

"I know, but . . ." I twist my wrist out of his grip. "We just started dating. I don't want you to think—"

"I know. I don't think that. I swear. Just touch me a little."

I let him put my hand over him again. This time he keeps his fingers pressed to mine as he thrusts into my palm. "You see what you do to me, Jane? God, I'm in pain."

He slides his other hand over my chest and pops one more button on my dress. "Did you wear this for me?" he asks as he exposes my black lace bra.

"Maybe," I whisper.

"I saw it when you leaned over in the office today and I knew it was for me." He pushes his fingers under the lace and finds my nipple. "Oh God, yes. Unzip me," he mutters.

"Steven. Anyone could walk by!"

"No one will walk by. And it's dark." He lets go of my hand and unzips his pants. "Just make me feel better," he whispers. "That's all. Please?" He takes out his penis and wraps my hand around it. "Make me feel good, Jane. Come on."

I give in with a whimper. He urges me on, telling me how hot this is, how good it is. He tells me to move faster. I'm slightly turned on by the idea that someone could be watching from a second-floor apartment, but Steven makes no move to make *me* feel better.

Finally he finishes with a curse, thrusting and thrusting into my fist.

"Oh God," I murmur, as if shocked at the outcome. Ha. The outcome.

A few seconds later Steven tucks himself away and zips up. I have nothing to clean up with and am forced to wipe my hand on my dress. "That was great," he sighs.

Yeah. A real crowd-pleaser. I bite my lip, then exhale slowly. "Are you sure?" I ask in a shaky voice.

"You're amazing," he assures me. "Really. I'll see you tomorrow, okay?"

"Oh. Okay. Sure."

"Hey." He pulls me in for a gentler kiss. "I'll watch and make sure you get inside. I can't really get out now. I'm in a sticky situation."

I laugh at his joke. "All right."

"I'll text you later, though."

"Promise?"

"I promise."

Smiling uncertainly, I say good night and get out. He turns on his lights so he can see me walk to my door. I wave and escape inside.

Once in my apartment, I wash my hands, put out food for the cat, and then check my window to see if his vehicle is gone. It is.

Steven made absolutely no move to get me off, so I feel no qualms about texting Luke. I wouldn't feel any qualms regardless, but I really do have the perfect justification, don't I?

Want to come over? I ask Luke.

He does.

CHAPTER 18

I prefer a king-size bed so it's easier for me to keep my distance if a man spends the night, but this place only accommodates a queen, and barely that. But Luke stays firmly on his side of the mattress after sex and I don't feel crowded. When the cat jumps onto the bed and settles down on the blanket between us, Luke laughs.

"You got her! She's gorgeous!"

"Thank you."

"What's her name?"

I shrug and rub my palm along her soft tail. "I don't know."

"She didn't have one at the shelter?"

I grimace. "They called her Bunny."

"That's cute!"

"No, it's awful. She's far too regal for a stupid name like that."

He scratches under her chin and she stretches to give him better access. "She *is* very regal." When he stops scratching, she butts his hand and rubs her cheek against him, marking him as another of her new possessions. He gives her more scratches. "Well, you have to name her."

"She's a cat. What does she care? She's not going to come when I call her. Not unless there's food."

"Good point."

"So you like cats?" I ask.

"Sure. I had one when I was little. What's not to like?"

Exactly.

"What about you? Did you have cats?"

"No. She's my first."

"Dogs?"

"Just junkyard dogs who lunged at everyone, including me."

"Yikes. That doesn't sound very fun."

"No. It wasn't. The dogs didn't seem to like the situation much either."

"Where did you grow up again? Oklahoma?"

I feel a jolt that he knows the truth. I must have told him in some offhand conversation during college. But it hardly matters. He already knows my real name and where I went to school. It's not as if I can disguise my identity from him.

"Yeah. Out in the boonies near the panhandle."

"I grew up in the boonies of Bemidji. It probably wasn't that different. More trees, though."

"And fewer tornados," I add.

"Yeah, and I've gotta be honest, I never had a junkyard dog."

I laugh. "Did you have a white picket fence?"

"Uh, we did, actually."

"Wow. Sounds like the American dream."

"To be honest, it really wasn't."

"Why not?" I'm curious now, but Luke goes silent, so maybe that was a question I wasn't supposed to ask. Sometimes I'm not sure of boundaries.

But then he decides to answer. "I don't know. It should have been. A middle-class life in the country. Nuclear family. Nobody ever hit me."

He leaves it at that, and I understand, at least a little. I didn't come from a broken home either. We were never middle-class by any means, but my parents were together. I got hit every once in a while, but no one ever beat the tar out of me, and that's the minimum standard for abuse in Oklahoma.

But those are surface issues. It's the *underneath* that makes you who you are.

It's your parents drinking with their trashy friends while all of them make fun of you for wetting your bed the night before. It's your mom cackling when the handsy guy who rents the back room asks when you're going to get titties. It's living alone for five days in first grade and wondering if your parents have finally decided they don't want to come back. It's your dad saying he'll send you to the Cherokee orphanage if he gets another letter from that stacked kindergarten teacher about your bad behavior.

Luke blows out a long breath. "Let's just say I only went back a couple of times after I left for college."

"Yeah," I whisper. "Me too."

"But now," he says, "now you have a cat." It's sweet and simple and true.

Luke reminds me a lot of Meg.

CHAPTER 19

Be nice.

That's what she used to tell me. Not often. Just when she needed me to be better. *Be nice, Jane. Just be nice, okay?*

And I would be nice. For her. For a little while. Long enough to listen to her problems and not tell her what she was doing wrong. Long enough to meet her new boyfriend and not scare him away.

She told me to be nice about Steven too. *We were drinking. We both said mean things. He's still a really good guy. Be nice, Jane.*

So I'd be nice and not remind her that he'd called her a stupid whore. I'd keep my mouth shut and not tell her it seemed like she believed all the terrible things he said.

I shouldn't have been so nice about him. Or maybe I should've been nicer to Meg? I don't know. But I did something wrong; that much is obvious.

I only came back to the States once while she was dating him. They'd just broken up, and she was a weeping, terrified mess. She seemed to think she couldn't go on without him. She was stupid, helpless, not good enough.

He'd kicked her out of his house again, and since she'd given up her apartment to live with him, she was sleeping in a friend's basement. I'd gathered her up, rented a cabin on the coast of Lake Superior, and we'd stayed there for two weeks.

But I'm not a nurturer. I can't heal people. I thought she was better when I returned to Malaysia, but my clumsy offerings of love—wine, s'mores, bad movies, sunburns, margaritas—they hadn't done the trick. A week later she was back with him and sending me texts about how great everything was now. How nice he was being. How happy she was.

I didn't speak to her for over a month. I was furious.

The next time he kicked her out, she was so embarrassed to tell me. She was ground down with humiliation. And all I could offer was *I told you so.*

She stopped telling me to be nice. And I couldn't remember.

CHAPTER 20

Hey, where are you?

I glance down at the text from Steven and imagine answering him honestly. I'm in a rental car in the Minneapolis suburbs, following GPS directions to your house. I smile a shark's smile and pull over to the curb in front of a row of 1980s ranch homes. It's 8:45 in the morning and freezing cold. A lone jogger bounces by in winter gear, but otherwise the neighborhood is quiet.

I called in sick, I respond.

Are you okay?

Sure. I just have a headache. And I felt . . . weird.

Weird?

After yesterday.

Why?

I shouldn't have done that with you.

Don't say that. I loved it! ☺

Ok, but . . . you never texted me. You said you would.

Sorry. I had a beer and fell asleep on the couch.

Well, I feel like a slut.

No no no! It was great.

I roll my eyes at his weak-ass assurance. Sure, it was great for him.

Ok. I have to go. I didn't sleep well last night.

Why don't I make you dinner tonight?
Will that make you feel better?

I dunno. Maybe.

I bet it will. I'll pick you up at 6. I might even bring flowers . . .

Flowers for a public hand job. What a bargain. He's a simple man, really, and I'm sending all the right signals. It's not that I don't want to have sex; it's that I'm worried he'll think badly of me afterward. This gives him access to sex *and* the ability to control me with it. What could be more perfect?

I throw the car in gear and pull back onto the quiet street. His house is half a mile farther into this sea of browning grass and falling leaves. But when I drive past Steven's house, there are no leaves on his lawn. His neighbors are ankle-deep in orange and yellow, but there are only a few stray leaves on his square of yard, as if he rakes every morning.

Steven really likes to keep up appearances. He doesn't want anyone to see his mess. I laugh as I drive one block over.

Feeling very satisfied with myself, I park and grab the satchel I packed this morning.

The cold is keeping everyone inside, but I'm not worried about being spotted trying to get into his house. I'm an average white woman.

Worst-case scenario, I'll wave and yell something self-deprecating about being dumb enough to lose the key, and that will be enough for the neighbors.

I reach Steven's house and head up his front walk to check under the welcome mat. When I don't find a hidden key, I walk around a corner to the gate of his privacy fence. I don't glance around. The more sure of myself I look, the less suspicious any witness will be.

Once the gate latches behind me, I'm free to slow down and look around. The backyard is just one tree, some grass, and a covered grill on a square stone patio. There's no dog to worry about, of course. Steven wouldn't put up with cleaning dog crap off his lawn.

I tried to teach myself to pick locks a long time ago, because it looked like fun, but it turns out I'm not great at it. Not enough patience. I was hoping to find a simple window lock to jimmy open, but I spot a sliding door in back, which is even better. All it needs is a quick slip of a bent metal file and I'm in. If I ever have to go on the run, maybe I'll make a good thief, at least when it comes to houses with patio doors.

The house is dead quiet and smells of bleach. The kitchen I walk into is spotless. Not high-end, though. It hasn't been renovated since it was built. The floor is old tile. I turn to survey the living room and immediately notice that the carpet in the rest of the house appears to be dark chocolate brown. Gross. But it's spotless as well, and I can see the vacuum lines as I step in.

Jeez, will I have to vacuum before I leave to hide my footprints? At least I know he'll be well groomed when we finally have sex. Not much to look forward to, but it's better than the alternative.

I give myself a tour of the rest of the house. He's using the first small bedroom as a workout room. I can't tell if it feels still and antiseptic because he never uses it or because he wipes the equipment down after each use. Mounted judo belts decorate the wall.

The brown carpet continues down a short hallway to another bedroom that appears to be half office, half storage. The last bedroom is the master. A big bed with an oak headboard dominates the floor. The only other furniture is a wide dresser with a mirror. And there's a big flat-screen TV on the wall, of course. His brown drapes and forest-green comforter give the impression that I'm in a tree house. It's pretty awful.

The attached bathroom is as clean as the rest of the place, but the tan tile continues the old 1980s look. Steven cares about appearances, but he definitely doesn't have an eye for design.

There's not much clutter in the bedroom, but I've lucked out. There's baseboard heating, but there are air-conditioning vents as well, and he won't be using those at this time of year.

I toss my satchel on the bed and unzip it to expose the equipment inside. None of it is legal in the US, not unless you're law enforcement. I bought it all in Malaysia and shipped it to a rental box here in Minneapolis.

I unpack two digital cameras the size of nine-volt batteries. The equipment doesn't have any storage but it transmits motion-activated audio and video to me via Wi-Fi, and I can back it all up on my laptop for leisurely viewing. The batteries hold a charge for nearly three months. I can't imagine I'll need to figure out how to replace them.

I've already synced the cameras up with my computer. The only problem will be accessing Steven's Wi-Fi. He definitely has a passcode. He's not the type to happily share bandwidth with his less fortunate neighbors.

I figure he has to give me access to his Wi-Fi if I spend enough time in his bedroom. It would be really rude to let a woman spend the night and not let her use the Wi-Fi, right? I pop open my laptop to check out the situation and find seven named networks. The one with the strongest signal is locked down tight and the name is just a random series of letters and numbers. The second Wi-Fi network is locked as well. But the third signal on the list has three bars of signal strength and isn't locked. This is very good luck. I don't need to rely on Steven's generosity after all.

I snort at the name of the network. FeelFreeToUseMyNanasWiFi. Poor Nana.

After I log in, I open the camera app to assign the network to both cameras. An image of the bedroom blinks to life on my laptop. A second image appears next to it, nearly identical. When I lean forward, the side of my head appears in both frames. Tiny moving status bars slide across the application's windows, letting me know I'm recording.

I'm up and running.

I turn toward the lenses and wave. "Hello, Jane." I know I'll laugh when I watch it later.

The multi-tool I've brought makes quick work of the vent screws, and I carefully tape the camera into position to peek between the slats. It's a wide shot of the whole room, but I adjust it a few times to make sure the bed is the center of the focus, then replace the vent.

Onward to the living room. There's a vent in the living room that faces the kitchen, so I unscrew it and set to work getting that camera positioned correctly. Once that's done, I test it by walking into the kitchen and saying "Hello again, Jane" in a normal speaking voice. I return and sit on the couch to greet myself once more. When I play back the video, I can hear myself clearly. The cameras were worth the exorbitant sticker price.

Before I leave, I go through Steven's dresser drawers, then his office file drawer. I find nothing. No secret offshore accounts, no love letters, not even a little tube of lubricant for jerking off. Everything is boring. It pisses me off.

Not all monsters are terrifying. Some of them are so tedious they'll just make you wish for death.

The worst part about Steven is that he doesn't have to be cruel. He wasn't born this way. He could choose to do better, choose to go to therapy and talk his cruelty away. Mine is hardwired from childhood, and even I try harder than he does.

He'll get away with it forever if I don't stop him. He'll treat woman after woman like utter shit. But let's be honest. I'm not doing it to protect those women. I just need him to pay for Meg. Then we'll be even.

"Even Steven," I say, and then I smile for the camera. Even Steven.

I look through closets until I find the vacuum, and I suck away all my tracks before I leave the house.

CHAPTER 21

When I first heard she'd died, I didn't even feel surprised. Maybe I was in shock. Maybe it wasn't real to me because I lived halfway around the world and never saw her anyway. Maybe it's just that I'm a monster.

Whatever the reason, I didn't feel much of anything except frustration. I'd told her that asshole didn't matter. I'd told her she'd be better off without him. And she clearly would have been if she'd given it time.

Shit, I'd even invited her to come to Kuala Lumpur and live with me for as long as she wanted. It seemed like the perfect solution. How could she possibly miss that loser if she was busy having an adventure in Malaysia with me? She was young and blond and she'd have been popular with the businessmen here.

But she'd decided to die instead.

After my frustration came anger. He'd called her a stupid bitch all the time, and maybe he'd been right, because Meg had believed him instead of me. *Him.* Some pissant nobody she'd known less than two years. She'd loved him so much that she'd taken herself away from *me*? Forever?

Fuck that.

Within a week, I'd decided that I hated her. That I'd never needed her and never would.

Then I received her letter.

Jane, it's me. I'm so, so sorry . . .

Whatever half-living thing there was inside me had opened up and I'd cried my eyes out. I'd sobbed. And screamed. And broken a lamp and a chair and several vases. I'd raged and cried, and that was when the grief had put its claws into my bones and settled down for a long meal.

CHAPTER 22

I gasp as Steven pulls into his driveway. "Oh my God, what a beautiful yard!"

"Thank you." The garage door rises and I see that the garage is perfectly clean, tools hung on walls and shelves neatly lined with boxes.

"Everything is so pretty. And it seems like such a great neighborhood."

"It's nice. There are a lot of older folks here, so there aren't too many asshole kids around. But the school district is one of the best, so home values are solid."

He's so cold and practical that I have trouble imagining what free spirit Meg saw in him. She never thought about home values or school districts during her walks around town. She liked pretty trim and brightly painted porches. But opposites attract, I suppose. His serious and responsible nature must have felt like safety to her.

She told me he was the best boyfriend she'd ever had. He had a job and a home. He paid for all their dates. He came from a good family. He wanted a better life for her.

I could see why she believed that at first. Compared to her previous boyfriends, he was a catch. She'd had a bad habit of collecting weirdos and taking care of them. She'd collected me, hadn't she?

Steven was so *strong*. That's what she said. He tricked her with that, and then he overwhelmed her completely.

She was proud of the way he'd revamped her finances and set up electronic payments on all her accounts. "I'm so bad with money," she started saying constantly.

I'd never heard her say that before. She'd seemed fine to me. She'd supported herself. Had her own apartment, her own car, her own life. After Steven it was always "He says I need to learn to be more responsible."

Whenever I snorted in response, she defended him. "I had two overdrafts last month, Jane! Two! I was so embarrassed when he found out. Do you know how much all those fees added up to? I'm so stupid."

"You're not stupid. And how did he even find out?"

"What do you mean?"

"Why does he know anything about your checking account?"

"He's balancing it for me now."

"Meg," I'd said flatly, "no. No way."

"Jane, come on! I'm terrible with numbers, and he's getting all my stuff in order for me. It's great."

"It's not great. You've been dating this guy for two months and now he has access to your bank account?"

She laughed. "What's he going to do? Wire himself twenty-five dollars and clean me out? I've got nothing."

I've got nothing, she said. But it wasn't true. She may not have had a savings account or a big spotless house or a perfectly raked yard, but she had warmth and friends and a heart.

Steven lost Meg, but somehow he still looks around at his neat suburban life and thinks he's winning.

"Is this a rental?" I ask as he unlocks the kitchen door.

"No way. A mortgage is an investment. Renting is just throwing money at someone else's bank account. Dumb as rocks."

"Well, sure, but a lot of us have to rent. You have to have a down payment to even think about buying. And you have to cover all the maintenance and taxes."

"You're covering the owner's taxes and all the maintenance on other units when you pay rent. You get that, right?"

"Whatever. I couldn't afford to buy anyway."

"That's why you need a better job, Jane. You'll never get ahead as a temp."

"I don't know. I'm used to living in apartments. And I don't need much space."

"You're thirty years old and you're just treading water and making someone else rich. You've never had a good family to teach you this stuff."

You've never had a good family. Who says that kind of thing?

"Yeah," I murmur. "Maybe you're right."

He turns on the lights and hangs his keys on a hook on the wall. I step into the kitchen and look around. "Wow, it's so nice."

"Thanks."

"You keep it so clean."

"You're not messy, are you? That drives me crazy."

"No, I'm not messy." Just to push his buttons, I take off my sweater and toss it onto a chair, then drop my purse on the kitchen table. His eyes go right to the mess I created and stay there. I'm very proud of myself for not laughing.

"So you're cooking for me?" I ask. "That's very romantic."

"I'm a pretty romantic guy."

I flash back to that night in his truck and don't say a word.

Steven washes his hands and tips his head toward the sliding glass door I broke into this morning. "Let me heat up the grill."

I did my best to latch the lock behind me when I left, but I'm not sure I got it hooked well, so I rush for the door while he's still moving toward it. "Oh, a real backyard! I've lived in apartments so long, I've forgotten what that's like!" I open the lock as I gush over his square of lawn. "Oh, brrrrr, it's getting cold out here."

"A beer and a warm grill will take care of that." He stops to give me a kiss in the doorway. "Hope you like steak."

"Of course," I respond as he steps out to fire up the propane.

"All right, we'll let that heat up. Let me get you a beer."

I follow him back inside and he pops open two beers and hands me one. Mine is light beer. His is a stout. I'm honestly beginning to think he doesn't like my weight.

He carries a couple of coasters into the living room and we sink into the giant cushions of his beige couch. The brown pillows really amp up the color theme of mud and shit. "This is nice," he murmurs as he tucks me under his arm and pulls me close.

"I think it's our two-week anniversary."

"Is it?"

I have no idea, but it's close enough, so I nod.

"Then happy anniversary, babe." With any other man, I'd be moving too fast, but I'm taking my cues from Meg. She claimed they were madly in love after only one week. And if Steven thinks I'm needy and desperately romantic, he'll read it as easy to control.

He kisses my cheek and settles into the couch with a satisfied sigh.

"Steven, can I ask you something?"

"Sure."

"When we were at the church, your dad mentioned unpleasantness . . ."

He shrugs and raises an eyebrow in question.

"He said how nice it was to meet me after all that *unpleasantness*."

"Oh. Right."

"What did he mean?"

He takes a hard swig from his beer and frowns as if it's filled his mouth with bitterness. The frown doesn't budge after he swallows. "Yeah. Well. My last girlfriend was a crazy bitch."

I'm ready for this. I don't smash him in the head with my beer. I don't even claw his face with my nails. Instead I just gasp a little as if I'm mildly dismayed. "Oh no!"

"Yeah. It was pretty bad."

"How so?"

He shrugs again. "Typical crazy female stuff."

"So she's a psycho? You're kind of freaking me out."

"No. I mean yeah. But you don't have to worry."

"She's not going to follow me home and slash my tires?"

He flashes a charming smile. "You don't have a car."

"You know what I mean. Should I be worried?"

"No."

"How can you be sure?"

"She killed herself." He says it without flinching. The words are straightforward and not tinged with the slightest haze of guilt.

"What?" My voice is tinged with all sorts of things and none of them are real. Shock. Doubt. Pity. Terror. I make my eyes wide and cover my parted lips with a shaky hand. "Steven. *What?*"

"Yeah. I broke up with her and she killed herself to get back at me."

"But . . . but . . . My God! She must have been . . ."

"A crazy damn bitch."

She loved this man. He never deserved it, but Meg loved him. She died for his love.

He'd kicked her out of his house again. Screamed at her that it was over. He'd told her to go fuck someone else so she'd know deep in her heart he was never going to touch her again. He'd thrown her things into the street. Not in front of his house, of course. That would have been embarrassing. No, he'd boxed up her belongings and dropped them on the curb outside her job to humiliate her in front of her coworkers.

Why? Because a man from work had called and invited her to his place. For a barbecue. Along with every other coworker. That was it. A man had called. But she'd been too friendly on the phone, apparently, and the man was taller and hotter than Steven, and that had been Meg's downfall.

Because she was a whore. Because she'd always been a whore. Because she was such a slut that she didn't even know how to behave appropriately around men.

Did you hear how you spoke to him? Did you hear your stupid giggling? It sounds like you two are already fucking. Sure, Meg, go over to his house and slut it up! I'll just stay here and work my ass off for everything we have. You're so fucked up and disrespectful. I can't believe I considered marrying you.

I know exactly what he said because she sent me screengrabs of the texts later that day.

I want to kill him right now. I want to break my bottle on his coffee table and stab him in the jugular and then drag him outside so I can press his face to the grill and burn him while he dies.

But I shake my head and keep my mouth covered.

"Let's not talk about her," he finally sighs.

"But . . . how long ago did it happen?"

"Last year," he answers curtly, but it's not true. It happened nine months ago, in the middle of February, when Meg couldn't face the long nights and gray days.

I told her a light therapy lamp would help her feel better. Apparently I was way off base.

"I don't want to talk about this," Steven mutters.

"But, Steven, this is a big deal! You must still be reeling."

"I prayed a lot. I got over it."

"But I don't understand why she killed herself. Did you break her heart? Were you cheating on her?"

"What? No way! I found out she was slutting around with guys at her job and I kicked her out. She realized she'd screwed up the best thing she'd ever had. When I wouldn't take her back, she wanted to punish me."

"By killing herself?"

His shoulders jerked up in a violent shrug. "She probably did it for attention. Figured she'd take a few pills and I'd come running back. I guess she fucked that up too."

He still wants to let everyone know Meg couldn't do anything right. She couldn't even die correctly. I swallow my rage and keep my frown soft and trembling.

"But you must have loved her," I say quietly, pretending I know what sympathy is. "You must be grieving."

I'm not sure if I've genuinely hit a nerve or if he realizes he's being callous, but Steven slumps a little. "I did love her. But she wasn't a good person. She was irresponsible and she slept around. I wanted to help her, but you can't help people who won't help themselves."

Meg was a great person. That's not sentimentality. I don't have that. She'd never been perfect, but she was kind, even to someone like me. "She must have had good qualities if you dated her."

"Yeah, she was fun," he offers. "And you know what they say about crazy girls with low self-esteem. They're great in bed."

He was her lover. Her boyfriend. He spoke at her funeral.

I didn't fly in for the service, but I heard about it from her mom. Steven had stood in front of God and country and said he'd tried to save her from her demons. He called her a light in his life. He wept and sobbed. Now all he has to say about his precious angel is that her low self-esteem made her great in bed. I should send the video of this little speech out to their mutual friends to watch.

He pushes up suddenly from the couch. "You want another beer?"

I've barely touched mine. I shake my head. Steven grabs another and drains half of it standing next to the fridge. He stares into the backyard for a while and I hope he's suffering at least a little. But whatever memories haunt him, he shakes them off and grabs the steak and a head of romaine from the fridge.

"I can make a salad," I offer.

"Wash your hands first," he says curtly.

"Are you a germophobe?" I tease.

"I don't like dirty people with no common sense." Oh, poor baby, I've made him angry with all my questions about Meg.

I pout as I take my beer into the kitchen. "I was going to wash my hands. I'm not stupid."

He grunts.

"You don't have to be mean."

"I'm not being mean; I'm telling the truth."

"By calling me dirty?"

"I didn't call you dirty. I said I don't like dirty people. If you're not dirty, then you don't need to worry about it, do you?"

Pretending to be hurt and chastened, I turn on the faucet and slowly wash my hands, marveling at this little play. In real life, I would have cut this man down to ribbons by now, but Meg must have put up with his tantrums. She must have tried harder and apologized and did her best to please him.

Why? Are we all just animals bound to relive our broken childhoods over and over? Is it that simple?

Meg's real father treated his family like shit before he left, and every stepdad and boyfriend who followed did the same. Her mom had spent her life pleasing loser men, and that was imprinted on Meg the way hunting skills are imprinted on young lions. *This is how you get through life. This is how you guarantee the species. Take abuse. Submit to men. Repeat, repeat, repeat.*

Meg broke the cycle, finally. She found a way out.

A hollow bang of glass cracks through the room when Steven throws his second bottle in the trash to join the first. I cringe as if I'm frightened by his obvious anger. "Do you have any tomatoes?" I ask as I carefully dry my hands.

"I don't like tomatoes."

"Oh."

"There's a cucumber in the fridge."

I guess that's his peace offering, so I dig the cucumber out of the crisper, then look through drawers until I find a knife. Steven leans against the counter and watches, a third beer in his hand.

"I told you I didn't want to talk about her," he finally says. A prompt if I've ever heard one.

I keep my eyes down, watching the knife blade glint in my hand. As much as I'd like to stab him right now, I can't kill him. Maybe no one saw me riding through the neighborhood in Steven's car, but there are texts between us. I suppose I could stab him and claim an intruder did it, but I'd have to set up some obvious motive. Score a pound of heroin and hide it in a dresser drawer. Claim the guy with the knife kept demanding payment. But setting up Steven as some middle-class drug dealer would take time.

Perhaps I could stab him and claim self-defense. Tell everyone he tried to rape me. But the police are skeptical of rape even when it's real. I was in his house, after all, showing off my bosom and letting him see my ankles. I can't cry rape now. They'd doubt every word and look deep into my background, and I don't have that kind of cover.

Damn.

I set the knife down. I nod. "I'm sorry," I whisper.

"What?"

"I'm sorry I pushed you about her. I just wanted to know what happened."

"And you call *me* mean?"

"It wasn't mean. I just—"

"You didn't care what I wanted," he snaps. "You just wanted details. Details that obviously hurt me."

"No. I thought we should talk about it. It's something important that happened to you."

"Yeah, it is, so have a little respect for once."

"I said I was sorry."

He watches me for a while before he shakes his head. "Jane." He sighs my name like a disappointment. "Maybe this is how you treat other men, but you're not going to treat me like crap. I'm not some loser you can push around. I have a good job, a nice house, a great life."

"I know you do. And I didn't mean—"

"I like you, Jane. I really do. But I don't need you. And I expect to be treated with respect."

"I wasn't being disrespectful!"

"Weren't you? I said no. Isn't that what women talk about all the damn time? I said no, and you kept pushing me."

"Steven, I'm sorry!" I make myself sound a little panicked. Just a little. That's what he wants. "I'm sorry, okay?"

He shrugs and downs his third beer before tossing it into the trash can. I jump as if the crash of glass is a slap. "I just wanted to have a nice evening with you," he mutters.

"I'm sorry," I say again. "Really. I shouldn't have pushed you."

"Yeah." He relaxes a little and his eyelids are heavier when his gaze falls to my cleavage.

I push off the island and move closer. "I was being a bitch."

"You were."

"Are you still mad?" I ask as I press into his body.

He shrugs again, but he puts his arms around me and stares down my dress.

"Don't be mad."

Instead of answering, he slips a hand over my chest and undoes an extra button. Now the fabric gapes open, exposing my black bra. With no warning at all, he shoves his hand into one of the cups and wrenches the whole thing down to expose my breast. He kisses me hard, kneading my flesh and trying to swallow all my breath. I let him push me up against the counter and grind his crotch against me. I guess this is forgiveness.

A button of my dress pops off and drops to the floor, rolling away with tiny clicks I can barely hear over his panting.

God, I hate these stupid dresses. They're weak and flimsy.

I hear the sound of his zipper and roll my eyes.

"Suck me," he whispers.

"Steven! I can't. You'll think—"

"Come on. I know you do it. You've done it plenty of times, right?"

"You'll think I'm a slut."

"I won't. Just do it. Come on." His hand is on my shoulder, pressing me down. This is how he'll forgive me. This is how I'll show respect for my big, strong man.

I pull back a little and he follows. I slide along the edge of the island. After a quick glance toward the vent in the living room, I let him push me to my knees.

"Oh yeah," he groans before I even touch him. "Do it."

It doesn't take long. He's primed on anger and frustration.

Afterward he drinks another beer and grills the steaks. I make the salad. The bodice of my dress gapes at the missing button. He's in a great mood, laughing and joking. He teases me about having a healthy appetite. I've done a good job making up for my bitchiness.

The steaks are surprisingly tasty.

At nine I yawn and tell him I'd better get home. He offers to pay for a ride.

Even I'm shocked by that. "Can't you drive me?"

"Sorry, baby. I've had too many beers."

"You could take me home and sleep over at my place."

He curls his lip. "The cat." I notice he doesn't ask me to stay here instead.

"Oh."

He kisses my hand. "I'll put the ride on my account."

Jeez, I feel like a princess.

I curl up against him and watch TV for a few more minutes while I wait for a stranger to drive me home. "This was nice," I whisper.

"Yeah," he agrees. "You're great, Jane." He kisses my head and gives me one last squeeze. "You're really great." His phone dings. My ride is here. He walks me to the door and waves.

And people say romance is dead.

CHAPTER 23

I've made sex tapes before, of course, but this is something different. It's like watching reality TV made just for me. I eat microwave popcorn and watch our little argument play out over and over. It's a fascinating class in manipulation, and Steven and I are both playing the game. Unfortunately for Steven, he's a rank amateur. His technique is clumsy and dumb and only works when emotions are involved.

Each time I see my glance at the camera, I giggle. Steven is completely absorbed in his penis and doesn't notice me breaking the fourth wall.

Arousal is a funny thing. I suppose when there's actual intimacy involved, arousal might bring you closer to the other person. Who knows. But in general it's a selfish state. Steven is turned on and all he can think about is getting more, more, more. Even afterward he doesn't notice that I turn and spit him out onto the clean floor. I hope he steps in it tomorrow morning.

I picture him hopping around on one foot, horrified and disgusted, and I laugh so hard my eyes water. Salt and butter coat my hands, so I wipe my face on my sleeve. I can't wait to review tomorrow's video.

After I left, Steven watched a little more TV and then went to bed. He brushed his teeth and washed his face, then put on two different moisturizers. I guess he's a little vain. Then he put on honest-to-God pajamas like he's Ward Cleaver. What a sicko.

I watch him sleep for ten minutes and then the camera feed ends. I back it up and watch it all again. At midnight I finally get to bed, but a text dings just as I turn off the light.

Still up?

It's Luke, and I would have welcomed this two hours ago, but even I'm too sleepy to be interested in a booty call right now. Barely, I answer.

Want to grab lunch tomorrow?

Lunch? I was expecting him to ask for a quick topless pic to help him get to sleep. I hesitate, frowning at the phone. Maybe it's just an opening gambit.

I can't.

Too busy? I can come over to Minneapolis if that helps.

I'm tempted, but I can't risk Steven seeing me with another man.

I'll probably eat at my desk.

Ok. Maybe another day?

Maybe.

There's a long pause and I think the conversation is over, but just as I'm setting my phone down, there's another text.

I don't want you to think this is all about sex for me.
It's not.

Hm. That's . . . interesting. I'm almost always certain of myself, but this is the type of interaction that can throw me off. Before I can think of an appropriate answer, he texts a follow-up.

You can probably tell by the way I've played hard to get.

I laugh at the stupid joke and finally respond.

Well, I think I'm starting to wear you down.

Maybe.

I have to admit, he intrigues me. I shouldn't spend time with him, but I like that he surprises me.

We'll see about lunch. Maybe Monday. Good night.

He signs off with a winky face. My cat jumps onto the bed and curls close. When I pet her, she stretches out and her heat presses all along my side.

Tonight . . . tonight I feel something that seems like true happiness, but it might just be satisfaction.

CHAPTER 24

I get up early to watch Steven get ready for work. The camera wakes up when he gets out of bed and stretches. I watch him tug up his ridiculous pajama bottoms before he heads to the bathroom. I hear him pee; then he tosses his pj's out the door and into a hamper. He wears a fresh pair every night, I guess. He probably irons them before stacking them neatly in his dresser drawer.

A glance at the dirty clothes lying on the floor of my bedroom makes me smile. It's too bad all my clothes are so pale and flowery. I'd love to wear a black shirt to work with gray cat hair all over the back of it. Still, that might be too much this early in our relationship. A deal breaker instead of a trigger for abuse.

I've already showered and dressed, so I wait impatiently as Steven gets ready. In the end I'm disappointed. Once dressed, he heads out the door, not even stopping for coffee in the kitchen. By the time he gets home from work, the puddle I left on his floor will be dry. I've missed my moment of slapstick comedy. Still, I feel certain he'll give me another chance.

I'm just finishing my last cup of coffee when my phone rings. Is Steven actually being considerate and giving me a morning-after call?

No, of course not. It's my mother. I put my phone down and ignore it. It's her second phone call in a week. Maybe I should turn off call forwarding so she can't reach me on this burner phone. She's becoming a nuisance.

A buzz indicates that she's left a message. Before I can listen to it, the phone vibrates with yet another call. It's my mother again. Jesus.

"What?" I snap when I answer.

"Daddy's had a stroke!" She always calls him Daddy. I haven't called him that since I was four. Even in kindergarten I could see he wasn't a hero who would fight monsters for me. He was a shiftless, immature loser with a massively overinflated ego and no sense of responsibility.

"Did you call 911?" I ask.

"We're at the hospital now." I hear the helplessness in her voice, but I feel no sympathy. She's always been helpless. Hapless. Unable to deal with life. Having a sociopath for a daughter was a boon for her. I started cold-bloodedly taking care of family business by fifth grade. "Okay. You're both on Medicare, right?"

"Yes! But they took him to the hospital up in Enid, and I don't know how I'm going to get back and forth. He could be here for weeks! If he makes it through."

"I just paid for a car repair, so I'm not sure what you mean."

"It's a two-hour drive! I'll have to find a place to stay, Jane. And I can't afford that. You know we're living check to check."

"Fine. I'll send a prepaid debit card."

"Can't you just set me up somewhere nice?"

"No. I'll send five hundred dollars, and you make it stretch." If I set her up, it'll be all room-service meals and valet parking. This isn't my first rodeo.

"Jane . . . Jane . . ." She's weeping now. "You should come on home and see your daddy. Just in case."

"In case of what?"

"In case he doesn't make it!"

"You've hardly said one word about his status, so I'm going to assume he's stable."

"He had a stroke!"

"Well, big surprise. He's been drinking hard and eating rich since the seventies. Was it a big one or a little one?"

"He's drooling, Jane! Slurring his words!"

I sigh. "Yeah, what do the doctors say?"

She hesitates, so I know she's trying to figure a way to frame it in the most dire terms. She once carried on for days about a "brain tumor" she had. I was six years old and still terrified of being sent to an orphanage. I knew damn well my father wasn't going to keep me if my mama died.

Four emergency room visits later, it turned out it was just a migraine. She got a lot of pain pills out of it though, so it was a win-win for her.

"Paralysis!" she finally warbles. "Daddy's right side is paralyzed! He can't hardly lift his foot!"

"Is it temporary or permanent?"

Uh-oh, I can tell by her silence that I've got her. "They . . . they say you can never be sure."

"But they think it's temporary?"

"Sure, but he's gonna need a wheelchair for now at least, Jane. We'll have to make updates to the house!"

She means the trailer. The latest trailer in a string of trailers, each one smaller and more run-down than the last. I don't think those aluminum doors are wide enough for a wheelchair, so a ramp won't do any good anyway. "I'm sure Ricky can help with that. He's pretty handy. No point throwing money into that heap."

"That's our home, you heartless bitch!"

"Then you'd better find a way to make it work. If it needs medical fixes, I'm sure Medicare will accommodate you."

"Family takes care of family." She's lost the helpless warble and moved straight into a hard, spitting screech. "But you wouldn't know anything about that, would you? Your own father is on his deathbed, and you could care less! There's a devil in you, you uppity cunt."

"You just cost yourself a hundred dollars," I say. "Care to try for more?"

"You!" she screams. "You evil little . . ." But she gets control of herself. She knows damn well that I'll cut her off without a dime. "Jane, I need that money." Helpless wheedling again. "How can I take care of Daddy if I can't stay close?"

"It's Enid. Four hundred dollars should go a long way. I'll send it today. Be sure to make it last."

I hang up. When the phone rings again, I switch it off. I feed my cat and grab my coat and some gloves. It's cold outside. When I step out of my apartment, I wish I'd brought a hat too. I'm thankful for the warmth of the convenience store when I stop to put $400 on a card. There's a post office on the way to work, but I'd rather steal a stamp from my company, so I walk on. I'm not worried she'll notice my mail is coming from Minneapolis. I travel for work, and my family doesn't even know who Meg was, much less why I'd be here.

I call the hospital before I get to the office and ask about my father. He's in room 223. I hang up before the call transfers. I don't want to speak to him. I just want to be sure my mother isn't running a scam. This was a little too close on the heels of that car repair.

Twenty minutes later the card is in the mail and I'm working on data entry. Steven walks through the room and catches my eye. He winks.

I ignore him and return my gaze to the computer. It's time to pull back a little and make him work for it. Maybe I'll grab lunch with Luke after all.

CHAPTER 25

Luke looks delighted to see me again. I'm not sure why. I only have thirty minutes, so we're definitely not going back to his place for a quickie.

"You said yes," he says as he meets me on the street in front of the restaurant. It's an Indian buffet I figure Steven would never stumble upon.

"I was tired of playing hard to get," I joke.

"Thanks for throwing me a bone."

He knows I don't have much time, so we head inside and get right in line with our plates. I load mine up with a little of everything and I notice Luke does the same. He even grabs an extra plate to hold naan for both of us, along with a few dipping sauces.

"How's your week going?" he asks as we find a table.

"Really good. I'm getting a lot of stuff done. How about you?"

"Same old, same old. How's the cat?"

"She's great."

"Does she have a name yet?"

I shrug. "I asked, but she's being pretty cagey."

"Cats, man."

We dig into our food. It's not the best Indian I've ever had, but the chicken is spicy and the naan is warm and fresh out of the oven, and that's good enough for me.

"I hear it's going to snow tonight," Luke says.

"Sure feels like it."

"Can I talk you into coming over to hide under the covers and watch a movie?"

I stare blankly at him for a moment. "You mean have sex, right?"

He turns bright red and coughs.

I can be charming. In fact, I'm really good at it. Small talk doesn't make me nervous, so I ask all the right questions and make people feel special and engaged. I'm good at lying and I enjoy it. It's an intricate, beautiful dance. But, like a dance, it takes concentration and effort, and pretending that I actually like that jackass Steven is draining me.

I don't want to lie right now. I don't want to be charming and warm and human. I just want to relax.

Luke gulps some water and recovers, though his cheeks are still pink. "No," he says. "I mean yes, maybe sex too."

I nod.

"But I was mostly asking about the movie."

I don't like movies as much as books. With books, the narrator explains what people are feeling and thinking, so I don't have to figure it out. But some movies are easier than others. "Okay. Something with action, maybe? Explosions?"

"The movie or the sex?" he asks, and I'm laughing again. Really laughing. He grins like he's proud of himself.

I grin back. "I meant both, obviously."

"I'll do my best."

"Then I'll see you at seven."

We finish our plates and go back for seconds. I get a big cup of rice pudding too. Luke doesn't notice or doesn't care.

I should be spending time manipulating Steven, but I'm so glad I met Luke for lunch instead. Something about this day has thrown me off, and I'm not sure what it is.

"My mom called this morning," I say abruptly. "She asked for money and I sent it. Why do I send her money when I don't even like her?"

"Guilt," Luke suggested immediately.

"I don't think that's it."

"It's a pretty strong emotion. We're supposed to care about our families no matter how bad they are. So even if you feel like you don't want to help, you've been told your whole life that you should."

That's true. I take my behavioral cues from others. It's my way of flying under the radar and fitting in.

"I don't *feel* guilty," I say, not sure how to explain that without telling the truth. "I mostly just want her to go away."

He nods. "Sure. You've learned that it's easier to give her what she wants."

"But if I don't give her what she wants, she'll eventually go away altogether, right? And that would be better. So why do I accommodate her?"

"Do you really want her to go away forever? It would be walking away from the first eighteen years of your life. We all want a foundation, I think, even if it's cracked and damaged. We want proof of where we came from even if we're running away from it."

"Maybe." Do I need a foundation? I feel like I'm utterly independent. But I obviously want something from those people. Am I still waiting to feel like I'm the same as other humans? That I have a family and connections and a heart? Do I keep my family in my life so I can pretend I'm normal?

"I haven't spoken to my mom in five years," Luke says, "but I still check her Facebook page. Same thing, I'm sure."

"Do you love her?" I ask out of curiosity.

"Yes. She's my mom." He shrugs and shakes his head. "We're all idiots, I guess."

"What did she do?" Even I understand this isn't a question I should ask. Not here and not now, but I want to know.

He sighs and finishes chewing a bite of food. "It's a long story. Suffice to say she's easily riled up."

He's already told me no one ever hit him, so I'm not sure what he means, but it's getting late, and he doesn't look like he wants to say more anyway.

"I'd better get going," I say. "Your place at seven?"

Luke stands when I do and says he'll get the check.

I feel calmer as I walk back to the office. A few fat snowflakes drift lazily from the sky, but nothing much happens after that. I hope it snows more later. I like the picture Luke has painted for me. A warm, cozy blanket, his leather couch and hot body, buildings exploding on the screen. I think it will feel real, and I don't get to feel real very often.

Steven is waiting for me when I get off the elevator. He herds me toward the break room, but there are two women eating there, so he moves farther down the hall toward the supply closet. "Where'd you go?" He keeps his voice low, but he's radiating secrets and scandal for anyone who sees us talking.

"Out," I answer.

"I was going to take you to lunch."

"Were you going to walk me back afterward or put me in a car by myself?"

"Oh, come on!" He tips his head back and rolls his eyes at the ceiling. "Are you kidding me? I'd had, like, four beers!"

It was six, actually. "Sure. I get it."

"You get it, but you're going to treat me like crap anyway?"

"I went out for lunch, Steven. How is that about you?"

"And the way you're acting now isn't about me?"

"How do you expect me to feel? I did . . . *that*, and you made me feel like a call girl afterward!"

"You said you needed to go! How is that my fault?"

"I don't just sleep with anyone, you know." I cover my face as if I'm crying. I can go through the motions, but I'm not always good at making my eyes water. "I'm a nice girl. I really am. And when we do those things . . . I just . . . Do you even *like* me?"

"Hey, come on. Don't cry. Of course I like you. I took you to my dad's church! You're being really silly about this. Maybe it's PMS."

"It's not PMS! I feel like . . . I feel like I'm being dirty."

"Come on. You've done that with other boyfriends."

"Yes, but . . . I don't even know if you're really my boyfriend."

"Of course I'm your boyfriend."

"You didn't ask me to spend the night."

"I'm sorry. I should have."

I sniff and let out a shuddery breath. "Really?"

"Really. I like you a lot, Jane. I don't want to make you feel that way."

Funny, because I can see he has an erection right now. My shame is a huge turn-on for old Steven. What a piece of work.

"You don't think I'm a slut?" I whisper.

Steven chuckles. "Would I take you to my dad's party if I thought you were a slut?"

I peek up between my fingers. "Are we going?"

"Yeah. It's tomorrow night. Are you free?" He asks that like he's teasing me. Like it's a joke that I might have something else to do.

I nod. "Yes."

"Good. And listen . . ." He glances over his shoulder to be sure no one else is in the hallway before he leans close. "Last night was so damn good, baby."

"Shh!"

"I hope it's not dirty if I'm your boyfriend, because . . ."

"It *is* dirty!" But I'm giggling a little now. "Stop it. You said you wanted a nice Christian girl, and I'm trying to live right."

"As long as you're trying, that's what counts."

"Yeah?"

"Yeah." He smiles down at me. "I talked you into it, so you don't have to feel bad."

"It's still a sin."

"It is, but you made your man happy, and that's part of living right, isn't it?"

"I guess."

He winks. "Want me to ask my dad about it?"

I squeal and shove him away. "You're awful."

"Maybe, but I got you to smile again. Feel better?"

"I do."

"So do you have time to see your new boyfriend tonight, sweetheart?"

He's teasing again, but I'll be busy having sex with another man tonight, so too bad. "I can't. I booked a haircut to make myself feel better."

Steven throws back his head and laughs. "Girls," he says with exasperation.

He won't notice that I didn't get a trim. He won't notice Luke's smell on me either. If I seem happier tomorrow, he'll assume it's because he's informed me we're officially going steady.

Girls. So easy to please.

CHAPTER 26

I haven't returned my rental car yet and it feels good to drive myself around for a change. I'm in control, even in the wet, heavy snow that starts falling before I get to Luke's condo. I spent my youth driving in Oklahoma ice storms and then Minnesota winters. Fresh snow is no problem for me.

Luke greets me with a kiss, and we order pizza and pile covers over our bodies on the couch as promised. He downloads a new action blockbuster I haven't seen, and I snuggle close to him. I don't get as close as another girl would, but my knee rests comfortably against his and his arm brushes mine every time he moves.

It feels nice and almost normal. But the truth is that I can't stop wondering what it should feel like and whether I'm acting the way a normal person would. We finish the pizza and have a couple of beers, but I can't lose myself in the movie. I can't be normal. I know there's only one way for me to stop pretending.

As a train derails in the movie and crashes into a high-rise, I slide my hand up Luke's thigh. He lets me tease him for a long while before he finally gives in with a deep groan and drags me onto his lap. Buildings fall on screen as we disappear beneath the covers. I finally stop thinking. Mostly.

The movie eventually goes silent. Luke strokes the sweat-damp hair from my face. He kisses my nose. "You should stay the night," he murmurs. "It's still snowing."

"I can't."

"Because you're seeing someone else?"

Instead of answering, I press my head to his chest and listen to the *thump thump* of his heart. The human body is such a strange puzzle of mechanical parts. So delicate and close to giving out at any moment. The tiniest weak link will bring everything tumbling down, yet we all walk around like we're unbreakable. It's odd.

"I just want to know if I have a chance," he says, the words rumbling through my cheek.

"I'm pretty confident I'm what's called a sure thing."

"You know that's not what I mean."

I cross my arms over his chest and raise my head to look at him. "Actually, I don't know. What *do* you mean?"

"I want to know if there's a chance for something serious."

"I'm only here temporarily."

"So you're definitely going back to Malaysia afterward?"

"Yes."

He raises an eyebrow. "You just adopted a cat. Can you take her overseas?"

"Probably."

"If you haven't even checked into it, I wonder if you're not so certain about your plans."

Is he right? I don't think so.

"Listen, I'm not saying let's be exclusive and start plotting out a future together. We've seen each other a few times now. I just want to know if you're about to get engaged to this other guy and start blocking my texts."

I actually snort at the idea that I would choose Steven and reject Luke. He smiles slowly at that, his eyes crinkling at the corners.

"I'm not about to get engaged and start blocking your texts."

"Okay, good. But it's still . . . complicated?"

He's not being too pushy, and I like that. He's not trying to claim me as his personal property after one week of sex. I can't tell him the truth, but I can offer him a reasonable lie.

"I'm seeing my boss. The guy who hired me for this project."

"Is it serious?"

"No. It's not serious. But breaking it off would cause tension I don't need. And you and I . . . we just met, Luke."

"Well, technically we are old friends."

He's teasing. His eyes are still smiling. His arms hold me loosely, as if he knows I may get up and leave at any moment, and he's fine with that.

"I'm not really a relationship type of girl," I tell him.

"How so?"

"I'm just not good at that stuff." I don't know how to say more than that, so I lay my head back on his chest.

"Because of your family?"

Well, yes. I suppose. The latest research on sociopathy hands some blame to genes and some to environment. My parents' behavior suggests pathological levels of selfishness and carelessness on both their parts. They combined their shitty genes and then ladled on hefty doses of neglect and emotional abuse, and here I am.

"My family is pretty special," I finally answer.

"Any more trouble from them?" he asks.

"Not tonight."

"Good." He kisses the top of my head and we lie comfortably together for a few minutes before I get restless and slide back to my side of the couch.

"You can stay," he says again.

I don't like staying. I prefer to leave as soon as the sex is done, yet I'm strangely lethargic and comfortable and I don't want to get dressed.

But we just finished having sex and it's not time for bed. "What would we do?"

"Anything. Watch another movie? Eat ice cream? Talk?"

I look around and spy a big bookshelf. "Could we just read?"

"Read?"

"Yes."

"Sure. You want to pick one of my books?"

"I have one with me."

Luke smiles. "Then we'll read."

"Okay, but we can still have ice cream."

"Obviously."

"And . . ." I glance toward his bathroom. "I noticed you have a big tub. I really miss my big bathtub in Malaysia."

He waves a hand. "Bathe away."

I might invite him to join me. I haven't decided yet. It might be more fun to let him listen to me splash around hot and naked and then tease the hell out of him until he grabs my wet body and throws me onto the bed.

But, for now, we both curl under the covers and read. I don't have to think of the right things to say and do. I can just observe others from the distance of the page. I relax and lose myself. Occasionally Luke strokes my foot. I feel like my cat. I like it.

CHAPTER 27

I get up early and sneak away before Luke wakes up. The spell is broken. I'm not a real girl and this coziness was only temporary.

I need to return the rental car today. I can afford to keep it as long as I like, but there's always the chance Steven will see me driving and ask questions.

He texted at 9:00 last night, but I ignored it. As soon as I get into my apartment, I text back. Sorry, I went to bed early. Just for fun I add: I fell asleep listening to Chicken Soup for the Woman's Soul. It's really good.

Hey! I'm just waking up. Wish you were here.

I could make you breakfast!

That's not really what I was thinking of.

I send back a goofy-faced emoji. Is that all you think about?

You're just so sexy, baby.

I think you need to learn more about resisting temptation.

Sure. Send me a pic and I'll see if I can stay strong.

Pervert!

Send a pic.

I'm not sending a pic! I'm seeing your family tonight!!!

I promise not to show them.

Shut up.

He sends me three pink heart emojis and I guess I'm supposed to melt at that. Whatever. I imagine sending Steven a pic of what Luke did to me after that bath last night, and I giggle so hard, I snort. If I did, Steven would break it off, but let's be honest, it would turn him on too.

I text him a big, fat red heart and tell him I'll see him later. Then I turn on my laptop and watch as he masturbates in bed.

He's looking at his phone as he furiously takes care of business, and I know damn well he isn't using our text conversation to get off. I wonder what kind of porn he's into. I'm sure he'll make me watch it at some point.

After he tugs his pajama pants back up, I review the night's videos. There's nothing interesting. He came home and changed into shorts before disappearing into his workout room. When he reappeared, he made a sandwich and then watched TV for a long time.

At 8:30 he got a phone call, and I listen to him counsel one of the parishioners, hoping there will be juicy details, but it's just a lot of scripture talk about walking alongside Jesus and being a rod of strength for his family even in a financial crisis.

Boring. Still, he's good at talking the talk. In fact, I think his religious beliefs are sincere. He seems to genuinely care about the parishioner on the other end of the phone. Steven's problem area is women. And hypocrisy.

I watch as Steven gets off the call and scrolls through something on his screen. God, I hope I learn something useful soon. I'm unsure about how to accelerate my plan, and I'm not used to uncertainty.

I should do some laundry and go grocery shopping, but I'm bored with the idea of chores and bored with watching Steven groom himself. I click around on my computer a little and then open my file full of Meg's pictures.

She sent me selfies all the time, but my folder is also full of photos she posted to Facebook. Photos of her laughing, smiling, looking sexy. There are photos of us together too, but I'm not worried Steven will recognize me from Meg's social media. When I'm myself, my hair is dark, nearly black, and my makeup as well. If he were a woman—or just a man who took care with others—he might recognize my features despite the frosty pink makeup and the lightened layers of grown-out bangs. Luke recognized me, after all. But Steven doesn't care about others enough to see the woman beneath the stupid pastel dresses and shimmery blush.

I click through the pictures, though I've long since memorized each one. Here's Meg in a bikini making a silly face. Here she is dressed up in snowboarding gear and beaming past her scarf. And here's a profile picture of her staring into the distance, looking a little sad and lost.

After she died, I backed up every photograph, because I was terrified I'd lose my phone and Meg would be gone forever.

I know she really is gone forever. I know that. She's no longer in the world, and all I have are pictures. So I'm alone.

I've been alone before. I walk away from people. I leave them behind. But I'm the one left behind now.

I open a picture of her grinning into the camera, her blond hair pulled by the wind into streamers that stand up from her head. It was taken at the lake on my last visit, and the next picture is both of us together. I'm tan and smiling, my arm around her, and she's leaning her head on my shoulder. Normally she shines next to me, but we were both trying to fake smiles that day. Me because it's what I know, and Meg because her heart was breaking over Steven.

I can still smell her shampoo as the wind whipped her hair over my face. It was a good day, a really good day, but not good enough, apparently.

I want it back.

If this is what love is, it's terrible. Why do people seek it out? And why have I ever wished to be like everyone else? Meg felt this pain when Steven stopped answering her calls. She felt this way when her grandfather died. I held her when she cried about it, though I'd been completely baffled by her weakness.

And that's what this is. Love. It's weakness. Vulnerability. It's waiting for an inevitable wound and then praying it will someday heal.

I don't pray, and I hate waiting.

I open the picture I've moved down to the very bottom of the file. It's a selfie of Meg. She's holding her phone out, arm stretched as far as it will go so she can get Steven in the picture too. She's kissing his cheek, her eyes crinkled with a smile while Steven smirks at the camera.

Me and my Sweetie! That's the caption she texted with the picture. Her Sweetie. The man who'd chipped slowly away at her unstable self-esteem the same way he was trying to do mine. Little comments about her looks, her intelligence, her choices, her hobbies. Pointed questions about her sex life. Then tiny approvals to soothe her hurt.

She'd gladly changed for him. She wore longer skirts and stopped going out with her single girlfriends. She brewed her own iced coffee so she wouldn't spend so much at Starbucks. She stopped working Saturday nights at the bar and grill even though she made the most tips then.

Too many drunk guys, she explained to me. *It's not really safe.* This from a girl who'd held her own working at a seedy nightclub at eighteen.

And, of course, she'd started going to church. She found God and discovered that she'd been living a wicked life of sin until then. Somehow the sinning with Steven didn't count. I'm sure he came up with a sound explanation for that, especially when he pushed her to her knees and told her to make him happy. She probably never even questioned it.

I stare into Steven's smirking face. The self-satisfied twist of his lips. The gleam of possession in his eyes.

He left her a voice mail while we were at the cabin. I listened to it after Meg dropped her phone and ran into the bathroom to sob.

Stop calling me. Stop texting me. We're not going to be together. I will never marry a stupid whore like you. I would never let you raise my kids. And don't call my dad again or I'll show him just how many slut pictures you texted me. Do you think he'll feel bad for you after he sees you spreading your legs like the piece of trash you are? You're an embarrassment. The world would be better off without you in it.

I open the camera feed on my laptop and watch Steven smooth gel into his hair. He's whistling. Once his hair looks perfect, he makes his bed and then dusts his hands as if he's finished a big project. He's so satisfied with his tidy little life.

I can't wait to watch it all crumble into a smoking pile of shit.

My cat appears and rubs her cheek against me in approval. She understands exactly. The kill is fun, but toying with your prey is really the best part.

CHAPTER 28

"Is this dress okay?" It's light gray and fitted. The skirt is knee-length, but the bodice shows off a little cleavage. I'm wearing a white cardigan over the dress and a delicate necklace: a gold filigree cross I bought this morning.

"It's fine, but leave the sweater on."

"Aw. I think it's pretty." I shrug the sweater off and wiggle my bare shoulders. Steven looks away from the stoplight to ogle my breasts.

"It is pretty, but this isn't some sleazy bar. Are you wearing a bra?"

"Yes!" I yelp. "It's just strapless. Jeez."

"Keep the sweater on."

"Fine." I pout. "I just . . . I thought you'd like it, that's all. It's a party."

He pats my knee and then rests his hand on my thigh. "I do like it, baby. You can model it for me later, all right? Without the sweater. Show me how pretty you feel."

I giggle and shove his hand away when he tries to slide it higher. "You're so bad."

"I am, but best behavior tonight, okay? There will be a lot of important people there."

"Got it."

"No drinking."

"Oh. Okay. If you think so."

"This isn't your normal crowd."

I nod as if I haven't been to multiple parties at the American embassy in Malaysia with dignitaries from all over the world. Yes, it's been all keggers and ragers for me. I hope I'll be able to keep my panties from falling off in the middle of a conversation about the local chamber of commerce.

Steven's been on his best behavior this week, charming and mostly kind, so things are proceeding nicely. I plan on sleeping with him tonight.

I turn to watch the world slide by through my window.

It's dusk, and the streetlights begin to flicker on. All the snow that fell this week has melted, but the weight of it pulled down most of the turning leaves, and the city looks bleak.

We get on the freeway and head out of town toward houses with bigger yards. By the time we reach Pastor Hepsworth's house, a little farther away than the church, the yards have turned into mini-estates, each big plot at least an acre of land. "Did you grow up here?" I ask.

"No, my dad bought this place when he remarried. I was twenty, so I lived here on and off during college, but I grew up just a few blocks from the church."

The houses closest to the church are big split-levels built in the early '80s, and I wonder if that's why he bought a similar-style house for himself.

"Your mom is in Rochester?" I ask.

"Yeah."

"Do you still see her a lot?"

"Not really. She made her choices."

"She's still your mom, though."

"She was a shitty mother."

"Oh no! I didn't realize. Was she . . . was she a drunk or something?"

"No, but she destroyed my dad and broke up her family. She doesn't get to come back around playing mommy now."

"Jesus teaches forgiveness, though."

"And God said to stone adulterers to death. I think not spending holidays with her seems like a good middle ground."

Yikes.

Steven takes my hand for a moment. "And when I have kids, I won't want them spending time around a woman who doesn't know anything about faithfulness or marriage. Would you?"

"I don't know. My mom has been divorced a couple of times, and she's a good person. She'll make a really good grandma."

"You're telling me that when your mom was dating and living the single life she exposed you to the best values?"

"I . . ." I've thought the same thing about Meg's mom, but it's not that simple. My parents let me live through hell, and they've never spent a night apart as far as I can tell.

"Exactly," Steven says. "You were probably molested, weren't you?"

He says it smugly. Oh, he's softened his voice to make it sound like sympathy, but I hear the self-righteous lilt at the end. He can tell I was trained from a young age to feel like crap about myself.

I duck my head and don't answer.

"Who was it?" he asks.

"Come on, Steven. I don't want to talk about that."

"Why?"

"It's shameful."

"You can tell me. If we're going to have a future, we have to be honest with each other. And God has already forgiven you. You know that."

"I know."

"It wasn't your fault your mom was living that way. Was it some boyfriend of hers?"

"No."

"Stepdad?"

I swallow hard and nod. "But it wasn't . . . it wasn't that bad, I guess. He just touched me. He didn't . . . you know . . ."

"How old were you?"

"Twelve."

"Jesus."

None of that's true. It wasn't a stepdad and it was far more than touching and I wasn't anywhere close to twelve. I was seven, and it was the gross man who'd rented a room in our double-wide that year. When my mom explained that he'd watch me when she and my dad were out, I was relieved. So relieved. I'd hated it when they up and disappeared for days at a time. But my relief at having another adult in the house didn't last more than a month.

So, by the time I was twelve, I'd already learned I could use my sexuality against men. I could use it against them or they'd use it against me.

Them or me, and it wasn't ever going to be me again.

"That's when I started going to church," I lie. "I knew something was wrong. I just wanted someone to protect me, and God was . . . Well, I started going to church with a friend from school, and it felt like God was the only good man in my life. I prayed so hard. And my stepdad eventually left."

Steven squeezes my hand. He turns into a long driveway and parks behind a line of shiny new cars. He lifts my hand and turns to me before he gives a kiss to my knuckles. "I'm good at protecting people, Jane."

I nod and press my lips tight together as if I'm trying not to tear up.

"And I'm a good man."

"I know."

"Maybe God brought me into your life to take care of you."

"Oh, Steven," I sigh. I drop my head and sniff, letting my breath shudder out of me. "That would be really, really nice."

"I know we've only been dating a few weeks, Jane, but it feels like I was called to take care of you. Guide you. I'm not like other guys you've dated. I believe in commitment. I believe in love and respect."

I breathe shakily and nod, keeping my face covered. "I love that about you."

"And my dad already likes you. That means the world to me."

"I like him too."

"Make me proud tonight, baby." He pulls me into a hug and kisses my cheek.

"I'll try."

"Good girl."

This was all Meg ever wanted. A nice man who'd protect her. A decent husband who would take care of his family and home. That had been her dream since childhood. I'd seen the notebooks she'd kept as a little girl, with pictures of wedding dresses and Victorian houses and adorably decorated nurseries. I teased her and she laughed about it, but she kept those notebooks her whole life.

Steven had dreamed those dreams with her. They spoke of marriage and how many kids they'd have. He told her how much he wanted to be the kind of father his own dad was. He even painted a picture of having their first son baptized in the United in Christ Church, the baby's head cleansed of sin by the hand of his own grandfather.

I have no idea if he believed in those dreams too or if he was just toying with her. I don't care. Either way, he built her up on good days and then used the fantasy of their future together to tear her to pieces when he was angry. He knew just what Meg wanted and he terrorized her with her own childhood dreams.

He thinks he knows what I want too. He thinks I'll do anything for it.

We walk through the dusk toward a big white house with a wrap-around porch. The lights glow with welcome and warmth. I can hear faint laughter from inside.

"Steven," I whisper, tugging him to a stop. It's time to make clear just how eager I am for the smallest bits of affection. He turns toward me and I gaze up at him, stars in my eyes. "I love you."

He smiles and cups my cheek, holding me tenderly for a moment before he gives me a gentle kiss. He doesn't reply in kind, but he does gaze fondly at me for a long time before putting his arm around my waist to lead me toward the front stairs. He looks pleased, and he should be. I'm vulnerable and he has the power.

The party is exactly what I expect. There's soft, vague music playing beneath the murmur of conversation. There's a room off the entry where everyone leaves their coats. Many square feet of middle-aged white people stretch out before us. I see a few children darting between the adults.

I stay close to Steven as he picks a trail through the guests. Most of them hold wineglasses, but I'm not allowed to touch. I will absolutely be imbibing in the bathroom within the hour. I'm not good at watching other people do things I want to do.

If I were really Low Self-esteem Jane, this party would feel magical. The Hepsworths probably call themselves upper-middle-class, but through the eyes of almost anyone else in this country, they're rich. The lights of an outdoor pool glint through a back window, and they can probably only use it a few months a year, if they bother using it at all. The floors are all hardwood and crowned with molding that looks like icing on a wedding cake. There's a dining room and a study and a media room, and of course a huge kitchen, complete with two sinks and a fridge that blends in with the cabinets.

This is the kind of life I can look forward to someday if I can just learn to be what Steven wants me to be. If I can please him, if I don't make him mad, if I live in the *right*.

Steven finds his father and raises a hand to hail him from across the room like a long-lost college buddy. As far as I know, Steven saw him on Wednesday for Bible study. They love each other excessively, and

I'm beginning to think their relationship may be my key to Steven's downfall.

"Dad!" We've worked our way through the crowd to Pastor Hepsworth for the requisite father-son hug and backslaps. I stand demurely aside.

"I see you brought your pretty friend," the pastor finally says.

I smile shyly. "Thank you for the invitation, Pastor Hepsworth."

"It's my pleasure, dear. I'm happy you could make it."

"You have a beautiful house. Steven was just telling me he didn't grow up here, but he got the chance to stay for a while during college."

"Yes, we lived a little more modestly when Steven was young, but the Lord does provide."

"He certainly does. And Steven can't speak highly enough of you, sir. I wish I'd had a father like you when I was growing up."

He nods sympathetically. "The world isn't what it used to be, I'm afraid."

"It sure isn't." I lean a bit closer and put my hand on his arm. "But I want you to know that the church was a sanctuary for me when I was a girl, and I know there must be a lot of young women who look up to you as a father figure. I know I would have." I nod earnestly and slide my hand down his arm. "Thank you so much for that."

His eyes actually look a little damp. He grasps my hand between both of his and squeezes. "That means the world to me. Steven, this girl is just a darling."

"She is," he agrees.

"Oh, stop now," I scold. "You're making me blush." He's not, but my words alone will make it true. I wrap my free hand over his for a moment and slide my fingers along his knuckles before he lets me go.

Steven grins proudly.

They start talking church business and I smile vacantly as though I'm not listening. I am.

Before I arrived in Minneapolis, I'd thought I could set Steven up for embezzlement and get him sent to prison, but I can't see a way to make that happen now. The business is a standard midlevel health insurance company with lots of moving parts and redundant safeguards. The accounting department is located at the headquarters in New Jersey, and all checks are cut there in a process that seems as laborious as childbirth. Steven doesn't have an expense account. He doesn't distribute payroll. He doesn't even shift money from department to department.

But the church . . . the church no doubt has looser accounting standards and probably a slush fund that pays the Hepsworth family expenses. I may be able to find a way to funnel some of that money into Steven's personal account. Or maybe just write him a few checks from their account. I'm not bad at forgery.

"Daniel's cabin is open next weekend if you're interested," I hear Steven's dad say, and Steven perks up.

"Are you kidding? I'd love to get out."

"Get out for what?" I ask.

"Deer," he says shortly, as if I've interrupted important talk.

"Oh no!" I cry. "You don't shoot them, do you?"

The men both laugh condescendingly. "Of course we shoot them," Steven says.

"But they're so cute!"

"They're also a nuisance. You know how many car accidents they cause every year?"

"But—"

"Where do you think your food comes from?" Steven asks. "The supermarket? It comes from animals that people kill."

"I know that." I pout a little, and Pastor Hepsworth reaches out to pat my arm.

"This is why men hunt and women don't."

Steven winks. "Maybe I should teach her how to hunt and toughen her up a little."

"No way," I protest, but then I see the opportunity I've been presented. "Although . . . I have always wanted to learn to shoot."

"Oh ho!" Pastor Hepsworth cries. "She gets better and better! Maybe you should give her some lessons."

"I could come to the cabin with you this weekend!" I suggest.

Steven clears his throat. "That wouldn't be appropriate, Jane."

Oops. I've painted myself as a woman who'd spend the night with a man she's dating. "Of course. I only meant—"

"Perhaps just a day at the range to start," Pastor Hepsworth suggests. "Or maybe fishing."

"Yes. Perhaps." We fall into an awkward silence. "Well," I murmur, "I think I'll find your wife and wish her a happy birthday."

"Good idea," Steven says, turning away from me to talk to his father again. I've been dismissed for my transgression. Such swift punishment.

I smile as I walk away. Steven truly doesn't want his father to see him as anything other than the perfect Christian son. I'm kind of surprised he ever let Meg move into his house in the first place, but she told me once that his family had no idea. He probably made her keep all her stuff in boxes in the storage room just in case his dad stopped by.

I know Steven will stick close to his father for a while at least, so I grab a glass of white wine from the caterer's bar and roam the rest of the house. I discover a big family room and another office, this one tucked at the end of a hallway near the laundry.

Slipping inside, I close and lock the office door behind me and turn on the light.

I sip my wine and methodically go through the drawers of the desk, but most of the documents are at least five years old. I do make one interesting find, though. Medical bills and records for an infertility specialist. Not exactly a big surprise when an older man is trying to knock up a younger wife. Still, I might be able to use it. I tuck the papers into my purse just in case.

I slip back out into the hallway and nearly run into one of the caterers coming through a back door. "Spanx," I complain. "They never stay up."

She laughs. "Yeah, I finally said screw it and stopped wearing them." I give her a high five.

After ditching my empty wineglass, I venture back toward the main crowd and finally spot Rhonda, the birthday girl.

She must dress for church like she's putting on armor, because she looks softer tonight. And younger. She really is just a few years older than Steven, and it makes sense that he stiffens when I call her his stepmother.

The jewel-green wrap dress she's wearing shows off her tight figure, and her makeup is more natural, though her mouth gleams with bright-red lipstick. There's no stiffness to her smile tonight, and I suspect the drink she holds isn't her first.

I wait until the gray-haired woman Rhonda is talking to drifts away, and then I approach. "Happy birthday, Mrs. Hepsworth." She turns to me with a blank smile. "I'm Jane," I remind her. "Steven's friend."

"Oh, of course. Jane. Thank you."

"This is such a beautiful house. Thank you for the invitation. I'm honored."

She lifts a shoulder, because she wasn't the one who invited me, after all. "Glad you could make it. Let me get you a drink." She raises a hand to one of the circulating caterers and snags a glass of red for me.

"I'm not sure I should, Mrs. Hepsworth."

"Oh for God's sake, call me Rhonda. We're the youngest women here."

I nod and take the wine. She's right, of course. It's her birthday, but these are all Robert Hepsworth's contemporaries, aside from the few children I've seen. Has she been isolated out here by her husband, a beautiful bird in a beautiful cage? It would make sense after the way his first marriage ended. He's not going to trust his tight young wife to wander the world free and easy.

"So you're dating Steven?" she asks.

"Yes." I sip my wine carefully, as if I'm not used to drinking.

She studies me for a moment, offering no praise for her stepson.

"It's so hard to find a good, upstanding man these days," I prompt her.

"Oh, indeed," she says, her smile spreading. "So very hard." She knocks back the rest of her wine and reaches toward another tray passing by. The caterer slows so she can exchange the empty glass for a full one; then Rhonda raises it in a tiny toast. "To the Hepsworth men," she drawls. "So upstanding."

She's definitely drunk, and apparently not one hundred percent happy with her husband. I use her offer of a toast to gulp half my wine. She does the same.

"Steven hasn't brought a girl around in quite a while. You must be pretty special."

"Oh, I'm not sure, but . . . but I like to think he—"

"You're vulnerable," she says. "A little lost."

"What?"

She laughs and waves her glass. "Nothing."

Well, she's got Steven's type pegged. Now I know why he doesn't seem to like her much. "Mrs. Hepsworth—"

"Rhonda," she snaps.

"Rhonda. Yes, I—"

"Jane." Steven says my name from behind me like a command. I'm supposed to snap to attention, and I do.

Despite the beer in his hand, he glares at the wineglass in mine. "I was just toasting Rhonda's birthday," I say quickly.

His angry gaze bounces between the two of us. "Happy birthday, Rhonda," he grinds out.

"Aw, thanks, Steven. So thoughtful." She tosses back the rest of her wine and hands him the empty glass. "I'd better go check on my husband."

"She's really nice," I say as soon as she's gone.

Steven sets Rhonda's glass on a table and rounds on me. "I asked you not to drink here."

"Rhonda handed me a glass and asked me to drink with her, and I didn't want to be rude."

"You didn't want to be rude to her, but you'll be rude to me by drinking?"

"I hardly had any. See?" I jerk the glass up too quickly and a little red wine sloshes over to land on the front of my white sweater. "Oh no. My sweater!"

"Now you're a sloppy drunk. At my dad's house. Great. Take that off before someone sees you."

"I'm not drunk," I assure him. "I only had a few sips." I struggle to undo the buttons of the sweater, nervous in the face of his angry disappointment. "I'm sorry," I say. "I didn't want to be rude on her birthday, that's all."

Once I have the sweater off, his eyes rake down my dress. "Great. You look like a fat slut, and I can't even take you home because we just got here."

Oh, Jesus, I'm a size ten. This guy really needs to get a grip. "Please don't say that," I whisper.

"I asked you to wear your sweater and not drink. That's it. Two simple things."

"Maybe Rhonda has a sweater I could borrow."

"As if you'd fit into hers."

"Steven, please don't be mean."

His eyes snap to mine as if he's heard that before. Meg probably said it a thousand times. "You're being mean to *me*," he growls.

"I'm sorry." I'm pleading now, reaching for his hand. "I'm sorry. The wine was just an accident. Please don't be mad. It's a nice party, and your dad is so sweet, and it's such a good night."

His shoulders soften a little. I'm saying all the right things, begging for forgiveness, complimenting his father, accepting responsibility.

"It's November," he mutters. "Why are you even wearing that dress?"

"I wore it for you. I thought it was pretty. That's all."

He nods and seems to simmer down. "At least it's not showing half your ass."

I slide a little closer. "We were toasting to you, you know."

"Who?"

"Me and Rhonda." That startles him. He frowns in the direction she went. "We were toasting the Hepsworth men."

He presses his lips together in a tight line and glares out at the room. Not what I expected.

"Was she part of the church? Is that how they met?"

"Yeah. She started working in the church office when she graduated from community college." Aw. A traditional May-December boss-and-secretary romance. How sweet and old-fashioned. Steven raises his bottle to his lips, but it's empty.

"Let me get you another beer, sweetie," I murmur. I take his empty and trot off to the kitchen to get my man a beverage. The birthday cake is sitting on the island. I count thirty-five candles. Steven is thirty-two. That means his father married a twenty-three-year-old when Steven was twenty, and she took a position of authority in the house. Steven obviously thinks she's some sort of grasping bitch, and she thinks he's an asshole. No reason they can't both be right.

I was going to spend the night at Steven's tonight, but I've screwed that up. Damn it. I want to move this relationship along, but he's already gotten the pleasure of degrading me about my looks and behavior. I can't be too easy a target or I'll be boring. It's a tightrope of misogyny.

Sex and humiliation are motivators for him, but his father's approval is the biggest one, and I can use that too. I find the pastor near a huge fireplace, and the fire is roaring. It's a cool night, but there are too many people packed in here, and he's sweating.

"Pastor Hepsworth, I was just getting Steven a beer. Would you like something to drink?"

His eyes slide over my shoulders, noting the change in wardrobe, but he doesn't leer. In fact, he offers a kind smile as he swipes a hand over his brow. "What a lovely offer, my dear. I'd love a whiskey soda."

"I'll be right back!"

I veer in Steven's direction to deliver the beer and a beaming smile. "I promised your dad a drink, so give me one second, baby."

He blinks. "My dad?"

Hurrying away, I find the makeshift bar at the corner of the dining room and ask for a whiskey soda, heavy on the whiskey. While I wait, I spy Steven making his way over to his father, though he has to stop every few feet to greet various guests.

He's all charm again, playing the very important deacon of United in Christ Church. I make it back to the pastor before Steven arrives.

"I mixed it for you myself," I say with a wink.

"Thank you, my dear." He sips and his eyebrows rise, but he drinks it quickly, still sweating from the fire.

"Can I ask you something about your work?" I ask with wide eyes.

"Of course."

"Do you work on your sermons all week? Or do you wait for them to come to you?"

He puffs up his chest a little and launches into a miniature sermon about being a vessel for the Lord's word. I hang on every word, letting him know how important he is. I nod and blink up at him with big eyes. He concentrates on each phrase. The words mean something to him. He's not a fraud—not in that way, anyway.

"My gosh, it's all just so intimidating," I breathe.

"Nonsense."

"You're so important. The work you do."

"If you open your heart to God, he flows through you. I am only a vessel, my dear. Are you coming to tomorrow's service?"

"I'll have to try to find a ride." I bite my lip and clasp my hands together. The motion pushes my breasts up, and his eyes stray there and he smiles a little before he looks away. "But I love the way you speak, so I'll try my best to come."

He pats my arm. "I'm sure Steven will bring you again."

"I hope so, sir. Another drink?" I wrap my hands around the glass and his fingers and ease the tumbler free.

"You don't have to . . . ," he starts, but he lets me take the drink away. I order the same again, and by the time I've returned, Steven is waiting with his father.

The pastor lights up when he spies me walking toward them. "Steven, I hope you're planning on bringing Miss Jane to church tomorrow."

"Well, I wasn't sure if—"

"You can't deny the word to one so eager to hear it."

"Very true," Steven agrees.

I smile shyly as I hand over the drink. "Pastor, you're so kind to me. But I'm not sure if Steven has time to—"

"Of course I do." Steven slides his arm around me and tucks me against his side. "Of course I do."

His father winks and takes another drink. I snuggle closer to his son. "Now I feel like I have two guardian angels watching over me."

"You've got a nice girl here, Steven."

"She's a sweetheart," he says, his voice gruff with pride at the praise.

I keep my fat slut mouth shut and smile up at him as if all is forgiven. This is his weakness, this love for his father, and I will find a way to crack it wide-open.

CHAPTER 29

Steven expected me to spend the night, I'm sure, but it was easy enough to get out of it. I told him I had my period. The end.

I woke up bright and early today and wore my most flowery dress to church. I'm not a VIP, so I don't get to sit with Steven in the front row, but I sit closer to the front this time, and I gaze up at Pastor Hepsworth throughout the service. Today he's speaking about generosity and charity . . . with a little homophobia thrown in, of course. Be kind and generous, but first to United in Christ Church and never to liberal organizations who don't discriminate against gays.

Another prejudice I'll never understand. Sex is apparently for procreation and not pleasure, and that's why gay sex is wrong, yet none of the men I've slept with have ever been in it for the babies. Strange.

Of course Steven nods along with the lecture, even though oral sodomy is clearly a favorite sport of his. I'm going to have to assume his dad likes it too, based on my own long-term studies of the general population.

I wonder if Meg started to believe this stuff. I can't imagine it. Meg had been a bit of a hippie, with love for everyone and anyone. Actually, she was a bit like Jesus Christ that way, accepting of all. I snicker and beam up at Pastor Hepsworth.

He hasn't been obviously lecherous with me, but there's no reason not to cover all my bases. Right now he's a father figure, and that fills him with a very satisfying pride. His leadership role in my life will make it easy for me to go to him for help. Advice and counseling—that kind of thing. I'll confess my transgressions to him and see what he has to say.

Even if he has good intentions, this man is excited by sin. And by younger women. He married a woman less than half his age, after all. Now she's just a wife, and being a husband at home isn't nearly as exciting as being a father figure in the office.

I have no idea if Pastor Hepsworth was kind to Meg or cruel. I don't care. He tells the members of his flock that women are devilish Jezebels tempting men into sin. He taught his son that. He made Steven into a monster, and despite his son's cruelty, Pastor Hepsworth is still proud of him.

Even if I had sympathy, he would deserve none of it. A man who stands up every Sunday to name other people as sinners shouldn't be susceptible to temptation at all. Live by the sword, die by the sword, my dear.

As Pastor Hepsworth's condemnation of godless liberals and socialists gets louder, I breathe faster and lick my lips, letting my mouth part slightly as I pant with excitement at his rousing speech. His eyes lock on me for a moment. I gaze in wonder. That's all the good pastor wants. A little worship from a young woman.

When he's done, I jump to my feet, clapping. I sing along to the final hymns, then hug the women seated on either side of me. It was a beautiful service. Everyone is glowing.

Instead of hanging back from the front of the crowd, this time I rush over to Rhonda. She's speaking to a brunette with two small children in tow.

I crouch down. "Hello! Didn't I see you at the birthday party last night?" They both nod a little shyly and stay close to their mother's legs. "I'm Jane."

Their mom nudges both of them. "Nice to meet you, Jane," they say in unison.

"Did you have fun at the party?"

The girl smiles and the boy nods. "We got cake," he says.

"Oh gosh, birthday cake is the best cake! The pink filling inside was my favorite part." Now they're grinning, and the girl excitedly tells the story of how she helped pick out a cake for her mommy's birthday. I listen, wide-eyed, and nod at every detail.

What can I say? Kids love me when I'm not being myself. I behave the way they imagine grown-ups should with children because I'm pretending to be an adult who likes kids. I give them what they think they want, same as I do with their parents.

"They are just adorable," I say to the mother before she bundles them up to take them outside.

Once she's gone, I lower my voice. "Rhonda, can I ask you something?"

"Sure."

"Did you know Steven's ex-girlfriend?"

Her brows rise, eyes brightening at the question. "Well. I . . ."

"He told me about her," I offer as assurance. "I know she . . . I mean, I know what happened."

"Tragic," Rhonda murmurs.

"I'm just worried, you know? I feel like he must still love her. They obviously had very intense feelings for each other."

Rhonda laughs. She actually laughs. "*Intense* is a good way to describe it."

"Do you think he still loves her?"

"I wouldn't worry too much about that." One corner of her mouth tips up in a tiny smirk, as if this is all very amusing to her. "Poor girl," she murmurs. I'm not sure if she's talking about me or Meg.

"Did you know her well?" I press.

One of her shoulders lifts. "Not well. My husband counseled her about their arguments, but she and I didn't spend much time together."

Oh, Meg. Going to your boyfriend's dad for advice about his abuse? What did the good pastor tell her?

Steven walks toward us, and Rhonda excuses herself. They really don't like to be in the same room together. He must have gotten drunk and called her a money-grubbing whore at some point. I can't wait to hear the story.

I gush to Steven about the church and his father, and once the place starts clearing out a little, I ask if they run the whole thing here in this building.

"We do. Dad's offices are in the back. And, of course, there's accounting and the communications office, along with the volunteer coordinators."

"Can I see it?" I'm practically clapping my hands with excitement.

"I'm not sure if—"

But his father is walking over now, eyebrows high in question.

"Jane wants to know if she can see the offices, but I don't know if—"

"Absolutely!" he booms. "Give her the grand tour."

"Oh, thank you, Pastor Hepsworth. You're such an inspiration." I dart close and give him a quick hug, then immediately pull back and apologize. "I'm so sorry."

He's chuckling, his cheeks still red from the rousing sermon. "Nonsense, my dear. Go enjoy the tour."

As we cross the grand hall of the church, I look back to see him smiling proudly at us. I give him a little wave and he waves back.

"I just can't believe you grew up like this," I whisper as we step through double doors into a wide hallway. "You must have felt so safe."

"My dad is the best. I really had a perfect childhood." His soft smile abruptly freezes. "Well, until my mom . . ."

"But it was good until then?"

"Yes. It was perfect." His voice roughens a little with grief.

Steven has no resiliency, I guess. He didn't learn about pain and disappointment until he was fifteen. Now every little letdown is a threat to him. Every weakness a sign of looming betrayal. I got a cat, so I need to be slapped down. Another man talked to Meg, so she had to be ground to smithereens. The smallest infraction might mean he's about to be humiliated and abandoned again.

Such a delicate flower, our Steven.

I know he didn't kill Meg. I know she killed herself. So is it fair that I blame him so thoroughly?

Well, first of all, life isn't fair, and Steven has had a hell of a lot more good fortune than Meg or I ever had. He's mad that his mom stepped off the path of righteousness after fifteen-plus years. My parents never once set foot on it or even tried. And Meg's father had been an example of moral frailty from the time she was born until the day he walked out on her forever when she was three. Just old enough to feel the loss.

So excuse me if I think Steven got a better deal.

My lack of sympathy aside, even if he didn't technically kill Meg, she would never, ever have killed herself if Steven hadn't tortured her. And it was torture. That constant push-pull of love and abuse. *I want you, I hate you, I love you, you're nothing.* Over and over again.

I've experienced it myself. I know it deeply. My parents were casual in their abuse. Unthinking. But Steven *wanted* Meg to crave his approval just so he could remove it as a form of punishment. He wanted her to hurt and hurt badly every single time he felt a moment's fear.

If he'd beaten her to death, it would be simple for everyone. But for me, this is still simple. Suicide was the method of her death, but this man was the *cause*. She'd struggled with anxiety in her life but she'd never been depressed. Not until Steven.

He shows me all the different offices, and I pretend to be rapt as I case the joint. There's not much here to go on, although the newsletter list could be helpful if I can get it. The door to the communications office is wide-open and unoccupied, and I assume it stays that way all the time.

The accounting office is locked tight. I wonder if the donations are stashed in there for the night. Churches aren't any more trusting than other businesses, so there must be a safe, either in the accounting department or in the pastor's personal office. I'm not a movie sociopath, just a regular one, so I wasn't born with any inherent safecracking abilities. Locks can't be manipulated the way people can.

The last stop on the tour is Pastor Hepsworth's personal office, and it's as grand as I expect. Not ostentatious but dark and woody and lined with bookshelves. Steven opens the door but does not cross the threshold.

A big walnut desk takes up a huge amount of floor space, and a tall leather chair sits behind it, awaiting the pastor's ass. The two chairs angled in front of the desk are much smaller, of course. He must loom over his guests as he gives counsel. Fair enough. He's the big man here.

I whisper in awe, "I'm imagining you playing under the desk as a little boy."

Steven laughs. "Not this desk and in a much smaller building, but yes."

"Christmas must be grand here."

Steven closes the door and smiles down at me. "I'm hoping you'll be here to see it."

I tip my head back and sigh. "Me too." I close my eyes when he kisses me. I melt. But modestly. Not into him but into the doorjamb behind me. He pulls back after a gentle peck on my lips, but he raises a hand to tenderly cup my cheek.

"I was proud of you today," he murmurs.

"You're so good to me."

"When will you be done with your . . . you know?"

My woman's curse? "In a few days."

"Good. Want to come over on Thursday?"

I duck my head shyly. We both know what he means. "That would be really nice," I whisper. "I mean, if you think it's okay."

"I think it's more than okay."

I don't get periods. I'm on a continuous cycle of birth control pills, so I'm in complete control of my hormones. But it's a good way to put Steven off whenever I want to. As far as he'll know, I bleed like a stuck pig every twenty days. It's not like he'd ever take the chance of coming in contact with my menstrual blood. Please.

Steven drives me home and I'm free for the entire afternoon. I play with my cat and then walk to the little Italian restaurant for an early dinner. I drink a whole carafe of wine by myself. It's heaven.

CHAPTER 30

Looks like it's the last warm day of fall.

I pause in my data entry and glance at my phone to read Luke's text.

A few seconds later a second one appears. Want to go to the zoo tonight?

The zoo? My hands hover over the keyboard as I frown at the bizarre question. Why would I want to go to the zoo? I'm not a child.

Not that I ever went to the zoo as a child either. There weren't a lot of zoos in the panhandle.

I text back three question marks.

The zoo is lit up for the holiday season starting in November. Supposed to be 50 degrees tonight. Go with me?

Maybe this is a thing that normal people do? I shrug and text back a yes, agreeing to meet him outside my apartment at 6:30.

Luke is one of those impulses I have trouble resisting. Being involved with him doesn't forward my mission here. In fact, it puts it in danger. Unfortunately I like a little danger. It quickens my blood the same way sex does. Otherwise, the world is too steady for me. Boring.

Maybe that's why so many sociopaths end up habitually hurting people, even killing them. It's not about the people; it's about the danger.

And there's a good chance Luke will get hurt here. When I leave, I'll go abruptly and I may very well leave a trail of crimes in my wake. No one knows I'm involved with Luke. He won't get pulled in. But he may find out and be hurt or frightened at how close we were. Or maybe he won't care. I'm not sure.

As I've said before, it's difficult to figure out how nice people work. I can manipulate Luke with sex, but a nice guy wants more than that, apparently. He wants to go to lunch and . . . and to *zoos*.

There's finally birthday cake in the office today, and I jump up from my desk when I see everyone else headed toward the far corner of the floor. It's Karen's birthday. I don't know Karen, but I sing along with the crowd and clap when she blows out the candles. Someone tries to hand me a piece of cake, but I pass it along and wait for a bigger slice. It's chocolate with white frosting, my favorite. Steven steps off the elevator just as I stuff a huge bite into my mouth. His eyebrows rise and then drop into a deep frown. I wish I had milk. There's nothing better than chocolate cake and ice-cold milk.

He joins the circle and stands next to me as he accepts his own piece. "Happy birthday, Karen!" he calls; then he nudges me and lowers his voice. "Are you skipping lunch?"

"No, why?"

"Really?" He shifts his eyes meaningfully to my cake.

"Lunch isn't for an hour."

"I know, but you just had cake on Saturday."

"So did you."

He rolls his eyes. "Whatever."

I try to pout while still chewing my next bite. "I'm not fat, and you're making me feel bad."

"I know you're not fat, baby, but you don't have a lot of wiggle room."

I take my cake back to my desk.

Once he's in his office, I text him. Was your ex-girlfriend skinnier than me?

I can actually hear him sigh from his office.

I told you she was crazy.

Yeah, but she had a hot body, right?

Sure.

He waits a few minutes, and when I don't respond, he texts, Don't pout. You know I think you're hot.

I text back a heart and finish my cake. I can't believe I'm saying this, but I'm really looking forward to going to the zoo.

CHAPTER 31

I have a few minutes to spare before heading downstairs to meet Luke, so I read through the papers I stole from the Hepsworths' desk on Saturday. I glanced over them yesterday, of course, but I was busy playing with my cat and then doing laundry and grocery shopping, and I get distracted easily.

Old Pastor Hepsworth has a low sperm count and decreased motility. He also has trouble regularly maintaining an erection long enough to ejaculate. Viagra was prescribed to good effect. The patient was counseled that a sperm donor could decrease the chances of miscarriage and birth defect due to the father's age. It doesn't say whether the patient heeded the advice.

I wonder if Rhonda is disappointed with the marriage she ended up with. I mean, it seems most people wind up disappointed with marriage one way or the other, but she made a clear exchange: wealth and prestige instead of a young husband. Fine. Pastor Hepsworth made his own deal: a young and beautiful wife instead of one more likely to stay satisfied and settled. An unspoken bargain between the two of them, I'm sure, but one they both agreed to.

I read through the records once more to be sure I haven't missed anything, then tuck the papers into the top shelf of my closet and grab my winter coat. It's pleasant in the sun today, but the light is already fading.

I wait on the sidewalk and wonder what Luke wants from me.

It's not like I've never been in a relationship. I've been infatuated a couple of times, but I've never loved any of my boyfriends. Does that make sense? I feel happy with them, but I don't trust. I don't want to live with a man or give up control. Why would I? Men lie. They lie right to my face, and it's not hard to spot. Do they think we don't know?

Women lie too. Everyone does, and we all see the falsehoods; the question is, Which of us are willing to lose ourselves enough to give another person a chance? I can't lose myself. I don't have enough feelings to fuel the fantasy or ignore the warnings.

My last relationship was with a married Lebanese executive in Malaysia. His lies were childish and weak, designed to bring me close enough for sex but keep me at the perfect distance. *You're so amazing, Jane, but I can't fall in love with you. I love my wife more than anyone in the world. She's everything to me.*

Ridiculous. He loved himself more than anyone in the world. But he turned me on like crazy, so I just smiled and pulled him back for more. He wouldn't leave his comfortable life for me, and I didn't want him to, so it worked nicely for a full year.

We never went to a zoo, though.

I lost interest in him after Meg died. I lost interest in everything.

He told me he loved me then. Finally. A last-ditch effort to get me back into his bed. I reminded him that he loved his wife. Maybe he does. The way other people love doesn't make much sense to me.

Why get married if you want to sleep with other people? Why stay if you suspect he's cheating and that hurts your feelings? Why fight and bicker and scream if the other person decides they're ready to go? If someone wants to leave, the only thing to do is move on. Find someone else. Have some pride.

Then again, I can't seem to follow my own advice with Meg. She wanted to leave and I still need her here, and I can't let her go. Maybe I'm more like everyone else than I think. Or maybe they're more like me.

Luke finally pulls up in his black Prius—no giant SUV for him—and I laugh to myself, because he really is better endowed than Steven.

That would make a good bumper sticker, actually. *My other car is a big penis.* My creative talents are wasted in law.

"Hey, there," he says when I get in. The car smells like apples and cinnamon and I look around in confusion until he picks up a Styrofoam cup from the console. "I got us hot cider."

"Oh. That's so sweet."

I take a sip and it's the perfect temperature. I'm on some kind of all-American date.

We start the drive in companionable silence. At least, it's companionable for me, but he could be uncomfortable. I watch for clues, but he seems relaxed.

"That was nice the other night," he says after a long while. "Reading with you."

"Oh!" I respond. "I got you a present!"

I grab a bag from my purse and open it to pull out a hardcover novel. "I saw it in the window of a bookstore, and he's an author you had on your shelf, so I thought . . ."

"Wow, Jane!"

"It's a signed copy."

"That's so nice! Thank you. And I don't have this one yet." He shifts his attention from the road to the book in quick little peeks to check out the cover. "You didn't have to get me anything."

Maybe not, but I used to buy Meg a lot of gifts. I'm never sure what else I'm contributing to a relationship. Practical advice for Meg. Sex for Luke. Heck, I would've given Meg sex too if she'd been interested. That's about all I know to give. So I buy presents. Everyone likes presents.

"Thank you." He squeezes my hand briefly and lets me go. "Is this music okay?"

"It's great." I don't care about music. I couldn't even really say what genre this is. Music is about emotion. It's not for people like me.

When I start seeing signs for the zoo, I realize we're way out near the Hepsworths' church. I'm unconcerned, though. I can't imagine I'll run into them at the zoo after dark. In the unlikely event I see the good pastor or his wife, I'll introduce Luke as my cousin. I'm certain he'd go along with it in front of strangers.

"I think I figured out that thing with my mom," I say before I even know why I'm saying it. It hasn't exactly been weighing on my mind, but I was reading through Meg's old emails this morning and it came to me.

"Which thing?" Luke asks.

"Why I keep accepting her calls when I don't even want to."

"Oh?"

"It's because it's what Meg wanted. She got upset when I said I was going to cut my mom from my life and move on. So I kept my family in my life. Because Meg wanted me to."

"Oh, Jane," he says quietly. "I'm so sorry you lost her. I know I said it before, but . . . even I can't believe she's gone, and I haven't seen her in almost ten years."

"Thank you."

"So you keep in touch with your mother for Meg's sake?"

"Yes. I think so." But Meg is dead now.

He squeezes my hand again. "I sent flowers to her grave. Did you see them?"

I shake my head. I've never been to Meg's grave.

"They were daisies. I thought . . . something cheerful, you know?"

"I think daisies sound perfect."

I'm surprised that he actually sent flowers. He'd said he would, but people say things like that all the time. In my experience, they rarely actually do them. I turn and study his face until he glances over. "What?" he asks with a faint smile.

"Nothing."

Nothing, because I'm not sure what to do with him.

It's fully dark by the time we get to the zoo. From the parking lot, I can see lights winking through the bare tree branches.

I wonder if Meg ever did this. It seems like something she would've liked.

My drink is cold now, but I finish it as we walk to the entrance. Luke pays for both of us and we follow the stream of people in, all of us bundled up in thick coats against the night chill. The cider tastes like fall on my tongue. I feel like I belong tonight.

Walking into the park, I expect Christmas decorations. Instead the lights are sculpted into the shapes of animals. I gaze up at a blue-and-orange monkey with a swinging tail.

"Where to first?" Luke asks, indicating a sign with arrows pointing in three different directions.

"Big cats," I answer immediately.

We head off in that direction, passing an exhibit with a sign that says BLACK BEAR. There's no bear in sight, or else he's hiding in a corner the overhead lights don't reach. I'm surprised to see that the space looks like a little mountain canyon with rocks and a stream.

"It's not what I expected," I say as we come to a similar-looking exhibit marked BROWN BEAR.

"The lights?"

"No, the zoo. I thought they were all in little cages. With bars, you know?"

Luke turns to look at me. "Haven't you ever been to a zoo?"

"No. This is my first time."

"Jane, that's crazy!"

I shrug. "Not a lot of zoos where I grew up."

"Then this is a special occasion. We're going to need to do everything. The carousel. Wax animal machine. Funnel cake."

"Hey, I've had funnel cake before!"

"But not *zoo* funnel cake."

"True."

"Come on. You have to read all the signs." He pulls me over to the brown bear description, but I still haven't seen any sign of life. I humor Luke and read the facts about each animal. Bears, foxes, wolves. The wolf is the first animal I spot. It's staring at me past the edges of a scraggly bush. I stare back until a paler wolf joins the first and they trot away together.

"That's pretty cool," I say.

"The big cats are just ahead."

I immediately abandon the wolves and hurry toward an archway decorated with tigers and lions. More faux landscapes await, but these exhibits are behind thick glass that rises up until it meets stiff netting that keeps the cats from finding a way out into the night.

The Bengal tiger is awake and prowling. I freeze in wonder at the sight. He moves exactly like my cat. Muscles slide under fur as his eyes scan his surroundings. Sleek, elegant, powerful—he's gorgeous and deadly.

His pupils turn briefly silver when they catch the light.

I'm shocked by the huge size of his paws and his massive head. He is a killer. Far more dangerous than I'll ever be.

I watch him slide between two tree trunks, and then he leaps up to a rock ledge with no effort at all. My God.

His keepers love him, I'm sure. They care for him each day, feeding him and tending any ills. They speak to him and throw him treats. Still, I can see in his piercing gaze that he would happily kill any one of them, given the chance. No, not any one of them. All of them.

That kind of thing isn't valued in a human, but we see the awesome beauty of it here, behind a cage, where it can't hurt us.

I will never be as dangerous as this animal, but I can move freely among people and they'll raise no alarm.

The tiger settles down and closes his eyes. We move on to a leopard, then a puma, then another tiger, slightly smaller than the first. All of them are gorgeous and fascinating.

I watch until I feel Luke getting restless beside me. He buys me cotton candy and leads me to the carousel. I'm dizzy with delight by the time we leave.

Luke fills up a little of the empty space inside me, and I see the world through his eyes, just as I did with Meg.

CHAPTER 32

Turns out that Steven was busy while I was out on my date. The little bastard is cheating on me.

Well, to be clear, he's trying to cheat on me, but the woman on the other end of the phone isn't interested in being his booty call. I click through to the earliest video from this evening to see who else he called.

He gets home from work and heads straight for his exercise room. He reappears forty-five minutes later to put a pot of water on the stove and then he disappears for what I assume is a quick shower, because he's wearing a different T-shirt and sweatpants when he emerges to dump a box of macaroni into the steaming pot. No booty calls so far. My man is still faithful.

He turns on a football game and sits at the kitchen table to eat his meal, but before he's done, he looks up, startled at something. He mutes the TV. I hear it then. The doorbell ringing.

Oh my gosh, it's Mr. and Mrs. Hepsworth!

Before I even see them, I hear Steven exclaim, "Dad!" with great joy. Then I hear the clap of male back patting before Steven leads his dad into the living room. Rhonda follows behind. No back pats for her.

"What are you doing out here?" Steven asks.

"Oh, we had an early dinner with that new minister from Brooklyn Park Christian. We were about to pass your exit and I realized we hadn't stopped by in months. Thought I'd drop in and see the new fence."

Steven's chest puffs out proudly at that, and he leads his father out to the patio. I hear a low murmur of conversation through the door. Rhonda stays inside, staring at her phone. I hope she has a hot online boyfriend to fill her days, but that's probably a bit risky for a preacher's wife.

Steven and his dad return and they discuss the new minister for a while. Rhonda faces away from them, straight into the camera, and I see her lip curl with contempt, though I'm not sure for what. Her husband? His son? This life she lives?

The pastor excuses himself to use the restroom, and as soon as he's gone, Steven's gaze goes to Rhonda. He glares at her back for a long moment before he finally approaches. "Stay the fuck away from Jane," he says, and I gasp and bounce with gleeful surprise. What the hell is this?

Rhonda rolls her eyes before she turns to face him. "What are you talking about?"

"Every time I turn around, you two are huddled up together gossiping. I don't want you influencing her."

"Influencing her to do what? Use her brain? She's even dumber than your last little piece."

"Just leave her alone."

"You think I give a shit who you date? She's the one who's trying to kiss my ass and get in good with Daddy. It's pitiful."

"I don't see you discouraging her."

"Yeah, because I couldn't care less."

"Don't fuck with me," he warns.

"My God, you're insane, you know that?" She swings back around toward the camera and raises her phone to dismiss him. A door opens offscreen and Steven moves away. I watch Rhonda's eyes slide to the side as if she's still wary of Steven's presence. When her husband returns, Rhonda heads straight for the front door.

"We'd better get going, darling," she says. She doesn't wait for him to agree before she leaves.

What in the world was *that*? I bounce again and clap my hands, then click back to the beginning so I can pay even closer attention.

Does Steven think she's going to tell me something I shouldn't know? Is it about him abusing Meg? It makes sense. Rhonda hates his guts; there's no reason she wouldn't want to sabotage a new relationship for him. I should see if I can get her alone for a cocktail. But this Jane isn't a drinks-with-the-girls kind of woman. Maybe coffee instead. Or tea.

Once they're gone, Steven is agitated, pacing back and forth across the kitchen, swiping his hand through his hair. He drinks two beers in quick succession. Then he gets out his phone.

He dials someone and gets no answer. I dig my phone from my purse and see that I missed a call from him at 8:30. He probably wanted to know if he could drop by for a quick curbside handy.

Setting down the phone, he turns the game back on, but a few minutes later he's back on the phone sending a short text. It wasn't to me. His phone buzzes. He texts again. He smiles a tight little smile and mutes the TV again to make a phone call.

"Hey," he says. "Long time no see."

He paces back to the bedroom and this is the video I saw a few minutes ago, phone already pressed to his ear and charming grin in place. "Come on, it wasn't like that. I just got busy with work."

Ah, this must be a girl who put out too quickly and never got a second date.

"Vanessa," he coos. He's supposed to sound sweet but he sounds whiny. "That's not true. Don't be mean about it. You were always such a sweetheart."

His grin flashes again. "Okay. Got it. That's good news, because I was calling to see if you're busy tonight . . . Nah, it's not that late. We could grab a drink somewhere. How about that pub?"

Whatever she says, Steven's smile fades and he rolls his eyes. "Yeah. Okay. Sure. Next time, then. Yeah, I'll call you."

He tosses his phone on the bed with a curse. God, he's really riled up. Is it just because he wanted to yell at Rhonda and call her names and he isn't allowed to? Now he needs another woman around to humiliate?

"Fucking bitch," he mutters, and I'm not sure if he's talking about Vanessa or Rhonda or all of us. Probably all of us.

He leaves the room for a few minutes, but before the camera can go to sleep, he's back. He turns off the lights and gets into bed with his phone. The screen lights up. I hear a woman speaking in Japanese, then the distinctive sound of spanking and weeping. Then the dulcet tones of porn sex, the woman high-pitched and desperate, the man guttural and in control.

I watch until he finishes, then I get out my cat's favorite feather toy and let her chase it around the living room. Every pounce, every twitch of her head, reminds me of that tiger. And of myself.

She finally flops onto the scarred wood floor with a yawn, and I do the same on the couch. It's been a long day, but in three days I'll be Steven's special girl, and I can't wait.

CHAPTER 33

My mom called again. I blocked her. Good riddance.

This time in Minneapolis is really helping me work out my issues. I feel more in touch with my feelings already.

That was a joke.

CHAPTER 34

It's Thursday and I feel like a girl getting ready for her wedding night. Instead of white, I wear black, of course. Steven's favorite black bra and a pair of transparent mesh panties. I've unbuttoned my delicate dress too far again, but whenever I catch Steven's eye across the office, I smile and look shyly down, a blushing bride.

He's practically strutting through the day. Tonight he'll accept the precious gift of my womanhood. If only this weren't an office romance, he could shout it to the world.

He leaves a few minutes before I do, but he's waiting by his truck when I come down. "Ready for dinner?" he asks with a wink.

I nod and duck my head as he opens my door. I can't quite meet his eyes.

"I'm making burgers," he says. "Sound good?" He closes the door on my quiet "Yes."

We pull out and he takes my hand. After kissing my knuckles, he laces his fingers through mine and holds my hand on his thigh. I play my part by not jerking my arm back to my side of the truck.

After a few minutes I clear my throat. "I'm not very good at it," I say in a rushed whisper.

"At what?" Steven shoots me a puzzled glance.

"I . . . I mean sex. I'm not really . . . It's hard for me to relax about it."

He huffs out a laugh and shakes his head. "It'll be great."

"I don't know."

"Listen, Jane." We're waiting in line at a long red light. He turns to me, raising my hand for another kiss. "I'm in love with you."

"Oh gosh. Steven! Oh my gosh! I love you too. I really do. I know it's only been a few weeks, but . . ."

"But it's something special. This isn't some cheap one-night stand like you've had before. It's going to mean something. All right?"

Wow. Can it ever really be special with a trashy girl like me? Stay tuned.

But this is what Meg wanted. I know that. She was so sick of dating. So sick of the constant grind. She wanted someone who'd tell her it was special. Someone to cuddle in the morning. Someone to hold hands with in the car.

My hand is sweaty and I desperately want it back, but I keep right on squeezing.

"Relax, baby," he murmurs. "It's gonna be so good."

I smile nervously, but I nod in agreement because I want to please him.

He glances toward my chest. "You wore that bra I like."

This time my smile is wide and sure. "I wanted to make you happy."

"Oh, I'm already feeling real happy, babe. Come here." I lean in and give him a kiss, but the light turns green and the car behind us honks. We giggle like teenagers and drive out of the city.

When we get to his house, Steven heads straight out to the grill. As soon as he's out the patio door, I grab two beers from the fridge, one stout and one light. After popping the tops off both, I drop four pills into the stout and swirl them around. It's bitter enough that he won't notice any difference.

When he comes back inside, I sidle up for a long, deep kiss, sucking lightly at his tongue until he groans. "Here, sweetie. I got you a beer."

"You're amazing."

He's in a great mood, nicer than he's ever been. "*I* should cook for *you* next time," I say.

"Yeah? What would you make for me?"

"Beef stroganoff?"

"Ick. Mushrooms."

"Okay, then . . . fried chicken."

"That sounds wonderful."

I don't know shit about fried chicken. "I promise to make all your favorites. I can't wait."

He clinks his beer against mine. "Drink up. We can't have you feeling uptight tonight, can we?"

I giggle and shake my head, then take a long pull on my beer as he supervises with a pleased smile. "Good girl."

"You're good at watching out for me," I purr.

"It's nice to find a woman who appreciates that."

"I do. I really like it. The way you take care of me." I lean up for another kiss and he pushes me back to the counter so he can press his hips to mine for a few seconds.

"God, you're hot."

I take another drink of beer as he leaves me to go to the fridge. "Cheese?" he asks. He sets cheese and ground beef on the counter, then leans back and finishes his first beer. I hope he swallowed all the pills in that last long pull.

He gets us both another beer and slides mine across the counter toward me even though I haven't finished the first.

"Maybe I could cook and you could have your dad and Rhonda over or something."

"That sounds nice, but we wouldn't want my dad to think we're shacking up or anything."

"Oh, right. Sorry."

"It was a sweet thought. You're going to make a great wife someday."

"Stop. Don't tease."

"I'm not teasing you, babe. I'd like to settle down soon, and I'd love it to be with a girl who wants to be a wife and not just a husband in a dress."

"I think it would be nice to be a wife. And a mom. My mom never got to stay home with me."

"Yeah, she probably put you right into day care, huh?"

"She had to work."

"Sure. But if you had a good, steady guy like me, you'd want to do it right, wouldn't you? Take care of our kids. Take care of my house."

His house. Of course. "I'd love that," I whisper.

He sets down his beer to frame my face with his hands, and the fingers on my left cheek are freezing and wet. I try my best to look dreamy. "You deserve that, Jane. You just need the right guy to make it happen."

"Is that you?" I ask softly.

"I think it could be. Are you the right girl?"

I sigh. "I hope so."

"Demure," he says, then kisses me gently. "Sweet." Another kiss. "Godly."

A strange thing to say when I can feel his erection against my belly, but everyone has their turn-ons.

"I love you," I murmur against his mouth.

He kisses me again, then heads out to cook up some red meat.

I take my second beer to the couch and put my feet up. We'll both enjoy this more if I'm tipsy. He'll feel like he's taking advantage of me, and I might be drunk enough to enjoy it.

The pills won't hit him for an hour. We'll have plenty of time to consummate our love.

Sure enough, we're done with our burgers in fifteen minutes and Steven is giving me a tour of his house. It's obviously going to end with his bedroom. I ooh and aah over the judo memorabilia and ask if I can come watch him spar sometime. "It must be so sexy," I purr, "watching you fight another man like that."

"Then you can definitely come watch sometime."

He leads me to the bedroom and begins edging me toward the bed as he kisses me. His hands go for the flimsy buttons of my dress, and I remember that I had to find a new button for that last one he popped. "Let me see you, baby," he whispers. He sits on the end of the mattress and unfastens two more buttons.

I ease my dress off my shoulders, still holding it up, as if I'm shy.

"That's it. Take it off."

I let it drop to the floor.

"Oh yeah. Look at you." He's still fully dressed, and if I were really as shy as I pretend to be, I'd feel vulnerable right now, presenting my body to him for approval. "God, these panties." He slides his hands around my back and straight down my underwear to cup my ass. "So hot," he whispers.

"You like them?"

"Hell yeah I do. Did you pick them out for me?"

I nod.

"A dirty little secret for your man?"

"That's right."

"Take off your bra."

I reach back and unclasp the strap, then cup the fabric to me and wait for him to push my hands aside. He does. He doesn't compliment my breasts; he just paws at them for a while. I know they're not exactly what he likes, but they're here, so good enough.

Surprise, surprise, there's not much foreplay. We climb under the covers and we have sex. I try for hesitant warmth, eager to please him even though I feel ashamed about it all.

He's not the worst I've had, but he's in the bottom quarter. Halfway decent lay, terrible lover. He doesn't even make a reluctant offer to go down on me.

Afterward I snuggle close and stroke the sparse hairs of his chest as if I can't get enough of touching him. One minute later he's snoring.

Unsure if it's the drugs or just a male postcoital nap, I say his name a few times. He grunts something as if he's trying to answer but can't rouse himself. I nudge him. He snorts and then settles back into a deep sleep.

The pills were only antihistamines, but allergy drugs are a surprisingly effective sedative when you mix them with alcohol. There are warnings about it on the package, but the mixture is one of my favorite antidotes to my own bouts of restlessness. I only take two, though, and I chase mine with cocktails instead of dropping them in beer. He'll hopefully sleep like an exhausted child for a good eight hours and wake pretty refreshed. Unless he has a heart condition.

I get up and walk naked through his house to retrieve his phone from the living room. I'll enjoy this video later, watching myself move free and languid like a feline through his rooms. I take the phone back to bed and use his limp hand to access the fingerprint lock. It's cozy here, and I settle beneath the sheets to explore his life as he sleeps deeply beside me.

Text messages first.

I read through several weeks' worth of conversations with his dad, but they're all wholesome as hell. Nothing good there, aside from access to his dad's number, which I transfer to my own phone.

There's no need to view my own conversations with him, so I move on to "Ted." It looks like Ted is his little brother. I don't remember hearing his name, but the texts are mostly about Dad, with Steven haranguing his brother for not bringing his kids to the church often enough. Ted wants to, but it's nearly an hour drive for them, and Bethenny is still struggling with the postpartum even though the little one is ten months old now.

Steven helpfully advises that spending time praying with Dad could go a long way toward helping her buck up. So understanding.

Then there's Vanessa, his failed booty call. He's deleted whatever messages he sent when they were seeing each other, and Monday's are just a version of "You up?"

Other than that, most of the texts are just verifications and reminders. He doesn't leave a trail.

I check his email, but it's only work stuff. I forward a couple of important documents to my anonymous email account, then delete the evidence from the sent folder. Maybe I can set him up for something after all.

After that, I forward his entire contact list to myself. Then I see the Tinder app icon on the second page of his phone. Score!

The profile photo doesn't show his face. He's a deacon, after all. Instead, it's a standard shirtless-in-the-mirror selfie with only the bottom half of his smirk showing. There are a couple more pics of his chest, taken when he was a little more tan and cut than he is now. Fair enough.

I click on *Profile* and find a few women he's been matched with, but most of them he's organized into lists. The top list is titled *Nice Tits*. There's also *Dateable*, *Slutty*, and *Hit That*.

Hit That has four women in it. They're all white with hair ranging from blond to light brown. He calls all of them "baby" in conversation, just like he calls me. Now I don't feel special.

The last contact with each of them was around April. He hooked up with all of these women almost immediately after Meg's death, as if he were trying to screw a demon away. Good. I hope he was roasting alive with guilt and regret.

I screenshot the interactions and send them to myself. The other lists are full of typical come-ons from Steven and a few topless shots from women. I capture those conversations too. Why not?

Steven starts to snore beside me.

Shooting him a grimace of annoyance, I close Tinder and open his photos. There aren't very many. Steven doesn't have an artist's eye for the world. There are more shirtless selfies of him, a few pics from the stands at a Minnesota Twins game last summer, snaps of him and his dad at some Christian conference together, a picture of a crack in the foundation of his house. There's also a picture of his erect penis, of course, the shot angled to make it look bigger than it is. All in all, no surprises.

Then I get to a selfie of him and Meg, similar to the one she sent me, but taken from a slightly different angle. There's also a pic of her wearing cutoff shorts and a tiny little tank top, holding out her hand and laughing. Next is a photo of her in a small boat, a light beer in one hand and a fishing pole in the other.

Hitting the back arrow, I find a separate folder of photos underneath the general file. When I click on these, rage turns my vision red. Red Meg. Red nudity. Red breasts and thighs. Red pictures of her from behind, being penetrated by Steven.

These are the pictures he threatened her with, likely after begging and cajoling and promising her the world in exchange for them. He wanted these photos and then he called her a dirty slut for providing them. They were proof that she wasn't good enough to even be alive.

I feel a wild urge to grab a knife and end this now. He's naked and helpless and out cold, and I could carve him into a puzzle of gore. By the time he wakes up enough to fight back, he'll be bleeding out, missing his throat or his balls, some crucial part now permanently fixed in a bloody, open-mouthed gape.

I stand and throw back the sheets to glare at his limp nudity. I hear my own panting.

This is love. This is *my* love, and it may be a dark, mean, greedy thing, but it is real. I feel it. I love Meg and I would kill for her. I *should* kill for her. All of this dancing around, all of this toying with him—it needs to end.

Before I've given myself permission, I'm in the kitchen, at the knife block, sliding out a medium-sized utility knife. People are scared by the big chef knives or meat cleavers, picturing those as murder weapons, but I want precision. I want to feel exactly what I'm severing inside him.

I return to stand over him again and measure all the hollowed spots of his body where no bone or muscle presses the skin. There, at his throat. Under his eyes. The spot just beneath his breastbone. The hollows of his hips right above the groin. Or the groin itself, all of it so squishy and unprotected from the danger I present. The insides of his thighs . . .

I lay the blade of the knife flat against his leg. He doesn't stir.

I slide it up, scraping the edge along his crisp hair. His balls are loose and heavy with satisfaction and sleep. Will he wake if I take them in a gentle grasp and lift them for a tiny metal kiss?

Smiling, I raise the knife and smooth it gently up his testicles and over his penis. The shaft stirs a little at the touch. Just a twitch. Then a slight thickening. His respiration stays the same, but his dick will take any kind of attention, even in sleep.

Pet me, it says. *Pet me with your knife.*

I slide it over him again, snickering at his stupid vulnerability. They're all stupid. Stupid and worthless.

He's not that deeply drugged. He could wake at any moment, but what do I care? At his first sign of protest, I'll slip the knife deep, and it will be too late for him.

But I'd rather take my time, so I lift the blade and move it higher.

His belly rises and falls in a slow rhythm like the skin of a toad's throat. Up and down. Up and down. I can almost hear him croaking.

I point the blade at the hollow between the bottom curves of his rib cage. The aorta is just there, unprotected by bone or gristle. I could pop it like a balloon and watch the blood shoot out with impressive pressure. It would paint me scarlet, but I'm already naked. A quick shower would clean me up.

I lower the knife until the next deep breath pushes his skin into the point. When he exhales, a tiny nick is revealed. Another inhalation, another little pinprick. I leave five behind. The first is bright red now.

I press my thumb to it and smear the faintest bow of blood across his skin. Finger painting.

What do I want to remove? I've never cut anyone before, and there are so many choices. His genitals for pointing his selfish body in Meg's direction. His eyes for the pictures he wanted and kept and used. His stupid tongue for all the evil words he beat her with. His treacherous, traitorous, ugly goddamn heart.

All of it.

I drag the blade over his penis again. And again. The metal makes a sweet chuffing sound against the skin as the shaft gently swells.

This is where I'll start. So Steven can wake up and look down with clear eyes and see that he's losing the center of his universe.

I angle the blade. I poise the tip to split his dick open from base to crown.

Except . . . I don't. I don't cut him.

I want this with every fiber of my being, but my heart rate has calmed and I know I can't. There's evidence of me everywhere. At work, in his phone, on surfaces here at his house and in his car. My DNA is all over his body and his bed. It's on the empty beer bottles and the crumpled napkins in the trash.

I've marked him as surely as a cat marks its possessions, and if I kill him this way, I'll never escape it. I could probably avoid capture, but I could never go back to my comfortable life.

I should have killed him the moment I stepped into town, but I was seduced by the fun of it, of invading his life and toying with him, making him into the ultimate fool.

Conceit is my greatest weakness. I know this. It's why I inserted myself into his world instead of keeping my distance. Because I wanted to *feel* him slide into my trap.

It's why I used my real first name instead of a complete alias. I wanted him to know it was *me* doing this to him. *Me*, even if he never connected the dots. *Me Jane*, as primitive as it was in the old Tarzan movies.

Good times indeed, but now there's a price to pay. I can't do what I want.

Damn it. I despise consequences.

But I reassure myself: it's only a momentary sacrifice. I'll find another way. He deserves to die. I can see that now. I'll find a way to take his worthless life without risking my own. I will. I whisper it aloud: "I'll find another way, Meg."

But I don't believe there's any part of Meg left in the universe to hear me, and the sad truth is she wouldn't want me to hurt him anyway. That won't dissuade me. This isn't about honoring her wishes. If she'd wanted a say in this, she should have stuck around.

I stare at him for another minute, letting my heart believe I could still kill him. Then I return the knife to the block and shut off the lights. I don't look at the pictures again because I can't risk the rage. But I can't allow him to ever look at the pictures again either. He killed her, and he used these photos as a murder weapon even as he delighted in jerking off to them.

I delete the entire folder. Then I climb into bed with Steven. He'll never know it was me. Even if he suspects, he'll assume I was only jealous.

I try to settle into bed, but I realize I'm aroused by my close brush with vengeance. So I masturbate, turned on by the idea of hurting him, turned on by the camera, turned on by the video I'll watch later of me hovering on the edge of murder.

When I'm finished, I tuck us both in and fall quickly asleep.

CHAPTER 35

I'm up before him in the morning, thanks to my not mixing drugs and alcohol. I shower and dress and put eggs and bacon on the stove before returning to the bedroom.

"Good morning, sleepyhead!"

He opens his eyes slowly. "Oh. Hey."

"I wasn't sure you were going to wake up. Sleep well?"

"I guess I did." He stretches hard.

"I'm cooking breakfast. It should be ready in two minutes."

I'm not a great cook, but I can handle breakfast, at least—not that I've made it for many men. Even if a guy sleeps over, I'm not looking to make him feel cherished.

Steven arrives at the table in sweatpants, rubbing a hand through his tousled hair. He sits down and waits while I find plates and silverware. The timer on his coffee maker kicks in and the machine begins brewing while I serve my lover his plate. Two eggs, three strips of bacon, and a little kiss on the mouth to add sweetness.

"Thanks, babe."

"You're welcome." It's easy to play the passive, clueless girlfriend this morning because I woke up with a plan. And I think it's a good one.

"God, I slept great," he says. "You really wore me out."

I giggle and serve myself one egg and two strips of bacon like the modest lady I am. "You seemed pretty satisfied."

He stretches again, then reaches down to scratch his bare belly. I hear the scritching of nails against skin and then he winces. "Huh."

"What's wrong?"

"Something bit me." He's hunched over, trying to get a good look at the little cuts I left in him.

I get close and crouch down. "Let me look." I make a show of peering at the tiny marks. "I'm not sure. It looks like maybe something bit you and then you scratched it while you were sleeping."

He shrugs and rubs his palm over the wounds.

"Or maybe I scratched you during . . . you know."

He grins. "The superhot sex?"

I mean, I'm not sure what his standard is for hot sex, but it's obviously pretty low. Still, I giggle and drop back into my chair to eat breakfast. When the machine stops brewing coffee, I pour us each a cup. I hum a little to show that taking care of him makes me so happy.

Before I can move away after delivering his cup, Steven snags my waist and pulls me onto his lap. "So," he murmurs into my ear, "it seemed like you relaxed after all."

I titter as he nuzzles my neck. "Maybe."

"Did you like it, baby?"

"I did. It was better with you than my ex."

"Hell yeah it was."

I know I shouldn't. I really know I shouldn't, but I didn't get to carve him open last night and I need a little fun to make up for that. "With him . . . with him it hurt sometimes because he was so big. I hated it."

Steven jerks back to glare at me and it's nearly impossible not to burst out laughing at his outrage.

"With you it was real nice." I try to relax into him with a dreamy sigh, but he's having none of it. He pushes me off his lap, his mouth twisting in a snarl.

"What a slutty thing to say."

"*What?* Why?"

"You're telling me about another guy's dick? Are you *kidding* me?"

"But I said I like yours better! It was a compliment!"

"You shouldn't even know the difference! But, oh, I forgot: you've had a few dozen inside you. You're running a slut survey of the world."

"Steven!" I make my chin shake. "Don't be mean! I liked it, and I don't always like it, so it was—"

"Oh, I'm being mean? You just threw some other man in my face the morning after we had sex. Do you think I wanted to know about that?"

"No. I—"

"Do you want to hear about my exes? Because my last girlfriend had a great rack. Way bigger than yours. And, yeah, she was skinnier than you too. Fucking hot."

"I'm sorry," I say quickly. "I'm sorry, okay? I shouldn't have said that."

"Whatever." He shoves his plate away and stalks to his bedroom to shower.

I lean against the table, laughing too hard to support my body weight. God, I hope he obsesses about my ex's penis for days. Weeks.

I finish my breakfast and steal his bacon, then scrape the remains of his eggs into the trash. I leave the dirty plates in the sink to give him one more thing to chastise me about later.

He's supposed to drop me off early so I can change clothes and put on makeup and still have time to get to work, but the shower keeps running and I figure he's now aiming to make me late. Whatever. I'm not super worried about my thirty-day evaluation. In fact, it's going to be very hard to drag myself into work today when all I want to do is watch the video of last night over and over again.

But I shouldn't. Each time I watch I'll hope for a different ending. I'll hope for blood and guts and joyful vengeance, and all I'll get is disappointment.

When Steven finally emerges to drive me home, I'm waiting with an insulated cup I found in the cupboard. "You didn't get to drink your coffee."

"Thanks." He still seems surly about his size issues, but he accepts the coffee and off we go.

As we drive, I spy a small lake at the edge of his neighborhood and recognize a great chance to put the first step of my plan into action. "Is it too cold to go fishing right now?" I ask.

"It's never too cold for fishing. If the lake freezes over, just drill a hole."

"I'd love to go sometime. Your dad suggested a fishing trip."

"Yeah. We could do that."

I watch him for a moment, then reach out to touch his shoulder. "Steven? Can I go to the cabin with you this weekend if I promise not to tell your dad?"

His eyes widen with surprise. "You really want to go that much?"

"I want to be with you. And I think it would be romantic. No one needs to know."

"If I take you, I won't have a hunting partner."

"I could hunt with you. I won't make any noise or anything, I promise."

"It seems like a bad idea. We'd be out in the woods all day. Where would you pee?"

I roll my eyes. "In the bushes. It's not that hard."

"I don't know."

"Pleeeease? You don't have to take me out while you hunt if you don't want to. I could just wait in the cabin for you." I circle his biceps with my hands and lean in to kiss his neck. "I love you and I want to like everything you like. I promise I'll make you happy you brought me."

He chuckles at that. "Oh yeah?"

"Yeah. You'll be very, very glad. Cross my heart." When I make the motion, his eyes fall to my breasts.

"Well, how can I pass that up?"

"Eee!" I kiss his cheek several times. "Can I go?"

"Can you be ready on Saturday morning bright and early?"

"Yes."

"You'll need to be all packed and ready to leave."

"Got it. I'll be ready. I promise."

"Bring some sexy underwear."

"You're so bad."

I feel better now. I have a plan and it's easy as pie. Go to a cabin in the woods. Kill him in the forest. Cover it up.

I even have several choices for how to carry this out. I can make it look like I stayed in the cabin and he accidentally shot himself while hunting. I can pretend he was teaching me how to use the rifle and I accidentally fired and killed him. I can stab him and bury his body somewhere deep in the woods, then find a way to get back to the city and pretend I never left.

It's an embarrassment of riches, really. So many possibilities.

It's crystal clear to me now. I wanted to destroy his world without putting myself in too much danger. But he has to die. I can't let him go on with his smug little life. Meg deserves more than that.

It's settled. Now I'll be able to enjoy last night's video with no regrets.

But I'll wait until after work. Probably.

CHAPTER 36

Luke's little brother is having an impromptu dinner party, and Luke wants me to come. I don't have time. I need to find some hunting gear at the secondhand store. I can afford to buy new, but I refuse to spend that much money on something so stupid. Plus, I really shouldn't leave any trace of my purchases. Better to hit the Salvation Army and pay cash.

Really, there's no point in me going to this party anyway. My fun with Luke is over. After this weekend I'll need to play the worried or grieving girlfriend full-time for a few weeks before I move on. I have to be back in Malaysia in a month.

I like Luke. A lot. He's great in bed and he makes me feel normal most of the time I'm with him. I'm not ready to give him up, but I have to.

Those are the reasons not to go to this party, but I still find myself saying yes. Have I mentioned that I'm bad at resisting my impulses?

In the hallway at work, I whisper to Steven that I can't see him tonight because I need to find a coat and boots. He makes a joke about women and shopping. I leave the office at 5:30 and head straight for the store.

The selection isn't great, but I find boots that almost fit and an ugly camouflage coat that is too large but more than warm enough for November. Good enough.

I put on tight jeans and a nearly sheer gray T-shirt, wind my hair into a tight bun, then accent it all with bright-red lipstick and diamond studs. I told Luke I'd meet him there at 7:30, so I call up a car on my phone and head downstairs.

By the time I arrive, I know Luke has been at his brother's for a good half hour, but as soon as I get out of the car, he is on the front steps of the little bungalow so I don't have to walk in by myself. He really is a good guy. It makes sense. That's why he can't see how bad I am.

I didn't have time to find him another gift, and I desperately wish I had something more in my hands than the bottle of wine I brought for his brother. But even when I don't present a gift, he seems happy to see me.

"You made it," he says, tugging me into a quick, hot kiss before he reaches to open the door.

"Thank you for thinking of me."

"Ha. I think about you too much, to be honest."

I grin at the attention and give him one more kiss as a reward.

"You look beautiful," he says.

"You have lipstick on your mouth."

He laughs and swipes his mouth across the sleeve of his dark-blue shirt. "Totally worth it."

Maybe he'll miss me when I'm gone. That will be something nice to imagine when I'm alone in a sterile apartment somewhere. Without Meg in my life there's no one who thinks about me, no one who wonders how I am.

Because I'm fine. I'm always fine. Not thrilled or anxious or joyful or heartbroken. Just fine. This grief is the most I've ever felt, and it will fade someday and I'll be fine again and no one will worry. But maybe Luke will be out there somewhere missing me and I'll be real for a few moments.

I hold his hand as we walk in as if I'm a normal girl.

Luke's little brother resembles him, just an inch shorter and a bit stockier. His name is Johnny and his husband is Isaiah. The couple look like two versions of the same man, one white and one black. They both have short hair nearly shorn on the sides, and both wear square tortoiseshell glasses. Their wedding pictures must be cute.

I'm introduced to everyone and I put on my best charming face. Uncertainty is not a normal state for me, but as dinner is served, I wonder what Johnny and Isaiah think of me.

Gay men are more likely to notice that I'm not quite right. Sometimes I'm in the middle of trying to soften them up with flirting when I realize that mask isn't a good fit for the moment. They can see the strings holding it in place.

Still, everyone likes flattery, regardless of sexuality, so I compliment their home and the cocktails and the dog.

Then I remember that it doesn't matter. This is my last date with Luke. I let myself relax and try to enjoy observing. A dinner party is a bit like a book: people tell stories and the listeners picture it in their minds, and I enjoy the prose and performance of it all.

There's an older gay couple at the end of the table, and they are a caricature of people who've been married too long. They finish each other's sentences and share each other's plates. One of them isn't eating carbs and the other doesn't like spinach, so they scrape and swap, clucking over the other's dietary quirks.

A heterosexual couple next to me hardly speak to each other at all, though they are lively with everyone else. I wonder why they stay together. Their arms never even touch accidentally. But they each tell hilarious stories about their work on local plays, and I like them both a lot for entertaining me. This is almost like a Christmas dinner, a little holiday for me before I have to get back to my darker side.

"You're quiet tonight," Luke whispers before dessert.

"I'm enjoying myself. I like your brother."

"That's you. He's pretty great. Don't you have a brother?"

"Yes. And he's not great at all."

Luke laughs and doesn't press the issue, and I'm glad. My brother was never a brother to me. He was a bully with shitty bully friends. When our parents would disappear, he didn't take care of me; he didn't even bother reassuring me. Instead, he'd say things like "Maybe they got tired of you being an ugly freak," and then he'd use the unsupervised time to stay out late and vandalize abandoned homes.

That was my brother. But Luke and Johnny seem close. Whatever they went through in their family forged sibling solidarity. Luke smiles at his little brother as if he's proud of him. That's nice.

I really wish this weren't our last night together. But Meg deserves to be avenged and I'll have to sacrifice to avenge her.

As dessert is served—apple bread pudding with rum sauce: yum—Johnny stands and taps his wineglass. I glance at Luke, but he gives an exaggerated shrug.

"Okay, I admit this is more than just a last-minute dinner party. We invited you guys here to announce some news." Johnny tugs Isaiah's hand to prompt him to stand up too, and their arms go around each other's waists as if that's their default. "A year ago, just after the wedding, we started the process of applying to adopt a baby—"

Luke's sharp gasp cuts through the other murmurs of surprise.

"It's been a long road, but . . . we've found a birth mother who really likes us, and we really like her, and . . . our baby will be born in February."

I turn to see Luke's reaction. He whispers, "Holy shit." His skin loses all color and his eyes go wide. I'm not sure he's happy. But then he smiles and everything about him lights up. Tears glisten in his eyes. "Jesus, brother," he says. "That's amazing."

He shoots to his feet and rounds the table to give both men big, squeezing hugs. "I'm going to be an uncle!"

Everyone laughs and congratulates him before crowding close for their own hugs. Johnny is openly crying. The joy in the room is palpable, even to me.

This is the kind of future I lost when I lost Meg. I try to soak up the love, though it doesn't belong to me. It heats my skin and even sinks a little deeper, the glow warming me briefly inside.

When Luke returns to my side, I hug him and tighten my hold when he squeezes me hard enough to squish the air out of my lungs.

"I'm going to be an *uncle*! For real!"

"That's so cool. You didn't have any idea?"

"None. He's good at keeping secrets, I guess. I'm just . . . wow. I wonder if I could coach a T-ball team. That would be cool, right? Whether it's a boy or girl, they'll like T-ball, won't they?"

I'm laughing at his wide-eyed wonder. "I have no idea."

"Yeah, I bet they will. Maybe I should buy a bigger place so the kid can come sleep over whenever they want."

"It will be a few years before you'd need more room, I think. I had no idea you were this into kids."

"I'm not! I mean, I never imagined I'd have my own, and since they're gay, having kids wasn't an assumption, but . . . God, Johnny will be a great dad, and Isaiah comes from a huge family, so . . . yeah. They're going to make a really great world for their kids."

"That's a lovely way to put it."

We're sitting again, and Luke is absently holding my hand and staring at his bread pudding as if he's seeing a million scenes playing out at once.

"You don't want kids?" I ask.

He shakes his head, then seems to snap out of his daze. His eyes dart up to meet mine. "I mean, if the woman I'm with really wants kids, I'd seriously think about it."

I laugh again at his obviousness. No point in explaining that I don't want kids. Luke will get the hint when I disappear.

Maybe he won't be the one person in the world who thinks of me after all. I can already tell that his universe will be too full of this tiny niece or nephew.

Isaiah and Johnny take their seats and we finally get to our desserts as they explain that the birth mother knows the sex of the baby but they want it to be a surprise. "The mother is a great girl," Isaiah says. "First in her family to go to college. She wants to work in criminal justice, maybe even go to law school."

Everyone at the party is vibrating with excitement. Everybody loves babies. I won't get to experience the wait or the arrival, but I'm glad that Luke gets this. A real family. He'll always have a place to go for Christmas.

That's nice for him. It would have been nice for me too. But he'll be much better at it. He'll be more involved, more in love with the experience. He won't just be leeching emotions from other people because he can't feel his own.

I take a bite of bread pudding and it's delicious. That joy will have to be enough for me.

CHAPTER 37

I call Steven at six in the morning to let him know I'm turning off my phone so I can be ready to get back to nature. He laughs at my silliness and says he'll pick me up at seven for the three-hour drive.

Of course I don't give a damn about getting back to nature, but I do care about leaving an electronic trail of texts and cell phone signals. The last thing I need is Steven texting me messages that could be used to ferret out the truth in a police investigation.

I leave my phone turned on and hide it in a dresser drawer in case I need to establish that I never left town. Then I pull an identical burner phone from its hiding place in the closet. No way am I going into the forest and not taking a phone. I may need to make a very convincing 911 call.

Speaking of, I've studied those. People say certain things during a real emergency and different kinds of things when they're faking it and covering up a crime. I've got this down. All of my worry and fear will be focused on Steven. I won't establish an alibi or theorize about what probably happened. I'll be confused and cooperative and so scared for him. I'll do exactly what the operator tells me, but I'll frantically beg for more help for him.

But I hope to avoid all that entirely. Best to keep it as simple as possible.

I pack the used boots and jacket I just bought, along with a hat and mittens. I choose two changes of clothes, flannel pajamas, and a nearly transparent black nightgown in case I need to distract him or just screw him to sleep. Then I add a few more things to my duffel bag: latex gloves, my pocketknife, duct tape, zip ties, a small flashlight, and a collapsible shovel I bought along with the hunting gear. He'll bring the gun, which is very thoughtful of him.

My flowery dress disguise won't cut it today, so I wear skinny jeans and a sweater and pull on half boots with a heel so he can make fun of me for being impractical.

I put out an extra-large bowl of water for my cat and enough dry food to last for two days. I'm just sitting down to play with her when I realize there's a bigger problem: if I need to go on the run, my cat will be trapped here alone. I don't know if I'd feel worried or guilty per se, but I definitely wouldn't like thinking about it. Shit.

I briefly consider smuggling her along on the hunting trip in my duffel bag. She might be quiet long enough to get an hour out of town, but Steven is so passionate in his hatred he could just leave us on the side of the road in retaliation. He might even decide to drive her all the way to the cabin and shoot her. I'd immediately kill him, of course, but that wouldn't bring my cat back.

What to do?

I close my eyes and ponder the options. If things go badly and I do have to disappear, there will be a good reason. I'll be under suspicion and the cops will come to the apartment regardless. So, at worst she'd be here for a week or so. Even if I jump the gun and run before the cops are looking for me, surely Luke will drop by to try to contact me. He would hear the cat meowing.

Decision made, I get up and put out another, larger bowl of dry food and a cake pan full of water. That should keep her going long enough to be discovered. I suppose if I were less selfish I'd leave a window open so she can escape, but I don't want to take the chance of losing her. She's mine, and I'll need entertainment while I lie low and play the worried girlfriend.

When I return to the couch, my cat is staring at her favorite feather toy, waiting for me to pick up the stick it hangs from and make it move. She gives me a croaky meow of impatience and her eyes flash silver when she turns in my direction. I wonder if the couch will be intact when I return. It's the first thing I'd destroy if I were her.

I play with her for fifteen minutes, admiring the vicious athleticism of her twisting, stretching body. I wish I could move like that. Wish I could suddenly expose curved claws above the little pink pads of my fingers. What a gift.

She eventually tires of me and slinks away to eat her breakfast and give herself a bath.

"Bye, cat," I say as she deserts me.

I still have fifteen minutes to waste. I get out the letter for an extra jolt of inspiration. It works.

CHAPTER 38

Jane, it's me. I'm so, so sorry.

I love you so much. You and my mom are the only people I don't want to leave, but I can't do this anymore.

Steven is my soul mate, and despite all our problems, I don't know how to do this without him. We were going to have a life, a house, a family. Now I have nothing.

Maybe that's what I deserve. He says I have nothing because I am nothing. It feels like he's right. It feels like I've spent my whole life falling down, and I'm too broken to get back up and try anymore. I'm afraid to do it without someone to love.

Please don't be mad at me, Jane. I'm so tired. I haven't stopped crying all week. I just want to stop crying. I know you won't understand that. You were always the strong one. The big sister I never had and always needed.

Please be strong for me now.

Thank you for letting me into your life. I should have listened to you about so many things.

I love you bunches, Jane. I love you always. Please forgive me.

Yours forever and ever,

Meg

CHAPTER 39

"Don't you want to come inside and show off your fancy boots?" Steven asks with a snide smile.

I slide lower in my seat in case anyone else pulls up on this side of the little general store. "I'm supposed to be a secret. You didn't tell anyone I was coming, right?"

"No."

"So what if the store owner knows your friend and tells him you brought a girl up here? He might tell your dad."

"Good point. I'll grab a few groceries and be right back."

"Get some ice cream!" I call out as he closes the door.

He gives me a disappointed look and shakes his head. Ice cream is only for girls who are a size four, I guess. I don't deserve it. The back of the truck is already full of beer and snacks, but Steven wants to grab bacon and eggs and some hot dogs for dinner. We're going to cook them over a fire. He was irritated when I called it a weenie roast, so I've said it at least three more times.

"Weenie roast," I say again, and giggle.

Despite the three hours on the road, I haven't quite decided how to kill him yet. There's no perfect option to keep me out of harm's way, and my brain is rebelling at the idea of self-sacrifice. It won't settle on a plan.

Or maybe I secretly have morals! But, no, that doesn't feel right. I want him dead.

The option that would cause the least suspicion would be burying him in the woods and then pretending I was never here. I'd get the most cover with this one. Steven would tragically disappear on a hunting trip, and the police would likely barely question me, if they got around to it at all. All my playacting would be for Steven's family, and it wouldn't be difficult to fool them.

But there are a couple of big problems with that plan. First, I'd have to find a way home without leaving a trail of evidence. Second, there's really no way for me to guarantee that no one has noticed me or will notice me. If the cops find out I lied about being here, I'd be screwed.

Still, it's my favorite option at this point, because I'm mostly out of the equation.

Another fairly good alternative is to kill and bury Steven in the woods, then call the sheriff tomorrow night when Steven doesn't return to the cabin. Hunters and hikers disappear all the time, and it's forecast to start snowing on Sunday. They'd never find his body in these thousands of acres of woods.

This plan would involve a lot of acting on my part, and my audience would be seasoned professionals. A challenge, but I think I'm up to it. I've been acting my whole life.

The identity I've created is solid enough for a quick background check. I'll just look like a girl who keeps to herself and has never had a brush with the law.

I don't think they'd dig deeper. For the first week or so, he'd only be a missing person, presumed lost in the woods, so they wouldn't focus on me. They'd be too busy searching for a man who could still be rescued.

And, really, I'm a woman he started dating three weeks ago. We're not married, I wouldn't benefit in any way from his death, and a motive more complicated than that would take a lot of imagination to conjure.

It's a decent plan.

The last option for killing Steven is my least favorite, but it might come down to opportunity. He teaches me to hunt and there's a terrible accident. These things happen when there are guns around. This scenario puts me in the spotlight, of course, but again, we've only been dating a few weeks; why in the world would I murder him?

This is an emergency-only option. I don't want that kind of investigation into my identity. It wouldn't hold up. But I still enjoy thinking about it. The shock on Steven's face as he realizes I've shot him. The fear and pain. I'd sit next to him and tell him the whole truth as he died. I'd make him apologize for Meg. I'd make him regret everything.

And then my hysteria as I race to a road and try to flag down a passerby! A kindly old sheriff would arrive and I'd offer a sobbing, stuttering confession. He'd likely believe it immediately because I'm a woman, and women are so dumb about guns and hunting and common sense. He has a granddaughter just like me, God bless her. Steven probably deserved it for handing his gun over to an idiot female, anyway. He was thinking with his dick instead of his brain.

It'd make a good TV episode.

Steven rounds the corner of the general store with a paper bag full of goodies and I wave happily.

"Did you get ice cream?" I ask once he's behind the wheel again.

"They didn't have any."

What a liar. "Thanks for bringing me with you. I'm so excited."

"You've said that about a million times."

"Because I'm excited, silly."

"I know, babe." He pats my thigh.

"Tonight's going to be so nice."

"Oh yeah?"

"I brought a little nightie I thought you might like."

"What does it look like?"

"It's a surprise."

He shoots me a hot look as he turns off the county road onto a dirt lane. "Is it black?"

"Yes."

"Short?"

"Yes."

"Mm. So you're going to dress up like a little whore for me?"

"Stop!" I smack him in the shoulder.

"You know I like it. As long as it's just for me."

"It is."

"You can model it. Show me how sexy you are. I'll take a few pictures."

"That is not going to happen!"

"We'll see what you say after a bottle of champagne."

"You brought champagne?" I squeal and clap my hands.

"First time bringing champagne on a hunting trip, that's for sure."

"You're so sweet."

"It'll be a great weekend, baby."

Yes, it definitely will.

The rest of the drive takes fifteen minutes, though I don't think we move more than two miles. The dirt road is deeply pitted and we bounce in and out of potholes until we finally turn off onto an even narrower path. The evergreens above us form a tunnel, and it occurs to me that Steven is moving through the large intestine of life now, heading right for the inglorious end.

Good. It's exactly what a shit like him deserves. I don't want to risk the life I've built for myself, but I'll stay strong for Meg. It's all she asked of me.

The cabin finally appears, and it's an anticlimactic sight. Just one room, I think, dwarfed by the giant trees that loom over the tiny wooden structure. It looks like the perfect place to make a man disappear.

"You'll need to wipe down the kitchen when we get inside. It's just one counter. There's a pump for water."

"Is that an *outhouse*?"

"Yeah, this isn't glamping," he says, sounding happy with my shock. "You said you wanted to go hunting."

"I did. I do."

"This is what it's like."

"It's great!" I lie, and he laughs. He wants me to hate it so he can tell me how soft I am. How inferior. He wants me to mince around in my high-heeled boots and scream over every spider I see. But I'm the spider here. And I've never minced.

Steven digs a key from under one of the stumps that circle a fire pit. The air smells like earth, as if there's no divide between land and sky. The whole place is a grave full of dead and dying plants and animals.

Here it doesn't matter if I have a soul or not. This dirt would absorb my flesh as easily as anyone else's. We're all portions for foxes, as the old Bible saying goes. Death rots all the soft parts of people away, and corpses don't have souls. In a hundred years no one will remember any of us or be able to tell our bones apart. I like that.

It seems the forest makes me morbid.

Steven unlocks the door and lets me step inside first, probably hoping I'll find it creepy. The windows are all shuttered and I hear a skittering sound in a corner.

There are two couches near a stone fireplace and two full-size beds against the other wall. This must be some cozy bro time when they come here in big packs.

"I'll bring in the bags," Steven says.

As instructed, I head for the wooden countertop that makes up the kitchen. There are some shelves above it and a metal sink with a drain. In place of the faucet, there's a pump. Under the sink, hidden behind a recycled calico curtain, I find cleaning spray and paper towels.

I wipe down the countertop and even the shelves above it.

"Thanks, babe," he says as he delivers a bag of groceries, and I glow with pride. "Here's the cooler." He slides it under the counter. "There's a block of ice in there, so it should stay cold all weekend. I'll keep the beer outside, since it's only supposed to get to forty-eight today. That should be cold enough."

I put the eggs, bacon, and hot dogs in the cooler along with the champagne. There are already condiments and snacks inside. Steven pops open a beer. "Once you finish unpacking, I'll teach you about the rifle."

If he gets drunk enough, maybe he'll just shoot himself. A girl can dream.

As I get the rest of the supplies unpacked, Steven starts a fire in the fireplace. I'm hoping the space will warm up quickly. I don't relish parading around in my see-through nightie in this freezing room.

He tells me to put on some real boots and meet him outside. I add another log to the fire as soon as he leaves, then switch out my cute boots for my used boots and tug on my big jacket and knit cap.

I bounce out the door, excited and a little scared about shooting my first gun.

Another lie, of course. I grew up in rural Oklahoma. My family weren't hunters, but there sure were a lot of varmints to shoot on the back side of our trailer. I've killed plenty of prairie dogs and field rats in my life. I'm not a dead shot, but I'm good enough. Deer offer a much larger target. So will Steven.

This is the beginning of the end for him, and as I take the rifle from his hand, I marvel that he's simply handing it over to me.

Steven gives me a bare-bones safety lecture, showing me how to unload the semiautomatic rifle and make sure the chamber is empty. Always treat it as if it's loaded. Never point it at others. Blah, blah, blah.

He demonstrates how to load a magazine, then takes aim at some old cans already pockmarked from bullets and set on top of a boulder. His form isn't bad, but his first shot misses.

I jump at the loud report, then clap my hands over my ears and scream.

"Come on, now. You're throwing me off."

"It's so loud!"

"It's a gun, Jane. It's going to make a loud noise."

It's going to make a big hole in your gut too, I think, but I mutter an apology and keep my hands over my ears for the second shot.

This time one of the cans goes flying and he grins, then fires again and again. Once all the cans are gone, he walks out and resets them on the boulder. "That's how you do it."

"Can I try now?"

He scoffs at my request but hands over the rifle. When I turn toward the cans, the barrel grazes right by him. For a moment he's in my sights.

"Hey! Don't point it at me! That's the first damn rule! How fucking stupid are you?"

"I'm sorry!"

"Jesus Christ. Is your finger on the trigger?"

Yes, it definitely is. "Oh, I'm really sorry, sweetie. I wasn't thinking."

"Well, use that worthless brain for once."

"Don't be mean."

"Mean? You just almost shot me! Don't you think that was a little fucking mean? I've only told you three goddamn things about shooting, and you can't even get those right!"

I raise my voice to a higher pitch, making my words tremble with panic. "I'm sorry, okay? I'm really sorry! I didn't mean it!" I can't shoot him here at the cabin, but the next time he turns his back, I'll point it right at him just for fun.

He rolls his eyes. "Yeah. All right. Don't do it again. And there's no crying on hunting trips, okay?"

I sniff and nod. "Okay. Don't be mad."

"I'm not mad. But pay attention. This isn't one of your ridiculous books. This is real life with real consequences."

It certainly is.

I nod and pretend I don't mind being talked to like a child. I remember how often Meg would tell me that she was just as bad as he was. *I say mean things too. I start arguments. I'm not innocent here.*

No. No one is innocent. But Steven escalates a thoughtless moment into deliberate cruelty every time. That was how he'd learned to respond to hurt: *Accidentally bump into my emotions and I will punch you as hard as I can.* It makes his pain go away, maybe. At the very least, he can feel as if he's won the interaction, and, boy, does he like winning. He needs to feel powerful to feel safe. Hey, I can understand that but I can't sympathize. That's not an emotion I can tap into.

He comes in close behind me to help me position the rifle correctly. His groin is pushed right up against my butt, of course. "You're not going to be able to cover your ears, you know."

"I know."

"I'll hold on and keep you safe," he murmurs, sliding his hands to my waist.

I sight through the scope and deliberately miss, letting the stock smack into my shoulder as the shot rings out. "Ow!"

"You need to keep it braced tightly against your shoulder or it's going to kick back. Try again."

"I don't think I want to."

"You have to try at least one more time, baby. I brought you all the way up here."

I sigh and shoot again, keeping it snug to my shoulder this time but purposely missing the can. "Steven! I did it!"

"Well, you shot a round, that's for sure."

"I think I got real close."

"How does it feel?"

"Fun." That's the truth. Maybe I'll find a shooting range in Malaysia and make this a hobby.

His hands slide a little higher, until he's grazing the bottoms of my breasts through the coat. "It's hot watching you shoot."

"Stop it." The words leave my mouth too sharply, but he doesn't notice. He just chuckles and I shoot once more, aiming a little closer. On the fourth shot I hit a can and whoop with joy. "I did it! I did it!"

"Good job, babe. But that doesn't mean you can hit a moving animal."

"No, but I can hit one that's not moving!"

"It'll be moving pretty fast by the time you get that fourth shot off."

"I just need to practice."

"Sure." He takes the rifle from me and loads a new magazine. "There you go. Try again."

He finally steps back and lets me shoot on my own. I take six more shots. On the last shots I'm really trying, and I hit the last two cans with no problem. If I do shoot Steven, he'll likely be pretty close. I'm not concerned I'll miss.

He takes the rifle from me and goes to set the cans again, apparently not trusting that I won't kill him while he's down there.

Smart move.

I could shoot him as soon as he gives the gun back to me and get this over with, but not here. A shooting accident in the woods would be better. I'm inexperienced and I saw movement and thought he was a deer.

If I just accidentally kill him standing right in front of me in this clearing, I could be charged with manslaughter or criminal negligence.

And if I'm going to bury his body somewhere and make him disappear, I can't have his guts and blood all over the yard. Even I won't be able to playact my way out of that one.

I fire off another ten shots or so, picturing Steven's face as the cans. Then he wants a turn. His turn goes on for a while. I shoot another few rounds, but he gets bored with sharing and suggests we stop for lunch. "It's almost noon already."

"Yay, weenie roast!" I yell. His face spasms in irritation, but I laugh because, come on, it's funny.

Steven makes a big show of cutting a couple of sticks off a nearby maple tree and whittling each end into a forked point using a pocketknife.

"Won't these get tree stuff on our hot dogs?" I ask as he hands me my stick.

He rolls his eyes. I imagine poking the stick in them.

"They're not, like, poisonous or anything?"

"No, Jane, they're not *poisonous*. Didn't any of the men your mom brought home ever take you camping?"

I shoot him a narrow look and he holds up his hands. "You know what I mean."

"No," I grumble as I stomp up the stairs to the cabin door, "they didn't take me camping."

"That's why women shouldn't have kids outside of marriage. Your real dad would have taught you this kind of stuff."

"Maybe. But men have kids outside of marriage too, you know. That's kind of how it works."

"But women should know better. They're the ones left with the children." Lucky men and stupid, irresponsible women. A tale as old as time.

Steven has done his whittling work, so he grabs another beer and puts his feet up on a rough block of wood that sits between the couches. I get the hot dogs and buns and condiments and paper plates. The fire has warmed the place up, at least, and I shed my big coat and boots.

"There are potato chips too," he calls out. I retrieve them, and he moves his feet so I can fit the chips on the makeshift table. Steven hands me his cooking stick. I kneel in front of the fire and cook our meal.

"This is nice," he says.

"The first dinner I've made for you!"

He laughs and chugs his beer. I grin with happiness as my cheeks flush from the fire. A tiny flash of movement catches my eye. A spider drops frantically from a high hearthstone to escape the heat. But it's hotter near the ground, unfortunately for the spider. It drops to the floor right in front of the flames, and I watch its legs curl in until it's just a little ball of drying meat. I don't squeal with fear once. I don't even blink.

When the weenies are roasted, I slide them onto buns and serve one to my man. He eats it quickly and asks for one more, but he does get up to fetch himself a beer from the doorstep. He gets me one too. As soon as our meal is finished, he announces that he's going out to get in a few hours of hunting before dusk.

"Hold on!" I cry. "Let me just get my coat and—"

"No. You stay here."

"But, Steven—"

"Not today. I need some peace."

He's out the door before I can think, stomping down the steps with his gun in hand.

Damn it. I shove my feet into my boots and scramble into my coat, but as I run for the door, one of the overlarge boots slides off and trips me. I have to stop and tie them to keep them on, and by the time I burst out of the front door, Steven has vanished.

I sprint around the back of the cabin to see if he's still somewhere here in the clearing, but he's gone and I don't spy any trailheads.

"Shit!" Maybe I'm not a jungle cat after all.

I walk down the dirt lane, one of my boots clomping sadly against the packed ground. I hope to find an obvious trail he might have taken, but all I see are a couple of narrow gaps in the trees. Even if I can make the right guess, it's not a great idea to silently stalk an armed hunter through the woods. Shooting me might make his life miserable for a while, but that's really not the way I want to go about it.

Okay, this is fine. I'll talk him into taking me with him tomorrow morning and I'll kill him the first chance I get.

But damn I hate making mistakes.

Don't believe the movies about us. Being a sociopath doesn't automatically make someone a genius at killing. I'm learning on the job here.

The good news is that I've made a decision. I've lost my chance to make this fast, so quickly making my way back to the city undetected will be too difficult. Option one is out. And option three—accidentally shooting my boyfriend in the woods—puts me under too much scrutiny and could result in charges.

It's going to have to be option two: kill Steven in the woods, bury him deep in the forest, and then report that he went out hunting and never returned. It's supposed to snow on Sunday night. I'll wait until the storm starts before I drive down to the general store to call authorities for help.

Hunters and hikers go missing all the time. Wherever I bury him, I'll tell them he set off from the cabin in the opposite direction. They'll search far and wide in the wrong part of the forest, and they'll find nothing. It will snow for half the week. He'll be impossible to track. Days will go by. Then weeks. I'll slowly fade out of the Hepsworth family's life. The end.

Satisfied, I head back to the cabin to settle onto the couch with the new book I brought. It's a sci-fi adventure packed with romance and war and intrigue. I love it.

When I look up again, fading sunlight is stretching across the plank floor from the back window, and I realize he's been out in the woods a long time. At least four hours.

Maybe he'll take care of this problem for me and never return, but I feel a sharp slash of irritation at the thought. I want to be the one to make him pay. I want to go to bed at night with the knowledge that I avenged Meg. That thought will keep me as warm and happy as my cat does.

I step outside and scan the woods around me. Gnats dance in shafts of sunlight. Birds scream at each other. There's a soft cooing somewhere nearby that sounds strangely like pigeons. But there's no Steven.

After a peek into the outhouse, I decide I'm better off going in the bushes. Amazing to me that men can see where they're aiming and what they're aiming with and they still can't hit the mark. The wood in there is soaked with old urine.

I walk into the trees and crouch. While I'm peeing, I catch movement from the corner of my eye. Steven has emerged from the other side of the woods and is walking toward the cabin. He can't see me in the deepening shadows, and I watch as he passes only twenty feet away. I smile at his stupid vulnerability and feel a jolt of near-sexual pleasure as I finish urinating.

After wiping with a tissue from my pocket, I stand up, but I don't head for the cabin. Instead I watch Steven go inside. I hear him talking to me as if I'm there. His eyes haven't adjusted to the change in light yet. I feel like I'm invisible. Powerful. Like he's a rat being run through a maze by a force he can't fathom.

A few seconds later he steps outside, blinking. He frowns, his head turning left and right and left again. He's lost me. Lost another one. Is he worried he'll find me hanging in the woods nearby?

"Jane?" He moves slowly down the steps as if he's not sure where he is. *"Jane!"*

I wish I had the gun. I can't shoot him here, but I could watch him through the scope, watch his pulse flutter in his throat. I could aim it at that quick heartbeat and pretend to pull the trigger.

He turns and hurries toward the outhouse. "Jane?" When he opens the door, nothing greets him but the smell of old piss.

Steven backs away and then turns in a slow circle, his gaze passing right over me. His furrowed brow suggests anger, but his mouth hangs open in confusion. When he finds himself facing the truck, he marches over and cups his hands to his eyes to look inside. I'm not there.

"Jane?" he calls again, taking a few steps toward the dirt road. He slows, then stops, at a complete loss.

Grinning at this game, I pick up a rock from the forest floor and throw it as hard as I can toward the far side of the clearing. He spins and stares toward the sharp crack of the rock hitting a tree. The stone rustles through the underbrush as it falls to the ground. Steven stares into the woods, but he doesn't move forward.

If I can get him to go out searching for me, I could kill him tonight. He left his rifle in the cabin, and I have my knife in my pocket. Sure, he's bigger than I am, but you never expect your sweet new girlfriend to step out of the woods and stab you in the throat.

But he's frozen. Afraid. Steven doesn't like this game as much as I do.

He stares into the woods for a long time before taking two backward steps toward the cabin. If he does plan to go out looking for me—and that's a big if—he wants to grab his gun first.

I throw another rock, and he cranes his head toward the sound. "Jane?"

I throw one more rock, aimed closer to one of the narrow trail openings in the trees. "Jane!" he calls with a little more irritation and a little less fear. "Where are you?" With only one sparing glance toward the cabin, he takes off for the trail.

I slip out of the trees and into the clearing. I draw the knife from my coat pocket and free the blade.

Moving slowly, I place my feet with care, avoiding twigs and leaves, setting my boots only on areas of bare dirt. I need to give him time to put a little distance between himself and the cabin.

I've pictured myself slitting his throat from behind, but that would spray blood everywhere, and we can't have that. Plus he's taller than I am. I wouldn't have the right leverage. Oh, well. I'll sneak up behind him and bury a quiet blade between the ribs. Almost as satisfying.

I'm halfway across the clearing and straining my ears for noise on the trail ahead. I hear a distant brushing sound; then he calls my name again. He's facing away from me, so I can't tell how far into the trees he is. I lean down and pick up another rock. I need to lead him deeper.

Concerned that I'll hit him with it, I whip the rock a little to the left.

"Jane?" I hear again. His stupid voice grates on my ears.

Gripping my knife more tightly, I move toward the tree line. The clearing is littered with leaves and sticks here. I watch my feet with each step. One loud snap and he'll hurry back to me.

The wind picks up suddenly and I use the chance to take five quick steps across the brittle leaves. I'm almost to the trees and the trail. The wind will cover my noise. I can rush up behind him and—

He's suddenly in the opening right in front of me. "Jane?"

I freeze.

His eyes widen as I stare at him. I don't know what I look like, but I'm definitely not wearing the sweet, submissive expression of his girlfriend. I think of my cat. The tiger at the zoo. Those cool, cruel eyes.

Then his gaze drops to the knife in my hand.

I could just jump forward and stab him before his surprise wears off. Thrust the knife right into his throat. I can almost feel it sinking in. But we're way too close to the cabin. I can't risk it. And his shocked expression is crumpling into suspicion.

I fix the mask back to my face and open my mouth in a frightened gasp. "Oh my God!"

"Jane . . . what are you doing?" His deep animal brain has finally registered the danger I present. He eyes the shiny blade warily. I imagine goose bumps spreading over his skin.

"I heard something!" I yelp. "I got scared!" I fling the knife aside and rush toward him.

He catches me automatically, though I notice his hands grip my arms and don't reach around to embrace me. He's not a stupid man. But I have an advantage. He'd never believe a woman can hold the upper hand. He's in charge here; I just need to remind him of that.

"I was scared," I whimper.

"Where were you?" he asks.

"What?"

"The cabin was empty. Where did you go?"

I make my voice quake and wobble. "I just went out for a quick walk."

"A walk?" I feel his muscles give a little, relaxing. His hands slide down my arms. "Christ, Jane, there are bears up here."

"I took a knife."

"A *knife*?" He finally sets me back and his jaw drops as he stares at me. "So you thought I was a bear and you were looking for me with a *knife*?" The scornful words echo against tree trunks. He's back in full form.

"Well, I didn't know it was a bear. I was just out for a walk and—"

"You don't have a gun and you don't know your way around here but you decided to go for a walk."

"I didn't go far. You were gone so long and I got bored."

He shakes his head in disgust. "Jesus, you're an idiot."

"You just went into the woods without a gun too."

"Yeah, and I was coming back to get it so I could find you!"

"Come on, sweetie. I'm sorry, okay? I didn't mean to scare you."

"You didn't scare me; it was just an idiotic thing to do! You're like a damn child."

"I didn't get lost and I didn't see any bears. I'm fine."

"Pure dumb luck, I'm sure. Good God, I need a beer."

"You said you brought champagne."

"Well, have at it."

He leaves me there and grabs a beer on his way inside. I blow out a long, tense breath as the door closes behind him.

He's shaken up, but I gave him a narrative he could believe. The narrative that's easiest for him to believe: I'm just a dumb, helpless woman.

But it was very nearly a fatal mistake. I let my guard down. I let him see the real me. For a moment he recognized the predator inside.

I shouldn't have strayed from the plan. "No more mistakes," I murmur aloud. There's a chance I could lose everything in my quest for revenge, but I have to keep that chance as small as possible.

Tonight I'll play my part perfectly, and he won't remember what he saw in my face today until he's bleeding out on the forest floor tomorrow. It'll be far too late for his animal brain to save him then.

I dig my knife from the fallen leaves, set my shoulders, and head back inside to make sure my man is too happy to think about anything but our blossoming love.

CHAPTER 40

He's guzzling his beer when I walk in.

"Did you see any deer?" I ask, trying to smooth things over. He gives a negative grunt. "Will you help me open the champagne?" This grunt sounds vaguely positive.

I pull the champagne from the cooler to peel off the foil and unwind the wire before delivering the bottle to Steven. He opens it the showy, stupid way, of course, pushing with his thumb until the cork shoots out and hits the ceiling. A good three sips of champagne are wasted in the foam that drips to the floor.

"I didn't see any glasses . . . ," I prompt.

He shrugs. "I must have forgotten. I think there's a mug under the sink."

Gross. I take a swig from the bottle instead. Steven's lip curls, but he pats the couch beside him. "Grab another beer for me?"

I get a beer and take another gulp of cheap sparkling wine, shivering at the way the alcohol is already seeping into my veins. I cuddle close to him and sigh.

"I was worried about you, babe," he says.

"I know. I'm sorry."

"I thought I was going to come home and find you in your sexy lingerie, and then I couldn't find you at all."

I giggle and take another drink.

"Why don't you put it on for me now?"

"It's not even dark yet!"

"When it gets dark, I won't be able to see it."

"Steven . . ."

"Come on. Be a good girl for me."

"I don't know. I'm feeling a little shy."

"I know. I like that about you. I like it even better when you're shy *and* naked." He nudges the champagne toward my lips, apparently past his disgust with my drinking from the bottle. "Have another drink."

I take another drink, totally enjoying the buzz. He kisses my neck. "Come on, baby. Put on your pretty outfit for me."

"Okay. All right. But you can't look while I'm changing."

"Promise."

I move behind the couch and change near the beds, shucking all my clothes shamelessly before I slip the nightgown over my head. The fine net material is nearly transparent. I don't bother putting on panties. He's going to love it.

"Close your eyes," I whisper before I move to stand in front of him. He opens his eyes before I give him permission and he groans loudly at the sight of me.

"Oh my God. You're so damn hot."

"You like it?"

"Hell yeah. Let me see the back." When I turn, I glance over my shoulder to see him tugging his phone from his jeans.

"What are you doing?" I scream as I shield myself.

"Taking a picture."

"No way!"

"Come on. I'm your boyfriend."

"No. No pictures!"

"You've never taken dirty pics before?"

"Never."

"Not even with your stepdad?"

"Steven! Oh my God! I can't believe you asked that!" What a shitty way to take a hard swipe at my confidence.

"I just thought those guys were really into pictures."

"I never . . . no. Absolutely not."

He puts the phone down. "Come here, babe."

I drop onto the couch beside him and pout.

"Listen. This is something special. I'm not going to show these to anyone. They're just for me. I think about you all the damn time and I want to be able to see the girl I love."

I shake my head.

"Okay. Then I'll delete them before we get back to town. Come on. Do this for me. It's such a turn-on." When I hesitate, he nuzzles my neck. "Don't you like making your man happy?"

"You know I do."

"I want to be the first," he murmurs. "The first guy you pose for."

I wonder if this is exactly what he said to Meg. It's a double betrayal—to talk a woman into this vulnerable intimacy, then use it as proof that she's beneath contempt. But I can't think about Meg now. I can't let my rage bubble up. I must be absolutely harmless tonight.

"You'd have to use my phone," I whisper. "Not yours."

"Okay. But maybe you'll send me some?"

"Maybe."

"Yeah, baby. Have another drink. Loosen up a little."

I don't mind taking photos, but I can't leave him with any evidence on his phone. Even if I make him delete them, who knows what the police will be able to recover? I swallow another gulp of champagne and move his phone to the other couch before getting mine.

He pokes around on it for a minute. "You don't take any photos? Not even selfies? I thought all girls loved selfies."

I stand in front of him, pretending to be self-conscious. "I don't have much memory. I have to transfer all my pictures to my computer to save space."

"I see. All right, baby. Smile for me."

I begin posing, giggling at his instructions. "Maybe you shouldn't get my face in the photos."

"I'll do my best. Turn around. Lift it up. Yeah. Now lean over a little. Hell yeah." I hear his zipper and he's breathing harder. "Touch yourself."

"Steven!"

"Come on. Move for me. Yeah, that's my good girl."

"Are you taking *video*?"

"Maybe."

"Steven!"

"Turn around and take it off." His voice is a little harder now.

I do as instructed, stumbling as if I'm drunk. "Nice," he grunts. "Real nice. You're good at this. My own personal little slut. Now touch them."

I cup my breasts and moan. I like showing off and I don't have to pretend to be turned on. I'll watch the video myself later.

He masturbates for a while, issuing instructions to me that I obey. It doesn't take long for him to order me to my knees. "Make me happy, baby."

"Don't record it," I say.

"I won't." But of course he will. I pretend to trust him anyway.

"I love you," I say, looking up at him with big eyes.

"I love you too," he mumbles. "I love you so much, babe." He moves my head where he wants it. "So much."

He thinks he's in control here, his hand pushing me down, his penis shoving into my throat. He thinks he's dominating me. But he's the vulnerable one, sliding his favorite part between my open jaws. My knees hurt on the dirty wood floor, but I fantasize about sinking my teeth deep into his shaft, ripping it off right at the root, and the time just flies by.

Afterward, I get him another beer and snuggle close. He doesn't return any favors. Big surprise.

But it doesn't matter. I'll take my satisfaction in knowing he's lost any sense of wariness now. A job well done.

CHAPTER 41

"You ever thought about getting a boob job?" he asks, the words slurring together. It's only seven, but I think he's had a whole twelve-pack at this point.

I push back and frown at him as if I'm offended. "What?"

"They're kind of small."

"They are not!"

"I mean, they're great and everything. Real pretty. But they could be bigger with your body type."

"I can't believe you'd say that!" I cover my bare breasts with my arm and reach for a blanket slung over the back of the couch like he's made me feel ashamed of my body. The fabric smells of dust and mildew. "Do you really like those big fake breasts?"

"Sure. My ex had them. They were great."

He's talking about Meg. She got them for herself as a graduation present after college. I filled her prescriptions and brought her take-out food for three days after the surgery. "You wish you were still with her, don't you?"

"No. I told you she was crazy. I'm just saying I think you'd look great with implants too."

"Well, I could never afford them, so this is a stupid conversation." I flop back on the couch and pout.

"Maybe I could help you out someday."

"You'd pay for *surgery*?"

He shrugs. "Maybe. I mean, they'd kind of belong to me, wouldn't they? A nice new toy."

"Whatever. Mine are fine the way they are." He's doing his best to undermine my confidence, so I pretend to seethe.

I wonder how many times he's had this conversation with women. I wonder if he looked at Meg's breast implants and saw a woman who'd already done the work for him. A two-for-one special: big boobs *and* body image issues!

I tried to talk Meg out of the implants, but not because I think there's anything wrong with them. Any advantage we can get in this world we should take. My objection was that I don't trust surgeons. Too many of them are like me. It's a wonderful profession for our kind. So much power and no fear about making mistakes. Great on that end of the scalpel, not always so great for the person on the table.

Still, I helped her through the recovery, and I'll probably get surgery myself when I get older and my breasts start to lose their shape. I can't let such useful tools get rusty. It's fascinating how helpless men are in the face of them.

"You know I think you're beautiful, baby," Steven murmurs into my ear.

"Do you?"

"Of course. You're my girl."

"What's your favorite thing about me?"

"You're sweet. And hot. You're a nice Christian girl. And my family likes you."

I turn eagerly to face him. "Do they really like me? Because I like them so much."

"My dad keeps telling me not to let you get away."

"Aw! He's so sweet. Do you think . . . if we . . . you know . . . if we ever got married . . . do you think I could call him Dad?"

"Yeah. Yeah, I think he'd really like that. And so would I."

"It'd be so nice to have a real family, Steven."

"It would make me happy to give that to you. A real home. A good dad."

"And Rhonda too. She's just so sweet."

He stiffens immediately and my pulse quickens. In the thrill of the hunt, I'd forgotten about his weird interaction with Rhonda. And this is the perfect time to press for details. Steven's words are running together, draping over themselves. He's drunker than I've ever seen him. I'll take every advantage I can. I'm not sure what wound Rhonda inflicted, but it's festering, and I want to poke at it.

"You know," I say breezily, "I was thinking I could get Rhonda's number from you and maybe we could have tea or something. Get to know each other better. A girls' day out."

"No."

"But if we really might get married someday—"

"No. I don't want you around her. She's a bad influence."

"Rhonda?" I crease my whole face up in confusion. "What are you talking about? She's your stepmom."

"She's a whore."

Good Lord, this again? We're everywhere. "Steven, she's nice. You shouldn't be so mean about her. She seems like a good wife and—"

He cuts me off with a loud snort. "She's a gold-digging slut! That's what she is."

"I don't understand. Did she cheat on your dad or something?"

"Yes."

"What?" I fail to keep the trill of delight from my voice, but he doesn't seem to hear it.

He growls deep in his throat. "Yeah. Everyone thinks she's such a perfect wife, but, believe me, she's a cheating whore."

"Wow. And . . . and your dad took her back?"

He shrugs. "They never broke up. My dad doesn't know anything about it."

Well. This is getting very interesting. "But, Steven . . . if your dad doesn't know, how could *you* know?"

His lips spread in a sneering, self-satisfied grin. "How do you think?"

Is he saying what I think he's saying? Delight shivers through my nerves at the possibility, but I pretend I don't understand. I shake my head, making sure I look upset. I'm worried for the family. Maybe a little scared.

Steven's grin fades. He takes a swig from the bottle and stares at the far wall for a minute before speaking. "Never mind."

"What do you mean? What happened?"

His eyelids dip in a slow blink. His head wobbles on his neck. "It was me," he slurs.

"What was you?"

"She cheated with me."

"What?" I gasp, hoping he's too drunk to hear the breathless glee in that word. It happened. It really happened, and I want to clap my hands and squeal.

I watch his mouth flash back to that proud sneer for a moment. "She begged me for it."

"Steven . . . no. That's not true."

"Oh, it's true."

"But you wouldn't have—"

He waves a hand. "I don't want to talk about it. Just stay away from her. She's evil."

"But how . . . ? I mean . . ." I want details, damn it. "My God, when did this happen?"

"I said I don't want to talk about it! Let's go to bed."

"It's not even eight—"

He kisses me then, pushing me down on the couch, and I realize he's completely turned on. He's between my legs and shoving down his jeans before I can say a word. As he pumps furiously into me, he keeps his eyes squeezed tightly closed, and I'm pretty sure he's picturing Rhonda.

Holy crap. Holy *crap*.

This is just . . . Wow.

I gawk up at the ceiling as he mutters something about how much I want it, how much I need it. He calls me a slut. I try not to take offense because I'm pretty sure he's talking to his stepmom.

This is just too delicious for words.

I won't have to kill anyone after all.

CHAPTER 42

I'm positively giddy by the time we pull away from the cabin on Sunday afternoon. I'm still enthusiastically hunting my prey, but Steven is grumpy because he never did bag that deer.

Last night I wanted to ask him a million questions about his affair with his stepmom, but he passed out immediately after sex and snored the whole night away on the couch. A lucky stroke, it turns out, because I could never have been patient, left to my own devices. But patience is key here. Patience is everything. His binge drinking is really working out great for me.

This morning he was out the door with his rifle at 7:00 a.m., and we immediately loaded up the car when he returned in the late afternoon, just as the snow started to fall. It's drifting gently through the trees as we bounce down the dirt road toward civilization. What a peaceful ending to this trip.

Steven wants a coffee, so we stop at the general store. I stay hidden in the car again, not that I care about being spotted at this point. Still, when he tells me to slide down, I halfheartedly slouch in my seat.

A car pulls in behind us as Steven rounds the corner and disappears. I have nothing to be on guard about now, so I pay no attention to the car door shutting behind me, but when the man walks past, I definitely take notice. I see a brown uniform and a face tipped down to look at me as he walks past.

He's frowning, likely wondering why I look like I'm trying to hide from him. I make a big show of yawning as if I want to catch a nap; then I sit up straight and give a little wave. He tips his head in acknowledgment when I smile, but his sharp eyes study me for five more seconds before he moves along.

I see that the patch on his arm says SHERIFF, not DEPUTY. This sheriff isn't exactly the kindly old man I'd pictured. He's forty-five at most, and he glances at the license plate of the truck before he follows Steven's path into the store.

Good God. I blow a long breath past my teeth. My arrogance might have been my downfall if I'd followed through on my plans to kill Steven. That man was not the country bumpkin I assumed I'd be dealing with. That was a man with a suspicious eye and a keen curiosity.

Steven reappears with a big Styrofoam cup of coffee. When he pulls out, I glance in the mirror to see the sheriff standing in the doorway, watching us leave.

Yeah. I would have been in trouble. I want revenge, but I do not want a life sentence. I feel like a damn lucky girl as we hit the highway. I'm not on my way to jail, and what I have planned now will be far more painful for Steven than death. It's a win-win.

I manage to keep my mouth shut the whole way home, and, boy, it isn't easy. Either Steven doesn't remember telling me about Rhonda, or he's just trying to avoid the subject, because he doesn't bring it up either.

When we get near the city, I ask if I can come over to his place tonight. When he responds with a grumpy "No," I'm genuinely disappointed. I want him drunk and spilling more details right *now*.

But this is for the best. I need to do a little planning.

I wave from the curb as he drives away; then I take the stairs two at a time and burst into my apartment, calling hello to my cat. She blinks sleepily at me from the couch as if she never noticed I was gone. Clearly she did fine without me. She lets me close enough for a few quick strokes of her soft fur, and then she scoots elegantly out of my reach and into the kitchen.

When I check the phone I left behind, I find three text messages from Luke and smile even harder at the sight of them. My cat didn't miss me, but someone did.

Want to go to dinner? he texted yesterday afternoon.

Then: Checking to make sure you got my text.

And finally: Now I'm just being annoying. Call me tomorrow if you're free?

I glance at the clock, but it's already after 8:00. Oh, well.

Popping open my laptop, I first search for everything I can find on Rhonda Hepsworth. Thousands of results appear almost instantaneously, and a quick study shows me that everything on the first few pages is related to the church. I open images and scroll through a few of those, but I see no sign of her wanton secrets here.

She wears the same overdone smile in each one. Her hair is perfect and her necklines modest.

When did this happen with Steven? And how? I'm absolutely dying to know, but he already told me he'd be busy catching up on church business for a couple of days. "Maybe we'll hang out next weekend," he'd said gruffly.

If I were truly a needy, dependent Jane, I'd be worried right now. He's obviously displeased and blowing me off, but my only irritation is that I won't be able to grill him about Rhonda for a while.

The truth is that he's embarrassed he didn't get to show off by bringing home a deer, so he's pissed at me for witnessing his failure. I told him I was proud of him anyway. That made a vein in his forehead stand out.

If only he'd taken me along on the hunt, he could have blamed his failure directly on me and my noise or female scent or something. Steven didn't plan ahead.

Tomorrow morning I'll start lobbying to go to Bible study on Wednesday night, followed up by some fornicating afterward. I need him to take me back to his house so he can get drunk again.

Returning to the hits on Rhonda Hepsworth, I click through to a church newsletter. Steven told me Rhonda had worked in the church offices before she married the pastor. If they keep all the archives online, maybe I can find her maiden name. But it's a bust. The archives only go back two years.

Still, it all must have been a big deal. Announcements. A grand wedding. I search for "Pastor Robert Hepsworth" and "Rhonda" and "engaged," and I've got it. A beautiful picture of young Rhonda Entenman and her new father figure posing for an engagement picture.

Her smile is more natural and her hair is less blond. She looks genuinely happy and could probably pass for eighteen instead of twenty-two. Good Pastor Hepsworth is positively glowing. The cuckold rises triumphant from his divorce! But still a cuckold, sadly.

Lucky for me, Rhonda has a pretty unique name, so I search her maiden name and here she is: listed on the graduation rolls for a community college, named as a regional champion in the javelin throw during high school . . . and pictured with quite a few red Solo cups on ancient Facebook posts.

Here she is in a bikini on a fishing boat, her arms around two other blondes. She's flashing a peace sign with one hand and holding a beer in the other. Her body is taut and tan, that unique blend of firm and soft that only comes with youth. I can see what the pastor liked about her. I can see what Steven liked too.

In another picture she's sitting on a boy's lap, skirt short and neckline low. He's smiling down at her cleavage while she laughs. She wasn't always into older men, it seems. She looks like an entirely average college student. How in the world did she get suckered into marrying Hepsworth?

But she probably wasn't suckered. She was an average girl dating average boys and going to a cheap community college. The pastor is the chief of his world, with lots of money and influence and a big house. Rhonda decided she was moving up and moving up quick.

Or maybe she was like Meg, looking desperately for a strong man to tell her what to do and wear and say, because she'd never had a dad around to be her moon and sun and anchor or whatever the hell good dads are supposed to be. I don't know anything about that. I've had affairs with far too many of those good dads. They're men, just men, the same as any other.

However it had happened, Rhonda became the pastor's wife, with the costume and performance that went with it, and it must not have been what she'd expected. Or maybe she just wanted to have her cake and eat it too. The father with all his money and power, and the son with his young body and filthy talk.

This is all so exciting.

I give up on my research on Rhonda and transfer the photos and video Steven took of me from my burner phone to my computer. I've already viewed it all several times, and, frankly, I don't look too bad even without implants.

I'm in the middle of deleting everything from the burner phone when I pause over one still shot. It's just my body, my head cut off below the chin. I'm naked, one hand sliding up my neck and the other at my side as if I don't know what to do with it. The only identifying mark is the filigree cross I wear at my neck. Other than the necklace, I'm completely exposed.

Still pumped up on mischief and adrenaline, I type in a number I stole from Steven's phone and text the picture with no message. Then I finish deleting the pics and remove the battery and SIM card from the phone to store everything in the dresser. I'll destroy it all when this is done.

Okay, I might keep a couple of the more flattering pictures. Every woman should have memories of her glory days once she's old and wrinkled. I'll add these to my collection.

Back on my old phone, I text Steven a quick I luv u! along with a bunch of pink hearts. He doesn't respond. Rude.

Then I text Luke. Sorry. I was out of town on a quick trip.

Only about thirty seconds pass before he responds. Something fun?

No. Just work.

I'm reading that book you got me. Thanks again. It's great.

I'm so glad you like it. I stare at my text for a while, trying to think what I should say, what he'd like me to say. Something to keep him interested now that I have a bit more time with him. I'm really missing your big bathtub tonight.

Just my big bathtub?

He's good at making me laugh. I send him a winky face.

Want to grab dinner tomorrow? he asks.

I do. I really do. Steven is ignoring me, so it shouldn't be any trouble at all, and I need to find a way to bide my time until Steven invites me back to his place again.

Plus I want to see Luke at least one last time.

I know I'm not real. Not really. But I feel more real with Luke, and now I won't have to give him up quite yet. It's a little gift dropped in my lap.

I tap out a quick text. Maybe we could read again. Order take out.

I'd love that.

Yeah. Me too. And, strangely, it's not just the sex I'm looking forward to. It's . . . everything. The couch, the books, the jokes. I'm not sure why, but it hardly matters. This will all be over soon, and I'll get back to my solitary sociopathic life in Kuala Lumpur. But I'll enjoy everything about Luke while I can.

CHAPTER 43

I'm stretched across Luke's couch, my feet on his lap. His warm hand absently holds one of my ankles, rising away each time he turns a page, then sliding back over my skin as if he likes the curve of my bones.

The loft is quiet but for the paper rustle of our books. Empty cartons of Thai food are spread across the coffee table, and we're lounging, full and sleepy like an old married couple.

"I'm leaving next week," I say into the silence.

His hand tightens in a quick spasm on my ankle. He sets the book down. "What?"

"The project is wrapping up." I don't know why I'm telling him. I planned to simply disappear. Am I trying to avoid hurting his feelings, or am I worried he'll contact the police if I go missing? It must be the latter. I don't worry about people's feelings.

"You're going?" He sounds stunned even though he knew this was coming.

"Yes." I add a cheerful note to my voice. "Back to Malaysia!"

"But . . . okay. Sure. Right."

I pick up my book again, my duty done. When I glance up, Luke is staring straight ahead as if I've shocked him. "The project is over," I say again, more softly this time.

"Yeah. I get it. I just thought . . . I don't know."

I nod. "We had a good time."

"Yes."

"There's still time for a few more rounds, you know." I nudge his thigh with my foot, but he doesn't laugh.

"I meant it when I said this wasn't just about sex for me."

Not sure how to respond, I fall silent.

He scrubs both hands through his hair. "You were the one who got away, you know? Now you're off again. I know I'll miss you, because I missed you the first time around."

I'm flattered. How can I not be? I only ever bought him a book. But it's the sex he'll really miss, of course. "Luke . . ." I shake my head. "I'm not good at relationships. I'm just . . . not."

He turns to study my face. "Not what?"

"I'm different," I try. "That's all. I'm not like other people."

"I know you're different."

"You do?"

"Sure. You're . . . I don't know . . . you're a little autistic or something?"

I've never thought of it that way, but I can see why he'd make that connection. As if my feelings are trapped inside instead of mostly nonexistent. "Something like that," I murmur. "So . . . yeah. I'd never make a good girlfriend. So you don't have to miss me. You're allowed to miss the sex, though." I nudge him again, but he doesn't even pretend to smile.

"I don't know how to say this without it sounding like an insult, but . . . I like whatever is wrong with you, Jane."

I shake my head, flustered in a way I rarely am. I feel the skin of my face heat as if even my body is confused.

He clears his throat and runs his fingers through his tousled hair. "Not wrong. I didn't mean that. Just different. You're always so calm."

"That's true, I guess."

"Being with you feels smooth. Steady. Like you're at peace."

"At peace?"

"I know it must be more complicated than that for you, but whatever it is, *I* feel at peace with you."

Most people don't notice that I'm different. I work hard at making sure I fit in. But sometimes perceptive people sense the coldness inside me, and they don't feel at peace. They feel nervous. They draw away. They watch closely, waiting for a strike, and that's exactly what they should do. There's nothing comforting about me.

"I don't understand," I say.

"My mom was . . ." Luke huffs out a laugh. "My mom was a cyclone. Up and down, always intense, always chaotic. When I was little, I'd ride my bike home from school, and my head would get tighter and tighter with each block I passed, wondering what was waiting for me when I got home. Maybe she made three dozen cookies and she wanted to have a movie marathon even though I had a big test the next day. Or maybe she tore all the books and clothes out of my closet because she walked in and got irritated by my mess. Whatever it was, I couldn't ignore it, because she *demanded* participation. She wanted our full attention. Always. It was exhausting. So fucking exhausting."

"So she was manic or bipolar or . . . ?"

"I don't know. She didn't think there was anything wrong with her, as far as I could ever tell, so there was never a diagnosis. She's never gotten help. And from the outside, everything looked perfect. Amazing Christmas decorations, fresh baked goods, new paint on the kitchen cupboards, our clothes perfectly ironed. But I hated that place. I hated being home. I could never, ever relax."

"I'm sorry."

"It was constant uncertainty. We were always on edge, waiting for her next idea or explosion or plan. All I wanted was some quiet."

"I bet." I'd lived with chaos too, though even that wasn't constant. Nothing was. You could never let your guard down. It was like being at war from the time you were born.

"Then my dad had a heart attack when I was in college. I know the stress of living with her killed him. I know it. But after the funeral all she could do was rage about how he'd left her. How selfish he was. She called him *selfish* for dying. We'd just lost our father, and it was all about her. It was always all about her."

"Is that when you stopped going back?"

"Yes."

"And your brother?"

"He still talks to her. He's nicer than I am, I guess."

"You might see her when her grandchild is born."

"Yeah. I'm older now. I'm hoping I can tune her out or keep some emotional distance."

"Maybe." I don't really believe this. People don't change.

His hand is around my ankle again, squeezing gently. "Whatever it is about you, Jane—whatever makes you different—I like that. The calm. The logic. Maybe you're a little cool sometimes, but that makes me happy. And if you leave, I'm going to miss it like crazy."

This is so strange. I don't know what to say to him. Lovers have said romantic things to me before. They've even declared love, but this is different. I never believed them. I could see why they were saying it and what they wanted. I knew they were lying to me or maybe to themselves.

But for some reason I believe Luke. And he's not even professing love; he's just saying that he *likes* me.

No one likes me. Not with Meg gone. No one *should* like me.

I have no idea what to do with this. People don't change, and that includes me. I couldn't settle down with a man if I wanted to. Could I? "I have a job," I say. "A life." But I don't have a life—not really. My real life died with Meg.

"I know you can't stay." He sighs and lets his head fall back on the couch. "I know that, but I really, really wish you could."

I like being with him the same way I liked being with Meg. I almost wish I could stay too.

"Maybe I can visit," I suggest. But he's a cute, nice guy. He'll find someone else, and he might not even be willing to cheat on her when I come to town. "We can stay in touch."

"Sure."

He's looking up at the ceiling, his thumb gliding absently over my skin. His eyes look sad and tired. I try to think of something to say that might cheer him up.

"Do you want to have sex?" I ask.

"Jane . . . you . . ." Luke squeezes his eyes shut and laughs. "Yes, damn it. Yes, I want to have sex."

I climb onto his lap and kiss him until he doesn't look sad anymore. It's all I know to do. And it works for a little while.

CHAPTER 44

It's finally Bible study night!

Steven agreed to bring me, but only after I cornered him in the hallway at work and started to cry.

"I haven't been ignoring you!" he insisted. "I've been busy, that's all."

Busy making me feel like worthless crap.

Anyway, my pleading worked its magic. I expressed regret for whatever imaginary infraction I'd committed, and now he can be nice to me again.

"Can I spend the night?" I asked in a quavering voice, and a pleased smile spread over his face.

"Of course you can spend the night, babe. And we can grab dinner on the drive out."

I'm back in his good graces.

Dinner was deli sandwiches eaten in a hurry, and Steven's breath smells like raw onions now, but I still feel like a princess as I hop out of his SUV and glide toward the big glass doors of the church. It's drizzling and miserable, and I take that as a good sign.

Once we're inside, I remove my bulky coat and unwind my scarf to expose my pink flowery dress and lace-trimmed neckline. Catching sight of myself in the glass entryway, I touch the gold cross nestled just below the hollow of my neck and smile.

Steven tells me to find a seat, and I pick one in the first row where the deacons normally sit during services. Tonight is less formal. No suits for the men and no hierarchical seating. It's almost seven, and fewer than a hundred people are gathered in the hall. Steven tells me we'll have a short service and then break up into smaller groups for discussion until 8:30. Then we'll go home and Steven will finally make me so, so happy.

When he enters the hall with his father, I wave in happy greeting. Pastor Hepsworth's gaze falls immediately to the cross at my neck. His mouth twitches into a frown, but he recovers and returns my wave. I clasp my hands in my lap and eagerly await the mini-sermon.

Steven joins me in the front row. He pats my hand. "It's nice having you here," he whispers.

"Thank you for bringing me," I whisper back. "I've missed you. It was nice being all alone with you last weekend."

"We'll be all alone tonight," he says with a wink.

"Stop!" I scold, covering my face in embarrassment. "Don't talk about that here!"

Steven grins. "You really are the perfect girl, Jane."

He's so sweet when he wants to be. Isn't that what Meg said all the time? *He's so good to me, Jane. I know we argue sometimes, but he's funny and cute and kind. Just give him a chance. You'll see.*

Pastor Hepsworth steps to the podium and begins speaking about forgiveness. I hope he's taking in his own message and really learning it, because he'll need to use it soon.

As he speaks, his gaze roams the crowd, and each time it strays over my section, his eyes move to my gold cross. I shouldn't have sent the picture. It was a wicked, pointless impulse. But I feel no regret, only giddy anticipation.

I don't need to seduce Pastor Hepsworth, but I like knowing that I could. His weakness is a little icing on my cake.

He only speaks for fifteen minutes, and then the crowd begins to break up into smaller groups. Steven leads his men's group away to one of the study rooms. I approach his father. "Pastor Hepsworth? Could I speak with you for a moment? I know you're very busy."

He watches me intently for a few seconds, looking for some clue. But I gaze innocently up at him until he cracks and settles his face into a gentle smile. "Of course, my dear. Come sit down with me." We move to the end of one of the pews as most of the people disperse to meeting rooms. The pastor takes a seat a foot away from me, but his eyes skip to my necklace for another quick look.

"Everything is going great with Steven, but I'm troubled by something that . . . Well, I guess it's not a secret . . ."

He nods, but his forehead crumples in confusion. "You can confide in me, my girl. You can trust in my absolute discretion."

"You won't tell Steven about this?"

The pastor clears his throat. "Not if you don't want me to."

"Thank you." I nod. "Okay . . ." I start as if I'm nervous. "I . . . I know about his ex-girlfriend. How she died."

He blinks as if he's surprised that's what I want to talk about, but he recovers quickly. "Ah, yes. Quite a tragedy."

"Sometimes I worry that he's not ready for another relationship. I think he blames himself for what happened."

He settles down finally, leaning back in the pew, ready to dispense godly advice. "It's normal for anyone to feel guilt after such an awful event."

"Yes, but he says he wasn't good to her."

"Nonsense! I counseled that girl myself and she was deeply troubled. Deeply."

Liar. Liar. Liar. Steven was the trouble in Meg's life. But I keep my face blank. "About what?"

"She'd lived quite a life of sin before she joined our church. She and Steven argued about her past, yes, but she still struggled to live in the right during her relationship with Steven."

"He says maybe he was too hard on her sometimes."

"A man's role is to lead his family, Jane. Do you believe that?"

"Yes, sir."

"Meg wasn't raised in the church, and she struggled to accept her role as a helpmate. Yes, they spoke of marriage, but she couldn't set aside her ideas of so-called liberation and feminism. She had demons, my dear. True, evil demons that tormented her and pushed her to sinful, reckless behavior."

Oh, Meg was the one sinning. Never Steven with his blow jobs and porn and Tinder hookups. He's just a man, after all. And so is his father.

"But we all sin, don't we?" I part my lips and raise my eyes to gaze up at him. "I'm a sinner too, Pastor Hepsworth. What if I have demons I can't escape? Am I still good enough for God? Am I good enough for Steven?"

He's staring at my mouth, then at that gold cross. "Is there something you want to tell me?" he prompts.

I shake my head.

The pastor takes a deep breath. He clears his throat again. Licks his lips. "Jane . . . did you text me last weekend?"

I shake my head harder.

"Perhaps you were reaching out for help."

"No, sir," I whisper.

"Jane."

"I don't know what you mean."

He watches sternly for a moment before sighing. "Well, if there's ever anything you need to confess or anything you need guidance with, you can come to me. My door is always open."

"I will."

When I don't say more, Pastor Hepsworth pats my hand, then slides both his hands around it to hold it. "Steven and I both tried to guide Meg, but, sadly, her demons were too much for her to bear. In the end she committed the ultimate sin by taking the life God gave her." Is that what he told his son? *There was nothing more we could have done.*

They could have been kind. Steven could have stopped stomping her into the ground every chance he got. His father could have counseled him to be gentle and understanding.

I swallow the bitter saliva pooling in my mouth and manage to rasp a question. "You don't think she's in hell, do you?"

"My child, suicide is something God can never forgive. She's damned for all eternity. But the rest of us still have time to save our own souls. And I can see what a good girl you are, Jane." His hands squeeze mine. "We are all sinners and we are all worthy of God's forgiveness. We have only to confess and ask for mercy. I will not judge you."

"Thank you, sir." I tug his hands up and hold them to my bosom. "Thank you so much. You've made me feel better."

His eyes are on his own fingers, resting against my cleavage. I smile as innocently as a mother cradling her babe.

No, there's no reason to seduce him. But after what he just said about Meg, is there any reason not to ruin him too? Just like Steven, his father blames Meg for everything.

Their day of disaster is near and their doom rushes upon them. Good old Deuteronomy.

This is hardly my first Bible study. I've already got the best parts memorized and I believe in them wholeheartedly. *Eye for eye, tooth for tooth.* But the rest is even better: *burn for burn, wound for wound, bruise for bruise.*

They're going to feel this for a long time.

CHAPTER 45

On our way home from church, I gasp at the sight of a liquor store. "Oh my gosh, I have the worst craving for a margarita right now! Could we stop and get some mix?"

"On a Wednesday night?"

"Is that too naughty?" I ask.

"I like you naughty." He pulls a quick U-turn and drives me back to the liquor store; then he lets me go in by myself. I grab tequila and margarita mix. Beer isn't going to cut it tonight. I need him drunk as a skunk.

He holds my hand for the rest of the drive, smiling because he can't wait to get me drunk and nasty. I know the feeling.

As soon as we get to his house, I mix up a pitcher of mild margaritas. When I pour his glass, I add extra tequila. Then a little more.

His eyes widen when he sips it. "Too strong?" I ask before taking a sip of mine. I close my eyes and hum with pleasure. "Mmmm. So good."

Steven laughs. "Not too strong for me, babe. Drink up."

He can't say his drink has too much tequila, because that would make him weaker than a woman. God, I hate this idiot. "Want to watch a little of the hockey game?" I ask.

He drops to the couch and switches it on. I hover for a moment, and as I expect, he drains the margarita quickly. He's used to downing beer after beer. He can't pace himself with hard liquor. I pluck the empty from his hand and rush to refill it.

"Thanks, babe," he says, eyes on the screen when I deliver a second drink. "You're the best."

"No, *you're* the best, sweetie." I snuggle close and watch the game with him. When I finish my first margarita, I offer to get him his third. I fill the glass about three-quarters of the way up and top it off with an inch of extra tequila. My glass is mostly ice.

"Want some chips, honey?" I call out. I find some tortilla chips and salsa and my man is so content. The salt and spice make him thirsty. I keep his glass full.

Within forty-five minutes he is red-faced and yelling at the TV as he finishes his fifth margarita. During the next commercial break, I mute the TV and turn to him.

"Steven . . . that wasn't true what you said about Rhonda, was it?"

"Huh?" The shift of topic is too sudden, and he grimaces with irritation as his gaze slides unsteadily toward me.

"You didn't really have an affair with her, did you?"

His eyes go comically wide. *"What?"*

My God, he was so drunk, he doesn't remember. "You told me about it, Steven. At the cabin."

He shakes his head hard, but the movement is too much for him in this state and he tips back, collapsing into the cushions.

I gently touch his hand. "Steven?"

"I don't want to talk about that."

"We need to talk about it. You had an affair with your own stepmom."

His mouth contorts with rage. "No. Don't call her that. She was, like, twenty-five years old. She was no one to me."

"But, Steven, she's your dad's—"

"Shut up. She's nothing more than a whore. That's all."

"I don't get it. What happened? Did you seduce her or something?"

"Me? You think *I* seduced *her*?"

"I don't know! I don't understand how this could have happened. She's your father's wife!"

I've brought the pitcher into the living room, and he refills his own drink now, spilling some on the coffee table. His hands shake. "She wasn't much of a damn wife," he mutters.

"So she . . . she seduced you?"

He snorts. "She was desperate."

"Desperate for what?"

"I'd just graduated from college and I moved in with them for a few months. I was living there, and . . . I don't know. I did a little snooping around. I didn't know much about her and I didn't trust her."

"What were you snooping for?"

"Whatever. Just anything. I figured she was a grasping little bitch. And she was. I found pills hidden under some clothes in the bottom drawer of her armoire. Birth control pills."

"So?"

"So they'd been married for almost two years, and she hadn't gotten pregnant yet, and they were seeing a fertility doctor."

"Oh."

"My father was torn up about it. He was upset that he couldn't get his young wife pregnant and he thought he was letting her down. The doctor said it was his fault. Low sperm count and all that. And she was taking birth control *the whole time*." Spittle flies from his mouth at this outrage. "I confronted her. Threw the pills in her face, and she begged me not to tell him."

"Did you tell him?"

He laughs. He's relaxing into the story now. He's proud of himself for taking advantage of this bitch. "No. She said she'd do anything to keep it quiet. Absolutely anything. So I told her to try her best. She got on her knees right there in my dad's bedroom and sucked me off."

"Steven! Oh my God! You . . . How could you do that? With your dad's *wife*?"

"I'm a man, Jane. I can't say no to that."

Holy cow, he is so warped.

"For the rest of the summer, she basically did anything I wanted. He'd been smart enough to make her sign a prenup. She would've walked away with nothing."

"So you betrayed your father with her over and over again?"

The smirk falls from his face. "I love my dad. Don't try to twist this around. She was already betraying him. She was already a terrible, lying, screwed-up wife. Just like my mom. All women are the same. You're all whores. My dad knows that too."

"I'm not a whore."

"Are you kidding? When I close my eyes, I can't tell the difference between you and Rhonda."

I should gasp and act offended and maybe cry a little. I don't bother. He's too drunk to notice the difference. "Did you love her?" I ask.

"Jesus, of course I didn't love her. I can't stand her. I just used what she was offering."

Yeah, he'd used her. But what he doesn't realize is she used him too. She'd conned her way into a prosperous marriage and Steven had found out, but Rhonda had come up with the perfect way to silence him. He couldn't expose her without breaking his father's heart. She'd tied him up in her secret and he could never escape it.

Maybe she's like me.

Or maybe not. Maybe she's just like everyone else in this world. She'd used Robert Hepsworth for money, and he'd used her for her young body and pretty face. She'd used Steven to ensure her continued prosperity, and he'd used her for sex and humiliation. So far they'd each come out pretty even. Now the tide was about to change, and they would all be swept out with it.

His eyes are bleary, the lids heavy, but he reaches for me. “Come ’ere.”

Oh, great, he wants to pretend I’m Rhonda again.

“I’m not in the mood,” I say.

“Come on. You wanted to know the truth and I told you. Don’t act pissed now.”

Strangely I’m not as excited about him calling me a whore as he is.

“Come on, babe,” he whines.

“No, this is serious, Steven. Your dad is a wonderful man.”

“I know he is,” Steven says softly. “He’s the best. He’s the best.” He makes a strange noise, and I realize he’s starting to cry. Good Lord. “I love my dad,” he says before breaking into sobs. *“I love my dad!”*

I’ve got no patience for this. “I know you do, sweetheart. Come on. Let’s go to bed.” I switch off the TV and tug him to his feet.

“It wasn’t my fault,” he slurs. A tear drips down his face and a trickle of snot leaks from his nose.

“I know. Get to bed. I’ll be right there. I just need to tidy up the kitchen first.”

He nods and stumbles toward the hallway.

I take the dishes to the kitchen, wipe down the coffee table, and call for a car. Then I do the dishes. I’m in the middle of writing Steven a note when his first snores echo down the hallway.

> *Dear Steven, I drank way too much and I’m afraid I’ll be sick in the morning, so I took a car home. See you at work, sweetie. Love you bunches.*

When I deliver it to his room, he’s lying facedown on the mattress, his jeans around his ankles. I drop the note on top of his bare ass and blow him a kiss.

I can’t waste any more time here tonight. I’ve got a recording to edit.

CHAPTER 46

I have a sense of déjà vu as I call in sick to work and walk to the car rental agency, but this time I ask for a full-size SUV. As I'm turning over my fraudulent driver's license to the clerk, Steven texts me.

> What the hell did we drink last night? I don't even remember going to bed.
>
> Tequila and lots of it.
>
> Are you sick?
>
> Yeah. So sick. In fact, I gotta go.

He responds with a frowny face. Yuck.

My Steven is a regular Florence Nightingale.

I drive my rental all the way out to Apple Valley this time. The church is quiet, though I can hear people in their offices working down the hall. Pastor Hepsworth's secretary isn't at her desk, so I knock on his closed office door.

"Yes?" he calls.

I open it a few inches and stick my head in.

"Jane?" he sits up straighter. "What are you doing here?"

"I wanted to apologize," I say.

He cocks his head, puzzled. "Apologize for what, my dear?"

"For lying to you yesterday."

"About what?"

"I don't want you to be angry . . ." I drop my head in shame.

"I promise I won't be angry. I'm here to help you in any way I can."

I swallow hard and raise my gaze to meet his. "You were right, sir. I . . . I did text you this weekend."

His gray eyebrows fly high. "The picture. It *was* you."

"Yes. It was me. I was . . . I was just scared to admit it to you, Pastor Hepsworth. I'm sorry."

"My word, Jane."

"I'm sorry. I don't know why I sent it! You're just such a great man, and I wanted . . . I wanted . . ." I break off and take a shuddering breath. "Can you forgive me for what I've done?"

He tilts his head a little, looking past me toward his secretary's desk. It's still empty. "Maybe you'd better come inside, my dear," he says, his voice deepening. "I think we need to have a talk."

"Yes, sir." I hit a button on my phone; then I slip into his office and close the door behind me.

CHAPTER 47

I've taken my time and really thought this out. I think audio is the way to go. Hidden video is just a little too menacing for the public to deal with. They might feel a twinge of sympathy for the subjects, and I don't want even a hint of softness to mar this day.

Also, it's really best if there's a buildup. Everybody likes a slow reveal. So I'm forcing myself to have patience and plan this out minute by minute. It's not easy.

On Friday I don't bother calling in sick to work. I'll never return there again. I spend the day packing up the few personal belongings from my apartment and loading them into the SUV. I close my cat into her carrier and I put her in the rental too; then I drive to the InterContinental Hotel in St. Paul and check into a suite. It has a great bathtub.

No cats are allowed in the hotel, of course, but I leave the maid a fifty every morning so she doesn't see anything, not even the litter box.

On Saturday I carefully set up a new email account through a relay server and enter all of the contacts I stole from Steven's phone. His siblings are in there, of course, and I assume a lot of his church members are too. I recognize two of the names as fellow deacons. I add some of his friends from work and all of his bosses.

I order room service. I sip champagne in the bathtub. I watch boats passing by on the river. What a relaxing day.

On Sunday I get up early and head to church. I'm not wearing a flowery dress today. Instead I wear jeans and a tight sweater. I put my hair up and slide on dark glasses. I stay in my car as people file into the building.

At 8:55 my email alert dings. Sunday service hasn't quite started yet, but Steven will be in place at the front of the hall with the other deacons. He won't be checking email or texts. He's busy setting a good example.

I open the email titled "Hepsworth Family Values Part One" and click on the attached audio file to listen to Steven telling me to pose for him, to touch myself, to get on my knees.

It's not that scandalous, really. I mean, it's pornographic, but mostly harmless. Nothing the other men inside the church wouldn't do, given half a chance.

And there's no video of Steven, no picture or visual evidence, so at most this file is something to titter over and discuss. I say his name several times in the recording, but he can deny it's him and a lot of people will give him the benefit of the doubt. That's fine.

Behind my vehicle, a man and his wife are hurrying across the parking lot when she stops dead in her tracks with her phone to her ear. She gapes openmouthed for a moment, then snaps the phone away from her ear. "Brent!" I hear her yell, but her husband is already at the church door, holding it open and waving her in.

Music rises up inside. The door closes as the woman rushes in, her hands waving as she tries to explain the email to her husband. Even with the doors closed, the muffled sound of the choir beginning to sing leaks past the glass. I get out of the SUV and stroll across the parking lot.

The vestibule is nearly deserted by the time I enter. A woman is on her feet, rocking a fussy baby in her arms. A little girl comes out of the bathroom and heads for the doors to the hall. Just as she's going inside a man stalks out of the doors, his phone to his ear, face stunned. A few seconds later another guy follows.

"What the hell is this?" he hisses.

Sliding my sunglasses off, I peek through the slowly closing door to the great hall. Most of the parishioners are singing along with the choir, but here and there I see pockets of people whispering. It's not enough of a disruption to stop the service, but it's enough to start a vibration of conversation.

I creep closer and prop open a door with my foot. Steven is oblivious at the front, his face raised toward his father, who stands at his lectern listening blissfully to the glorious music behind him.

Steven sings along. His world is still intact. He can't see the cracks working through the foundation beneath him. I watch the scene for a little while. The people closest to the front are the most pious and obedient and none of them know yet, but the back rows are aflutter.

My email dings again. I hear the buzz of one of the other phones in the vestibule. I can't stop the chuckle that rises in my throat.

The Hepsworth Family Values Part Two file is a little more scandalous. In fact, it's downright disgraceful. Steven sounds so arrogant, so drunkenly pleased with himself as he tells the story of his sordid affair with his stepmom, the pastor's wife, the matron of this faithful, pious community. Oh, Steven. How could you? How could you betray your father this way?

I cut out his tearful regret at the end, of course. He can express that on his own if he wants to. And he will want to, I'm sure.

An actual screech gurgles up from the crowd. Several people stand up. I back away from the doors and let them shut, but they soon swing open again. The choir is still singing, but most of the congregation has realized that something terrible is happening. Some have phones pressed to their ears, but most are huddled in groups in the pews, communicating in frantic gestures and rumbles of words over the music.

The doors stay open almost continuously now as people trickle out. The choir begins a new song, but the sound is weakening as the people in the choir begin craning their necks at the jumbled audience.

I spy Steven standing at the front of the room, turning in a slow circle, totally confused by the uproar. Pastor Hepsworth looks mildly concerned and moderately puzzled, but he still has no idea what's coming.

As more people surge into the vestibule, the roar becomes deafening. Just before I turn to walk out, there's a break in the crowd and I see Steven approaching his father at the lectern, his brows drawn down in concern. In that sweet moment his gaze touches mine. His eyes widen. I smile at him.

Jane? I see him mouth in confusion. I let my smile widen to a grin. I let him see my pure, heartfelt joy. I hope he'll remember this smile for the rest of his life. Then I wave and turn to walk away.

As I reach the door, I hear a dozen more phones buzz. My email dings. I head to my vehicle and start the engine.

Safe in the warmth of my big black SUV, I listen to the last audio file. Hepsworth Family Values Part Three is a real barn burner.

Is that Pastor Hepsworth, *our* Pastor Hepsworth, telling a woman to lie down on his desk? My God, is he praying for her as he takes her in his church office? Is she . . . ? Oh my God, is she calling him *Daddy* and begging for forgiveness for her sins?

I giggle over that. I'd really played that part up, and he'd loved it, groaning and growling with pleasure at my subservience, calling me his sweet girl as he pounded me. My performance sounds so sincere. I do my best work when I know there's an audience. And what an audience it is.

A woman bolts from the church, sobbing. She's the only one fleeing so far. Most of them will stick around for quite a while to watch this play out.

It's not every day you get to see a man destroyed. It's not every day you get to watch a whole family burn. This isn't one isolated incident. This isn't a simple transgression that can be forgiven.

I roll down my window. The music has stopped. Now the church rumbles as if boulders are tumbling through it. It's the sound of a mob.

I sit in my car and watch for a long time. People begin to drift out, all of them upset and angry and betrayed. Even some of the men are crying.

I hear shouting through the glass. The children's Bible study classes are led out to the grassy area beside the church as if a fire alarm has gone off. The teachers want to get them far away from the flames of scandal. They lead the kids in a round of "Jesus Loves Me," but then one of the teachers breaks into sobs and runs back inside. The children grow quiet for a moment until they're finally allowed to wander over to the church playground.

When a few more worshippers bolt through the vestibule doors into the parking lot, I decide to leave before the traffic gets too bad.

My work here is finally done.

CHAPTER 48

Steven is crying again. I pop a room service nacho into my mouth and put my feet up on the hotel desk to watch tiny Steven on my monitor as he paces around his kitchen island.

"I told you I don't know!" he yells into his phone. "She's just someone I met at work. I don't know why she would do this! I went to her place, and I . . . I think it's empty. I think maybe . . ."

Steven rubs his face, then shakes his head as the person on the other end of the line says something. "I know. I know. Just . . . will you please ask Dad to call me? He won't answer my calls and I . . . I . . . I don't know how he is. Ted, please! Please, I was drunk and I didn't know what I was saying. *Please!*"

He slides down to the floor and curls up into a ball to sob. I guess Ted didn't have anything helpful to contribute.

I turn off the sound and watch Steven lie in a heap for a few minutes before he pushes himself up and stumbles to the fridge for another beer. I pick through the last of my nachos with a sigh. It's not that I'm not enjoying myself, but it's been three days, and his weeping is getting a little boring.

All I've thought about for months is getting revenge, and now I have it.

On Monday, Steven's company suggested he take a leave of absence. I'm not sure they have grounds to fire him, but there's no doubt they won't let him come back. No one wants to look a man in the face after they've listened to him get a blow job and brag about sleeping with his stepmom.

On Tuesday he kept leaving the house and then returning. Leaving and returning. It seems he was driving to his father's house, but no one would answer the door. He apparently stopped by my apartment as well, but the lights aren't on and no one is home. I like to imagine him banging on the door and furiously screaming my name. I hope the old barfly down the hall read him the riot act and told him to get lost.

It's Wednesday now and I guess I've seen all I need to see. Amazingly he doesn't seem to suspect that there might be cameras in his house. The audio files really fooled him. Any American can make a secret recording on a smartphone these days. Privacy is an illusion, and people have accepted that, though it hasn't made them any more discreet. Please see recordings number one, two, and three.

What I've done is nothing close to murder, but I've still braced myself for some sort of danger. Minnesota is a one-party-consent state for recording, but I assume I could be charged with other minor crimes, like stalking or fraud. Invasion of privacy. Even revenge porn, if they've put that on the books yet. But if anyone has called the police, I haven't heard about it. Maybe the Hepsworths don't want more attention. If this went to trial, it would be a huge national hit.

So now I'm feeling a little . . . deflated. I'm not sure what to do with myself.

Don't get me wrong, I'm satisfied. It's not quite an eye for an eye, but it's darn close.

On the monitor, Steven puts his phone to his ear. I turn the sound back on in time to hear him rasp my name. "Jane? You'd better call me back, you evil bitch. Who are you? *Who the fuck are you? Why did you do this?*" He hangs up and starts crying again.

I blow him a kiss. "That was all for Meg, sweetie. Love you bunches." That was how Meg always signed off on emails. I guess Steven never noticed.

I want to tell him. I desperately want him to know that this was all for Meg. I would have if I'd stabbed him in the woods. I'd have whispered it in his ear over and over again. But I've let him live, and now I can't offer him the relief of knowing.

Because it would be a relief. To know who I was and why I did it. Steven would be able to blame it all on Meg. Hang another sign on her corpse and tell himself that none of this was his fault. It was all that crazy bitch Meg and her crazy bitch friend.

No, this way is better. Let him wonder for the rest of his life. Let him look into every shadow and worry I'm waiting to hurt him again. Let him believe that any woman might destroy him at any time.

I'll know I did it all for Meg and that will have to be enough.

Meg.

I still miss her. Revenge hasn't eased that. I guess I hoped I might wake up Monday morning and feel better. But every morning I wake up and she is still gone and I am still hollow.

I haven't eased the terrible loss. I haven't made that better. Is there any way to do that? I know what other people do. Is that the secret? To pretend to grieve like a real person?

I close the laptop and grab my coat and keys. This is something I didn't want to do, which means I should probably do it.

It only takes fifteen minutes to get to my destination. She's been so close this whole time.

I park along the narrow, twisting road and walk between stones and trees until I come to her grave. The marker is tiny. I guess there wasn't money for anything grand. I should have thought of that. I should have offered to pay for something pretty.

Megan Peterson, beloved daughter.

I wish it said more. I wish it sang her praises. That she was pretty, yes, but that her smile made her absolutely glow. That she was kind to everyone, even those of us who were broken. That she never tired of helping her friends, though she finally grew too tired to save herself.

"I miss you," I say. Then I stand silent.

I don't believe in prayer. I know she's not listening. I have no idea why I've come. Still, I stand there for a long time. I think maybe I'll cry, but I don't. It's just me, alone, empty as ever.

"Meg," I finally whisper. "It's not what you would have wanted, but I made him pay for hurting you. I made him hurt too. Because I love you, Meg. I know I love you. You're all I ever had."

Meg doesn't answer, and I'm empty and dry.

I wish Luke were here with me. He would have told me to bring flowers.

I'm sure he's been texting and calling, but I destroyed that phone on Friday. I thought I'd leave in a couple of days. I thought I'd have to. It's time to go home.

But home to what?

My big apartment, my big job, the big parties where I meet men I can use for a week or two? There's no Meg waiting to hear what I've been up to. No one I can call and gossip with. No plans to make for visits. No silly surprise greeting cards to remind me that someone somewhere truly cares about me.

I don't have a Meg anymore. But . . . maybe I could have a Luke.

It's just now dawning on me that I can stay if I want. Stay here in this city that's so perfect in the summer and too cold and quiet in the winter. In this place that reminds me of Meg. In the only place I've ever felt any sense of family.

If no one files any charges, then I have nothing to fear. I'm free. Even if I run into Steven on the street one day, I'll just smile with a lot of teeth and watch his face pale. But we don't really run in the same circles.

I could be nearly real here, at least for a little while. Luke doesn't know me the way Meg did. He probably never will. But he knows that I'm different. And he *likes* it. He might even learn to whisper "Be nice, Jane" just when I need it.

Or maybe there's a chance I could be really *real* in this life. Is that possible? I've never imagined it before.

I enjoy Luke. I like him. And, more than that, I trust him. Maybe that would be enough for me to be in a true relationship. If I can predict his actions and intentions, perhaps I could really understand him in a way I've never understood other humans. Maybe I could love and be loved.

But maybe not. I pull up a list of flights to Kuala Lumpur and I wonder.

CHAPTER 49

I get my hair dyed back to its usual midnight brown at a very expensive salon. I have it cut into a sleek shoulder-length bob with a straight line of bangs that fall just to my eyebrows. I go shopping to buy tight skirts and knee-high boots and four shades of red lipstick, each darker and bloodier than the last. I feel almost myself again. Whenever I pass a mirror, I smile and say, "Hello, Jane."

I'm back.

Even the Hepsworth family might not recognize me if I walked right into their church and said hi. My cat isn't fooled, though. When I return to the suite after my transformation is complete, she barely glances up from her perch in the window.

But maybe Luke will be more impressed.

It's been more than a week since we've spoken. He probably thinks I've left the country. Will he be happy to see me? Will he be happy I've stayed?

Yes. Yes, I'm sure he will.

I retrieve the $1,200 watch I bought him from the room's safe. I wrap it in shimmery gold paper and tuck it into my purse, then smooth down my hair and set off to see him.

If I can make him love me, if I can make him want me to stay, then I'll do my very best to love him back.

CHAPTER 50

"I don't get it." I peek over the crowd of shoulders to get another look at the squishy brown face. "Is she cute?"

"Yes!" Luke assures me. "She's gorgeous! She's perfect."

"I'm pretty sure she's squashed beyond all help."

He covers his mouth with a hand to hide his laughter. "Don't let anyone else hear you say that. My niece is definitely the most beautiful newborn in the world."

"Sure, that may be fair. They're all really weird-looking."

Luke holds his phone high to take another picture.

Three of Isaiah's sisters have held the baby, and now it's Uncle Luke's turn. I take his phone from him so I can snap a dozen pictures of him with his first niece. I still don't think she's cute, but Luke is definitely adorable. The whole crowd is oohing and aahing over his crooked grin and tear-filled eyes.

He looks down at tiny Holly, and suddenly her eyes open a little and she focuses on his face. The family swoons and a dozen cameras click. Luke beams at her. "Look at that. She likes me. Hello, little Holly. Hello."

Once she closes her eyes again, he gestures toward me and I shake my head. I don't want to hold the baby, so he hands Holly to one of Isaiah's brothers.

"Sorry," he says as he wipes tears from his cheek. "I'm a mess." I shake my head. I don't understand babies, but this is like the touching end of a TV season, and I understand that. This is the wrap-up that brings the whole cast together and makes the viewer sigh.

It's a happy ending. Even for me.

I have a place here now. I have Luke's family. His friends. It's more than I've ever had before.

I'd say I can be myself with Luke, but I'm still not quite sure what my self is. Sometimes I feel real, but mostly I feel like I'm just enjoying a good TV show.

That's okay, though. That's enough for now. I often felt the same way with Meg. I can make this work. I love Luke. And I'm learning to take care of him in my own way.

I still keep an eye on Steven, of course. Not literally. The camera batteries ran out a month after I blew his world to smithereens.

I wasn't checking in often at that point, but I knew he still hadn't spoken to his father, and his brother had cut him off too. The family is broken apart and divided. Pastor Hepsworth has lost his firstborn son. And his wife. And his authority. Steven has lost his hero and his career and everything he held dear in the world.

In January he sold his house and moved to Omaha, Nebraska. He's an assistant manager at a fast-food place there. He'll work his way up to manager, I'm sure, and he'll be a big man in a little world again. But he'll never, ever be the same. He'll never feel safe.

Good.

The church closed for two months and then reopened under the guidance of one of the other deacons. It has a new name and a new sign, and any mention of the Hepsworth family has been wiped from the website and newsletter.

Just like me, they never existed.

When I drive by on Sunday mornings, the church parking lot isn't nearly as full as it used to be. I hope every time someone mentions the weakness of women, the parishioners all picture the behavior of the Hepsworth men. I hope they imagine it in great detail.

Rhonda filed for divorce. It's not final yet, but she moved to Florida already.

Pastor Hepsworth is working at a call center. He goes by plain old Robert now. I bet no one calls him "Daddy" anymore either.

None of them are dead, so I'd say they're all just fine. They're better off than Meg, aren't they?

Today is February seventeenth. It's been a full year since she died. My grief has grown more muffled, finally. These days I only feel it when I take it out to remember her.

Someday soon I think it might leave forever, but I'm spending the day with Luke's family, the way I should have spent time with hers, so tonight I'll go home to the condo I rent near Luke's place and I'll watch my videos. I'll watch myself with Steven. I'll play over and over the scene of him lying naked and vulnerable under my blade and I'll let myself imagine that I killed him then. It helps the sorrow.

Luke is doing great, at least. We've only been a couple for a few months now, so he doesn't miss being with a real girl yet. Someday he might.

And me? Well. I'm fine. I sold my place in Kuala Lumpur. My cat likes the new condo. I'm working in a downtown Minneapolis law firm under my real name. It's a good place for me. I like the office politics and I'm great at negotiation. I love knowing I won, and I almost always win.

And I have Luke now. He's mine the way that Meg was, and I'll never let anyone hurt him.

I'm content. In fact, I'm happy. Really happy. I feel almost peaceful.

The door to the private family hospital room opens, and Luke's mother walks in to meet her first grandchild. When I catch her eye, her delighted smile fades. She wants to glare at me, but she only looks away and pastes her smile back in place.

She's been hanging around a lot. Helping Isaiah and Johnny set up a nursery. Inserting herself into their lives. She tried to weasel back into Luke's life too, but he found it very upsetting, so I drove up to her place in Bemidji for a little chat, just one girl to another. She was quite surprised to wake up and find me standing over her bed, but I think I got through to her.

I love Luke the way I loved Meg, and I've learned my lesson. I am the strong one. It's my job to protect. I see that now.

She offers Luke a quick wave from across the room, but she stays close to Johnny and the baby. I know she'll be on her best behavior. I know she won't ever upset Luke again.

I love him, so I've made sure of it.

ABOUT THE AUTHOR

Victoria Helen Stone (nom de plume of *USA Today* bestselling romance novelist Victoria Dahl) is the author of *Evelyn, After* and *Half Past*. Born and educated in the Midwest, she finished her first manuscript just after college. In 2016, she was the recipient of the American Library Association's prestigious Reading List Award. After publishing more than twenty-five books, she has taken a turn toward the darker side of genre fiction.

Having escaped the plains of her youth, she now resides with her family in a small town high in the Rocky Mountains, where she enjoys hiking, snowshoeing, and not skiing (too dangerous). For more on the author and her work, visit www.VictoriaHelenStone.com and www.VictoriaDahl.com.